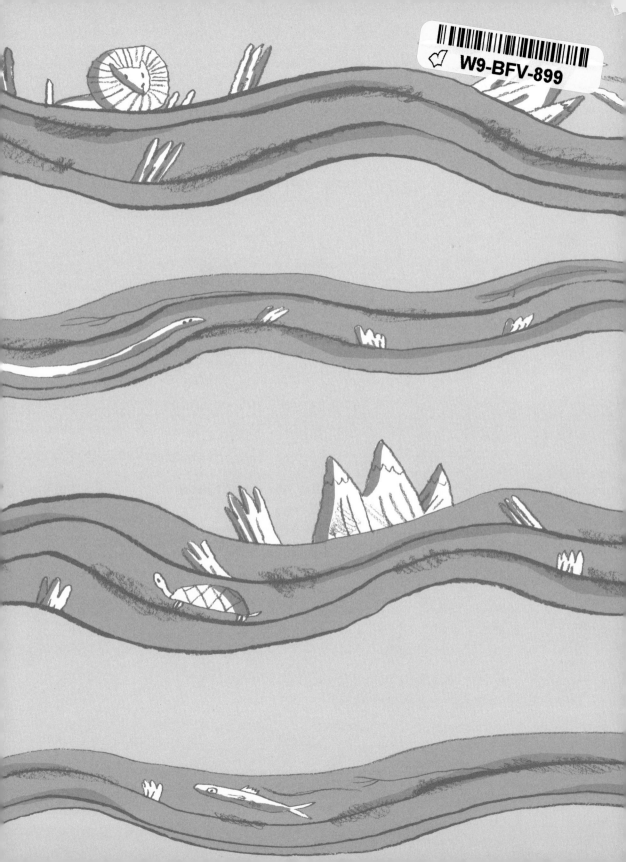

W9-BFV-899

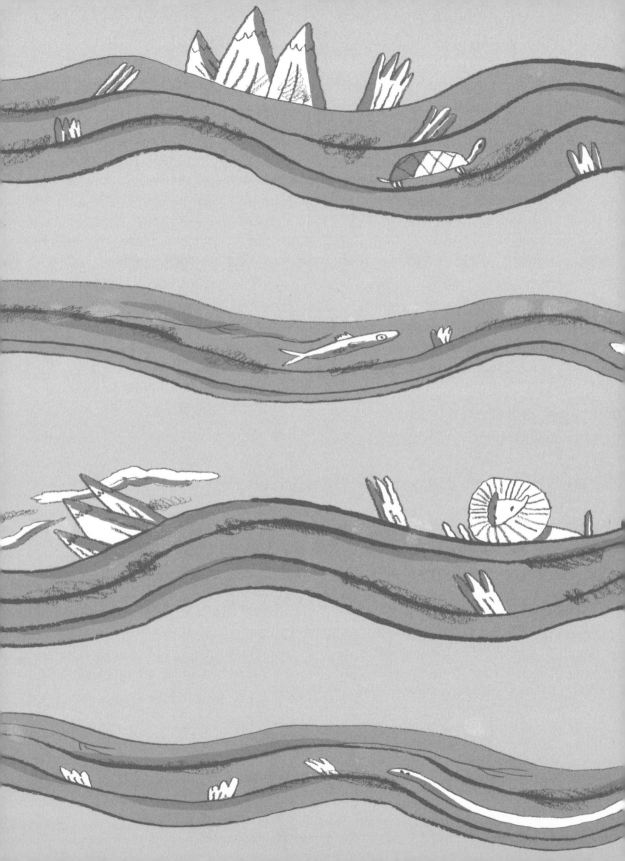

TALES OF GREAT GODDESSES

GAIA

GODDESS OF EARTH

LIBRARY OF CONGRESS CONTROL NUMBER 2021945981

ISBN 978-1-4197-4861-5

TEXT © 2022 IMOGEN GREENBERG
ILLUSTRATIONS © 2022 ISABEL GREENBERG
BOOK DESIGN BY MAX TEMESCU AND JADE RECTOR

PUBLISHED IN 2022 BY AMULET BOOKS, AN IMPRINT OF ABRAMS.
ALL RIGHTS RESERVED. NO PORTION OF THIS BOOK MAY BE REPRODUCED,
STORED IN A RETRIEVAL SYSTEM, OR TRANSMITTED IN ANY FORM OR
BY ANY MEANS, MECHANICAL, ELECTRONIC, PHOTOCOPYING, RECORDING,
OR OTHERWISE, WITHOUT WRITTEN PERMISSION FROM THE PUBLISHER.

PRINTED AND BOUND IN CHINA
10 9 8 7 6 5 4 3 2 1

AMULET BOOKS ARE AVAILABLE AT SPECIAL DISCOUNTS WHEN PURCHASED
IN QUANTITY FOR PREMIUMS AND PROMOTIONS AS WELL AS FUNDRAISING
OR EDUCATIONAL USE. SPECIAL EDITIONS CAN ALSO BE CREATED TO
SPECIFICATION. FOR DETAILS, CONTACT SPECIALSALES@ABRAMSBOOKS.COM
OR THE ADDRESS BELOW.

AMULET BOOKS® IS A REGISTERED TRADEMARK OF HARRY N. ABRAMS, INC.

ABRAMS The Art of Books
195 Broadway, New York, NY 10007
abramsbooks.com

TALES OF GREAT GODDESSES

GAIA

GODDESS OF EARTH

IMOGEN AND ISABEL GREENBERG

AMULET BOOKS • NEW YORK

FOR FRIEDA

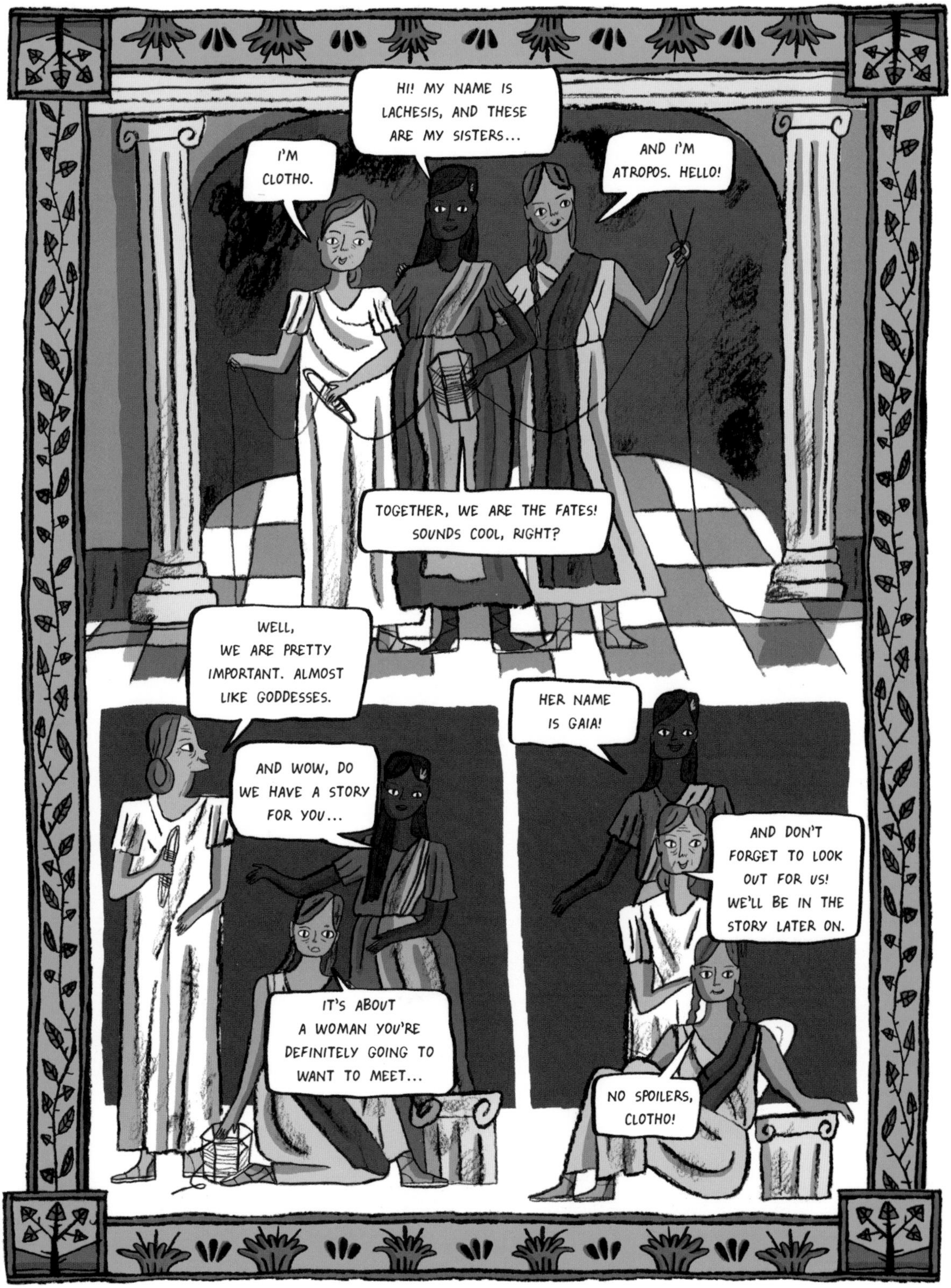
HI! MY NAME IS LACHESIS, AND THESE ARE MY SISTERS...
I'M CLOTHO.
AND I'M ATROPOS. HELLO!
TOGETHER, WE ARE THE FATES! SOUNDS COOL, RIGHT?
WELL, WE ARE PRETTY IMPORTANT. ALMOST LIKE GODDESSES.
AND WOW, DO WE HAVE A STORY FOR YOU...
IT'S ABOUT A WOMAN YOU'RE DEFINITELY GOING TO WANT TO MEET...
HER NAME IS GAIA!
AND DON'T FORGET TO LOOK OUT FOR US! WE'LL BE IN THE STORY LATER ON.
NO SPOILERS, CLOTHO!

IN THIS

BOOK YOU

WILL MEET

GODS AND GODDESSES

GAIA

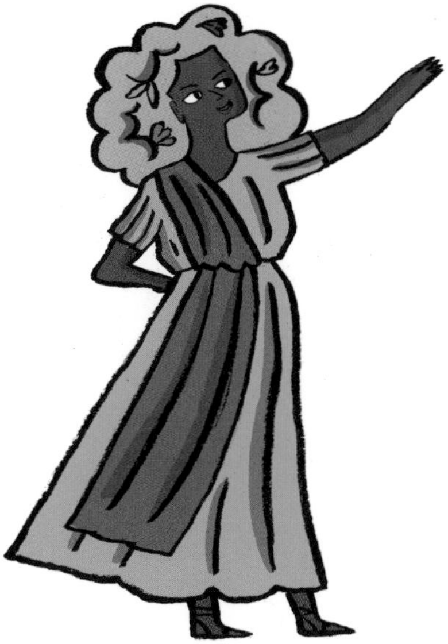

GAIA WAS THE GODDESS OF EARTH, WHO CREATED THE UNIVERSE AND THE WORLD—FROM THE LAND TO THE SEA TO ALL THE PLANTS AND CREATURES ON IT. SHE WANTED THE TITANS, GODS, AND MORTALS TO LIVE IN PEACE TOGETHER AND KEEP THE EARTH SAFE FROM HARM.

OURANOS

OURANOS WAS GAIA'S HUSBAND AND THE
LEADER OF THE TITANS. THE GOD OF THE SKY,
HE THOUGHT HE SHOULD RULE OVER ALL THE
EARTH AND THE MORTALS ON IT.

SELENE

GAIA'S GRANDDAUGHTER AND GODDESS
OF THE MOON, SELENE HELPED CARRY THE
MOON ACROSS THE SKY, IN HER CHARIOT
WITH MILK-WHITE HORSES, TO TURN THE DAY
INTO NIGHT. BUT SHE COULDN'T HELP BUT BE
COMPETITIVE WITH HER BROTHER, HELIOS.

HELIOS

HELIOS WAS GAIA'S GRANDSON AND THE GOD
OF THE SUN. NOT WANTING TO BE OUTSHONE BY
HIS SISTER SELENE, HE BROUGHT THE SUN AND
THE MORNING IN A FANCY CHARIOT WITH FOUR
HORSES WHO GALLOPED ACROSS THE SKY.

EOS

SISTER TO SELENE AND HELIOS, EOS WAS
THE GODDESS OF THE DAWN—AND THE ONLY
ONE WHO COULD KEEP HER SIBLINGS FROM
FIGHTING TOO MUCH.

CRONUS

OURANOS AND GAIA'S YOUNGEST SON, CRONUS
WAS BOLD AND CUNNING AND HELPED TO FREE
GAIA WHEN OURANOS CHAINED HER UP. BUT ONCE
CRONUS ROSE TO POWER, HE BECAME PARANOID OF
HIS OWN CHILDREN—AND TRIED TO EAT THEM SO
THAT THEY'D NEVER BE ABLE TO OVERTHROW HIM!

RHEA WAS THE WIFE OF CRONUS AND THE GODDESS
OF MOTHERHOOD. SHE WAS ALSO THE MOTHER
OF THE OLYMPIANS: HESTIA, DEMETER, HERA, ZEUS,
POSEIDON, AND HADES. SHE WORKED WITH GAIA TO
HELP TRICK HER HUSBAND AND SAVE HER YOUNGEST
SON, ZEUS, FROM GETTING EATEN.

ZEUS

THE YOUNGEST SON OF CRONUS AND RHEA,
ZEUS WAS THE GOD OF THE SKY AND THUNDER.
ONCE HE GREW UP, HE OVERTHREW CRONUS AND
FREED HIS SIBLINGS. HE BECAME THE LEADER OF
THIS NEW GROUP OF GODS AND GODDESSES,
KNOWN AS THE OLYMPIANS—AND HE'D DO
ANYTHING TO STAY IN CHARGE!

DEMIGODS, MORTALS, AND MORE!

THE FATES

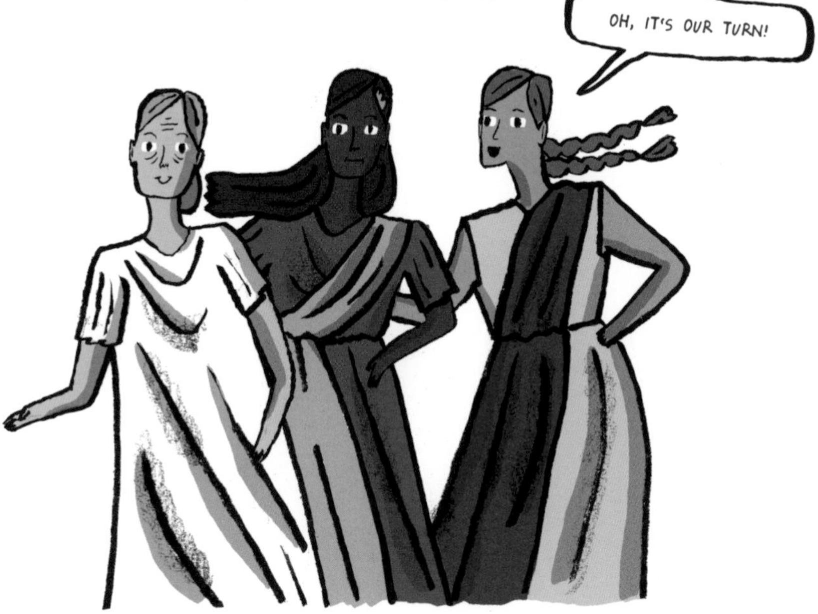
OH, IT'S OUR TURN!

THE FATES WERE THREE SISTERS—CLOTHO, LACHESIS, AND ATROPOS—WHO PICKED UP THE THREADS OF CHAOS AND SPUN SENSE INTO THE UNIVERSE. THEY CREATED THE STORIES AND DESTINIES OF ALL THOSE ON EARTH AND ATOP MOUNT OLYMPUS.

HERCULES

HERCULES WAS A DEMIGOD WHO WAS RECRUITED
BY THE OLYMPIANS TO BE A HERO. ZEUS USED HIS
POWERS TO MAKE HERCULES BIG AND STRONG SO
THAT HE WAS ABLE TO PROTECT MOUNT OLYMPUS
FROM THE GIANTS.

PORPHYRION

PORPHYRION WAS ONE OF THE GIANTS WHO
TRIED TO HELP GAIA BY LEADING A REBELLION
AGAINST ZEUS AND THE OLYMPIANS.

ALKYONEUS

ALKYONEUS WAS THE OTHER GIANT WHO HELPED
TO LEAD THE REBELLION. ON THE WAY UP TO
MOUNT OLYMPUS, HE WAS STRUCK BY ONE OF
HERCULES'S ARROWS, FELL TO EARTH, AND DIED.

TYPHON

CREATED BY GAIA IN THE GLOOM OF THE
UNDERWORLD, TYPHON WAS THE GREATEST GIANT
WHO EVER WALKED THE EARTH. HE WAS TALLER
THAN THE MOUNTAINS, HAD A HUNDRED SERPENT
HEADS, AND HAD WINGS THAT STRETCHED FROM
THE FARTHEST WEST TO THE MOST DISTANT EAST.

THE FURIES

THE FURIES WERE THREE FEROCIOUS WOMEN—
ALECTO, MEGAERA, AND TISIPHONE—WHO FOUGHT
FOR JUSTICE AMONG THE GODS AND MORTALS.

PART 1

The Earth's Beginning

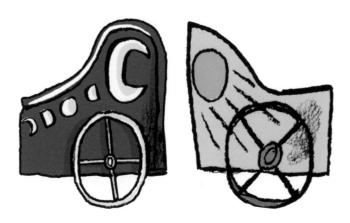

LONG AGO, GAIA CREATED THE EARTH AND THE UNIVERSE AND THE INFINITE SPACE BEYOND IT. SHE CLOSED HER EYES, AND THE TURNING EARTH CAME INTO EXISTENCE. THE SALTY SEA MET THE LUSH LAND, AND THE SKY STRETCHED OVERHEAD.

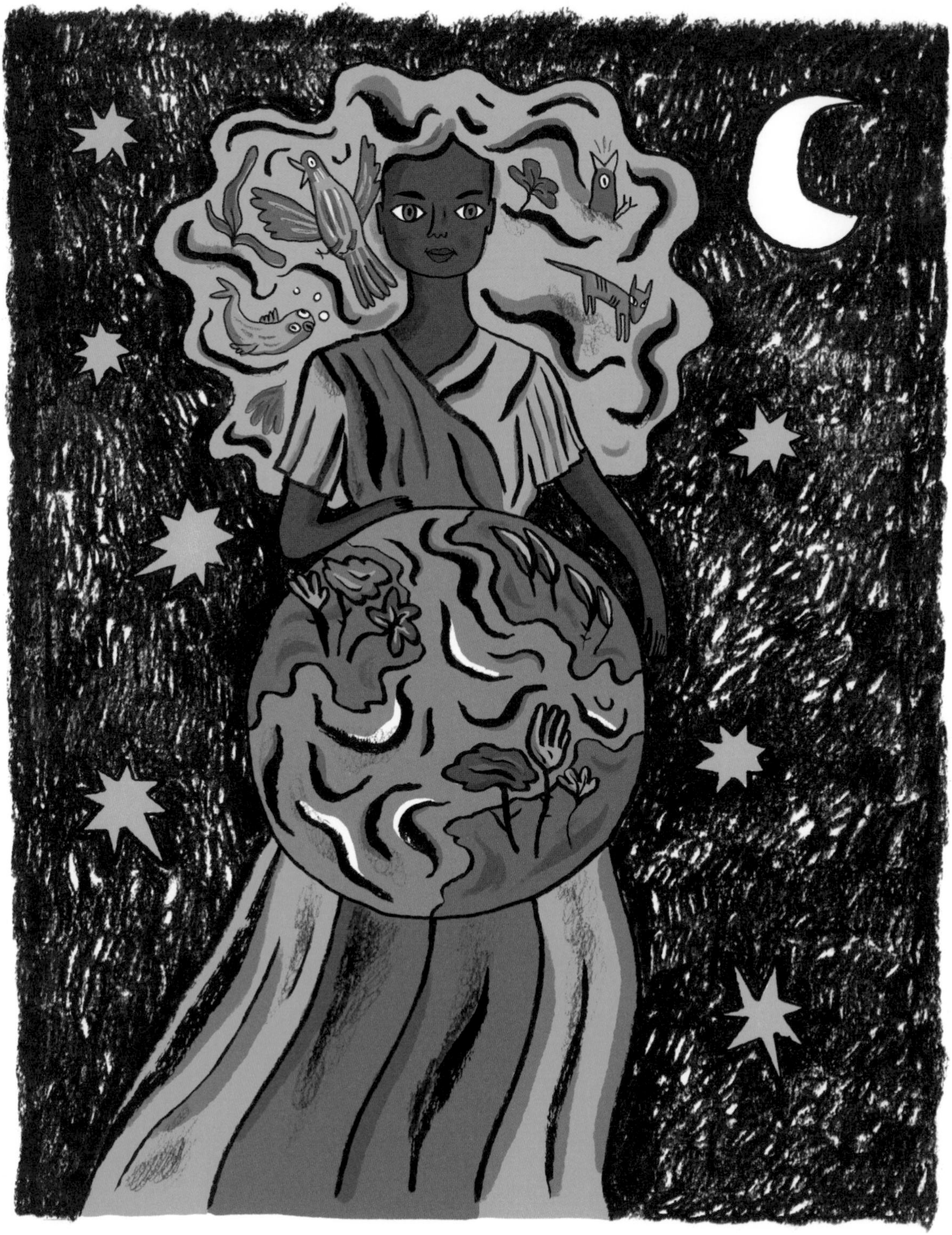

HER HUSBAND, OURANOS, WAS THE HEAD OF THEIR FAMILY—A GROUP OF ANCIENT GODS WHO CALLED THEMSELVES THE TITANS. HE CAME TO SEE WHAT GAIA HAD MADE.

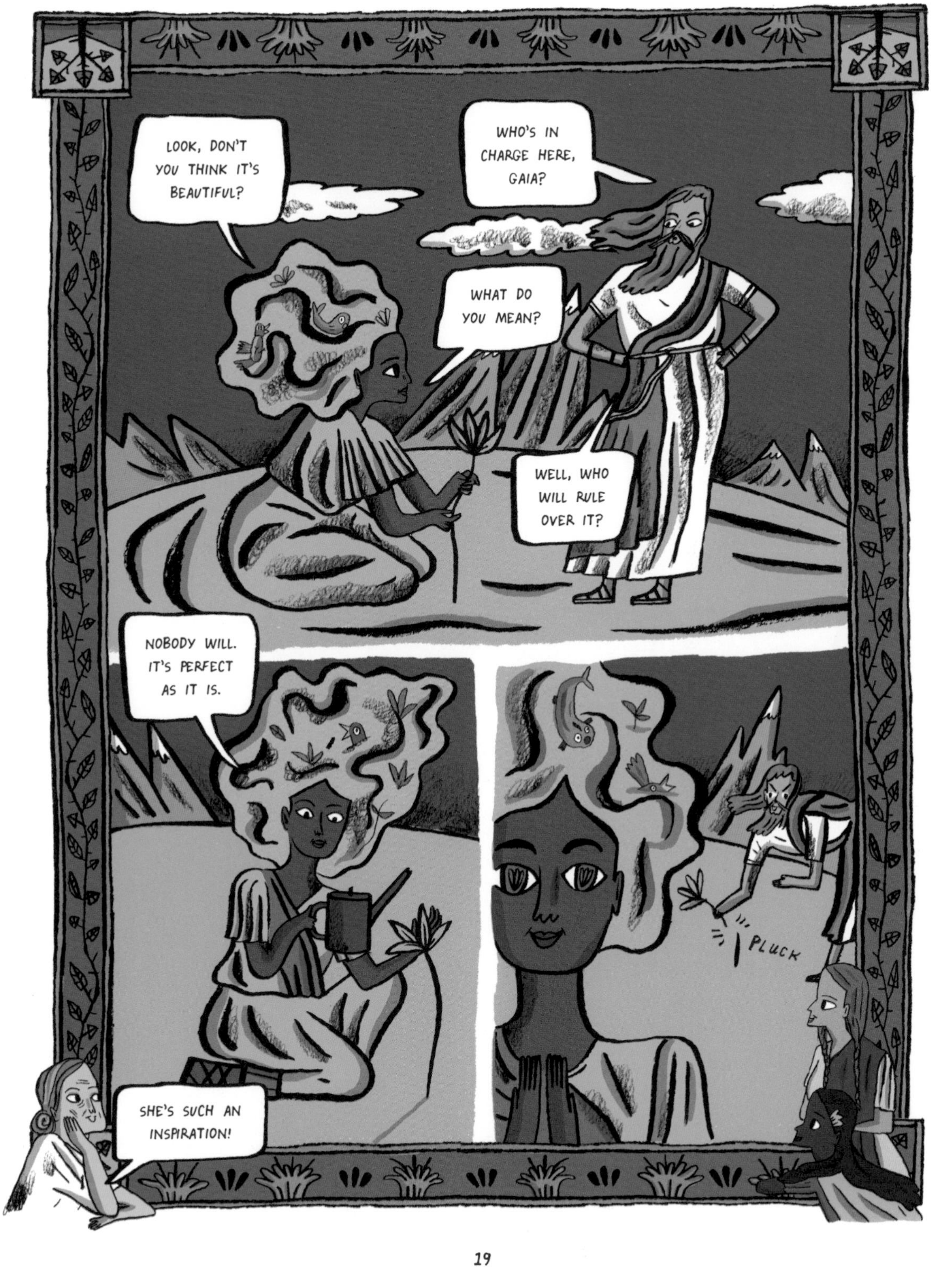
LOOK, DON'T YOU THINK IT'S BEAUTIFUL?
WHO'S IN CHARGE HERE, GAIA?
WHAT DO YOU MEAN?
WELL, WHO WILL RULE OVER IT?
NOBODY WILL. IT'S PERFECT AS IT IS.
PLUCK
SHE'S SUCH AN INSPIRATION!

GAIA TRAVELED THROUGH THE NEW LAND, PERFECTING IT.
SHE CALLED FORTH THE TREES, AND THEY STRETCHED THEIR BRANCHES TO THE SKY.

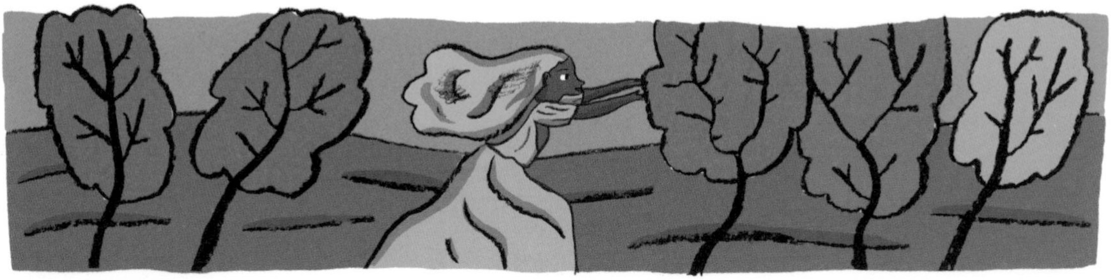

SHE SUMMONED WATERFALLS AND SENT THEM TUMBLING OVER CLIFFS. SHE CREATED THE TIDES THAT SLOSHED ON THE SHORE.

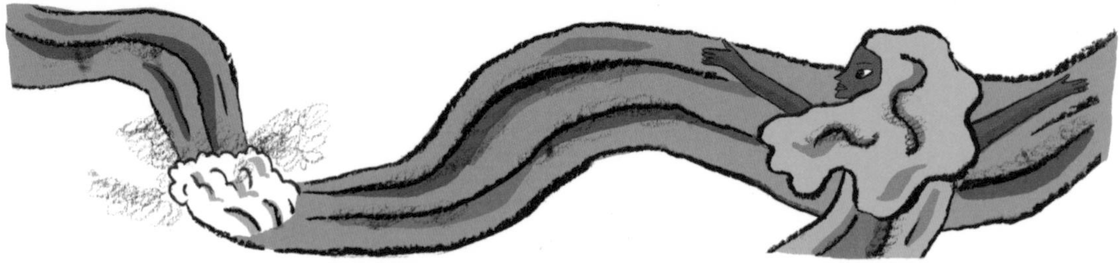

INTO THIS WORLD, SHE LET LOOSE THE ANIMALS—

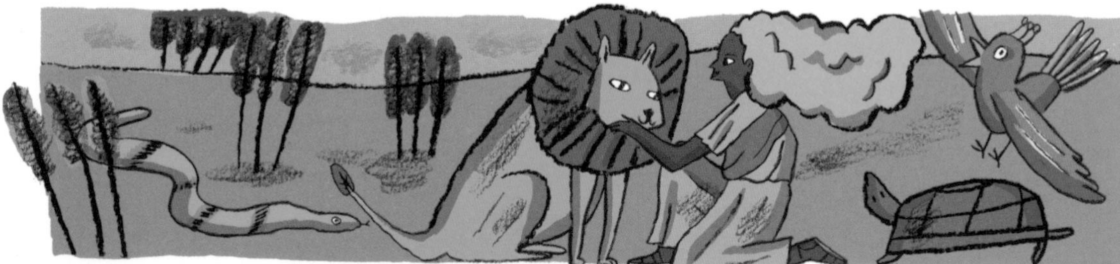

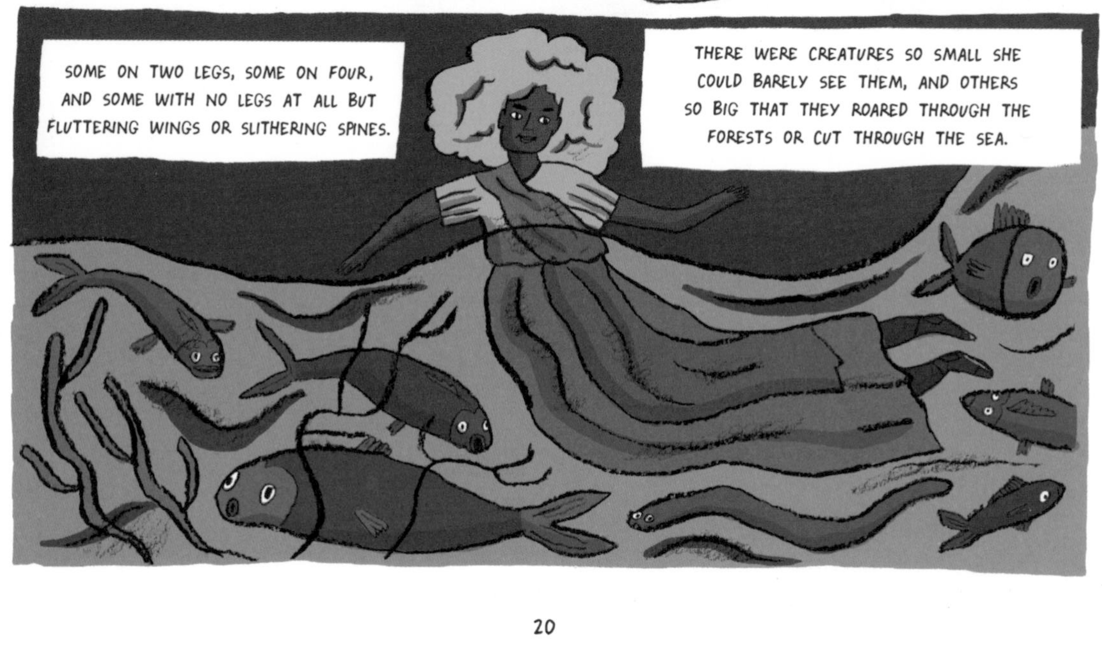
SOME ON TWO LEGS, SOME ON FOUR, AND SOME WITH NO LEGS AT ALL BUT FLUTTERING WINGS OR SLITHERING SPINES.
THERE WERE CREATURES SO SMALL SHE COULD BARELY SEE THEM, AND OTHERS SO BIG THAT THEY ROARED THROUGH THE FORESTS OR CUT THROUGH THE SEA.

THEN GAIA CREATED MORTALS.
SHE WATCHED AS THEY TOOK THE LAND SHE HAD GIVEN THEM, CULTIVATING IT, CHERISHING IT, AND MAKING IT THEIR OWN. THEY BUILT HOMES AND MARKETS AND TEMPLES. SHE BECAME QUITE FOND OF THEM.

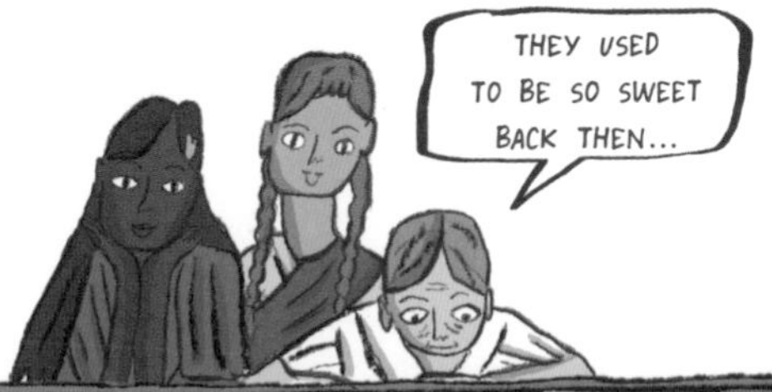
THEY USED TO BE SO SWEET BACK THEN...

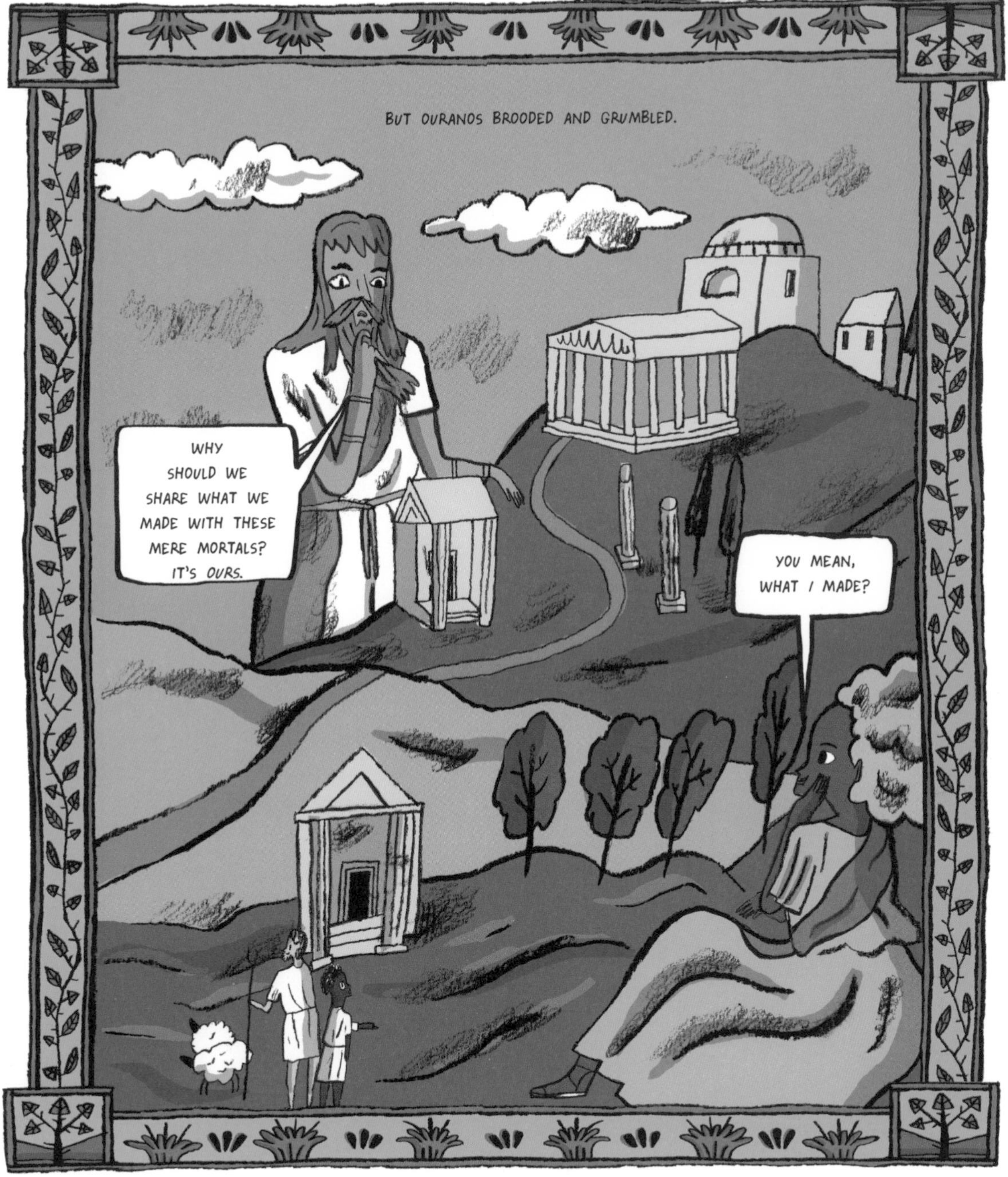
BUT OURANOS BROODED AND GRUMBLED.
WHY SHOULD WE SHARE WHAT WE MADE WITH THESE MERE MORTALS? IT'S *OURS*.
YOU MEAN, WHAT *I* MADE?

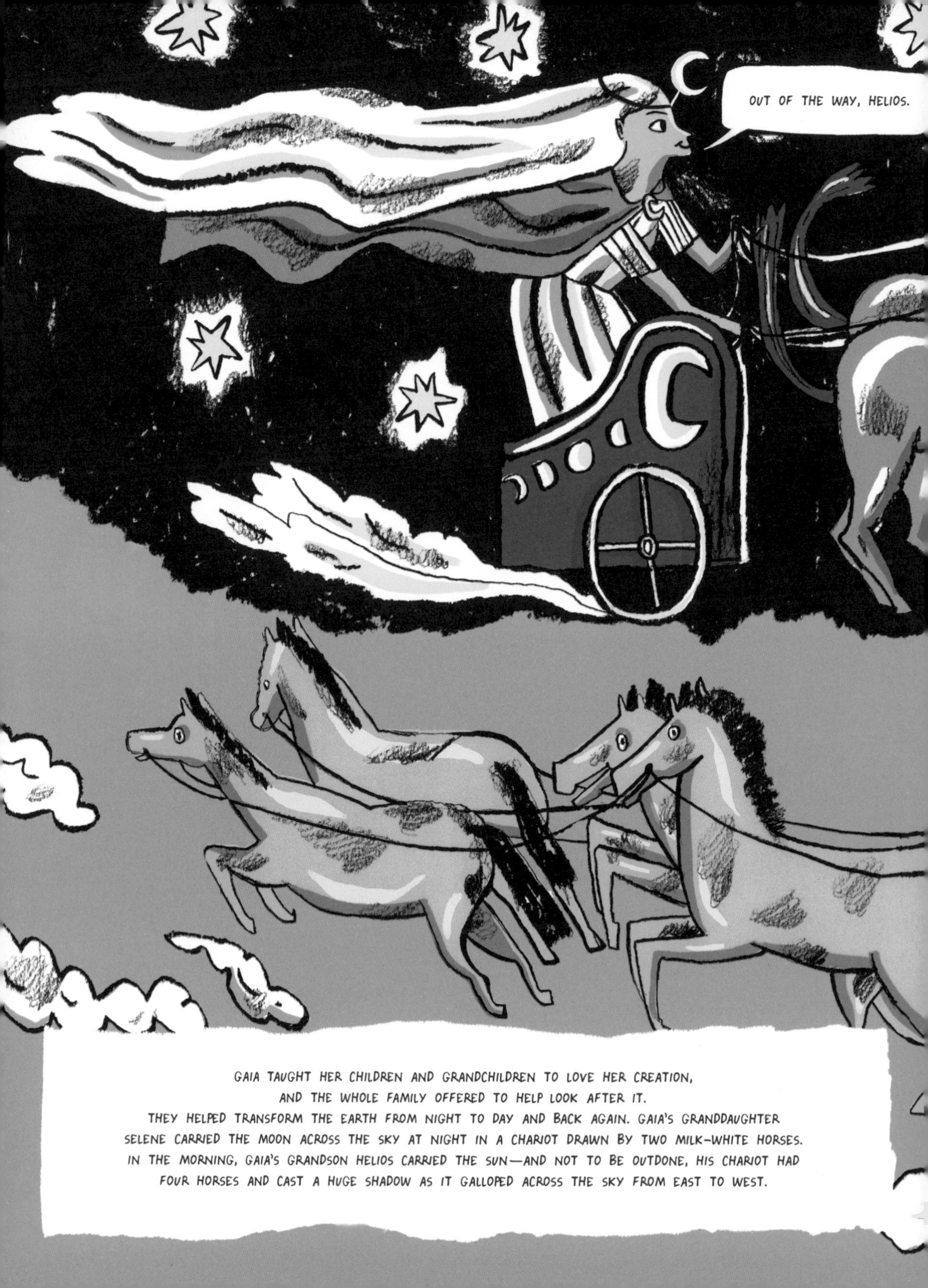
OUT OF THE WAY, HELIOS.

GAIA TAUGHT HER CHILDREN AND GRANDCHILDREN TO LOVE HER CREATION, AND THE WHOLE FAMILY OFFERED TO HELP LOOK AFTER IT. THEY HELPED TRANSFORM THE EARTH FROM NIGHT TO DAY AND BACK AGAIN. GAIA'S GRANDDAUGHTER SELENE CARRIED THE MOON ACROSS THE SKY AT NIGHT IN A CHARIOT DRAWN BY TWO MILK-WHITE HORSES. IN THE MORNING, GAIA'S GRANDSON HELIOS CARRIED THE SUN—AND NOT TO BE OUTDONE, HIS CHARIOT HAD FOUR HORSES AND CAST A HUGE SHADOW AS IT GALLOPED ACROSS THE SKY FROM EAST TO WEST.

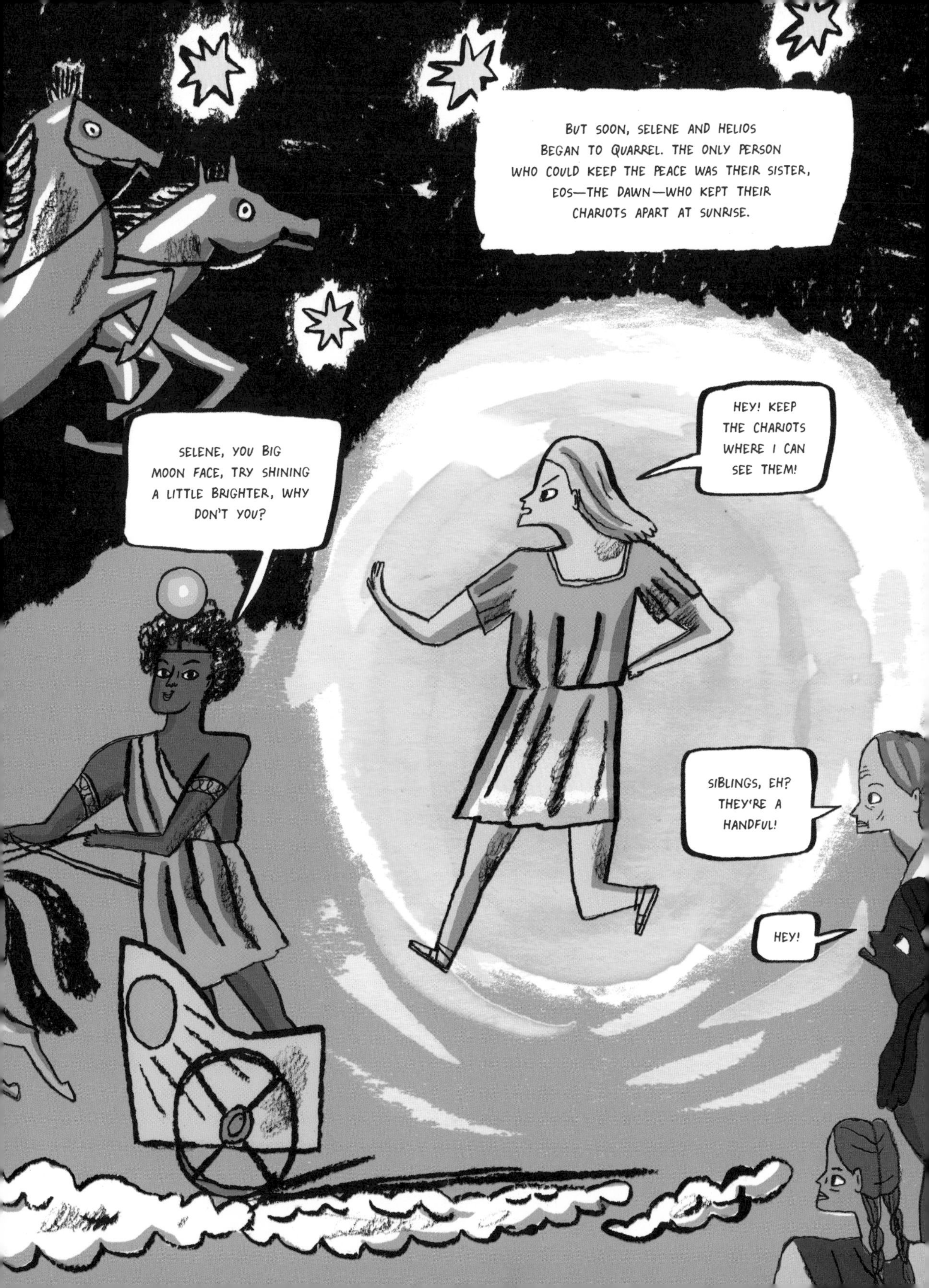
BUT SOON, SELENE AND HELIOS BEGAN TO QUARREL. THE ONLY PERSON WHO COULD KEEP THE PEACE WAS THEIR SISTER, EOS—THE DAWN—WHO KEPT THEIR CHARIOTS APART AT SUNRISE.
SELENE, YOU BIG MOON FACE, TRY SHINING A LITTLE BRIGHTER, WHY DON'T YOU?
HEY! KEEP THE CHARIOTS WHERE I CAN SEE THEM!
SIBLINGS, EH? THEY'RE A HANDFUL!
HEY!

IT SEEMED AS THOUGH OURANOS'S BAD MOOD HAD SEEPED INTO GAIA'S WORLD. THE PEACEFUL TURN OF DAYS HAD BECOME AN ARGUMENT AS HELIOS AND SELENE FOUGHT FOR CONTROL. WHEN HELIOS WON, THE DAYS WERE LONG AND EXHAUSTING. BUT OTHER TIMES, SELENE DRAGGED THE DARKNESS OF NIGHT ON AND ON.

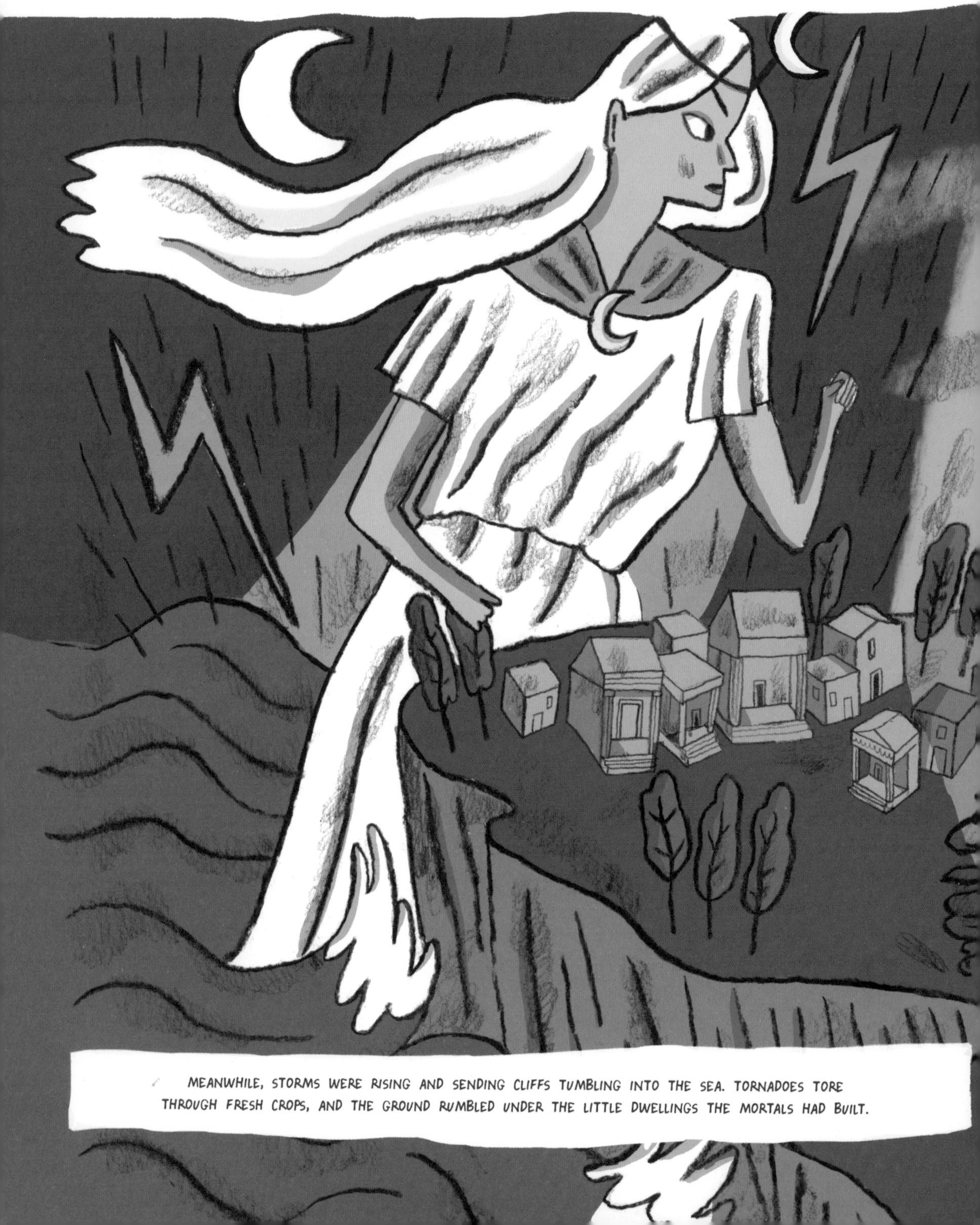

MEANWHILE, STORMS WERE RISING AND SENDING CLIFFS TUMBLING INTO THE SEA. TORNADOES TORE THROUGH FRESH CROPS, AND THE GROUND RUMBLED UNDER THE LITTLE DWELLINGS THE MORTALS HAD BUILT.

THE MORTALS WERE DISTRAUGHT. THE ANIMALS HID IN CONFUSION. THE WORLD HAD ALWAYS BEEN GOOD TO THEM. SOMETHING WAS WRONG. ECHOING IN THE DISTANCE, SOMEWHERE FAR AWAY, A DRUMBEAT OF CHAOS STARTED TO BEAT.

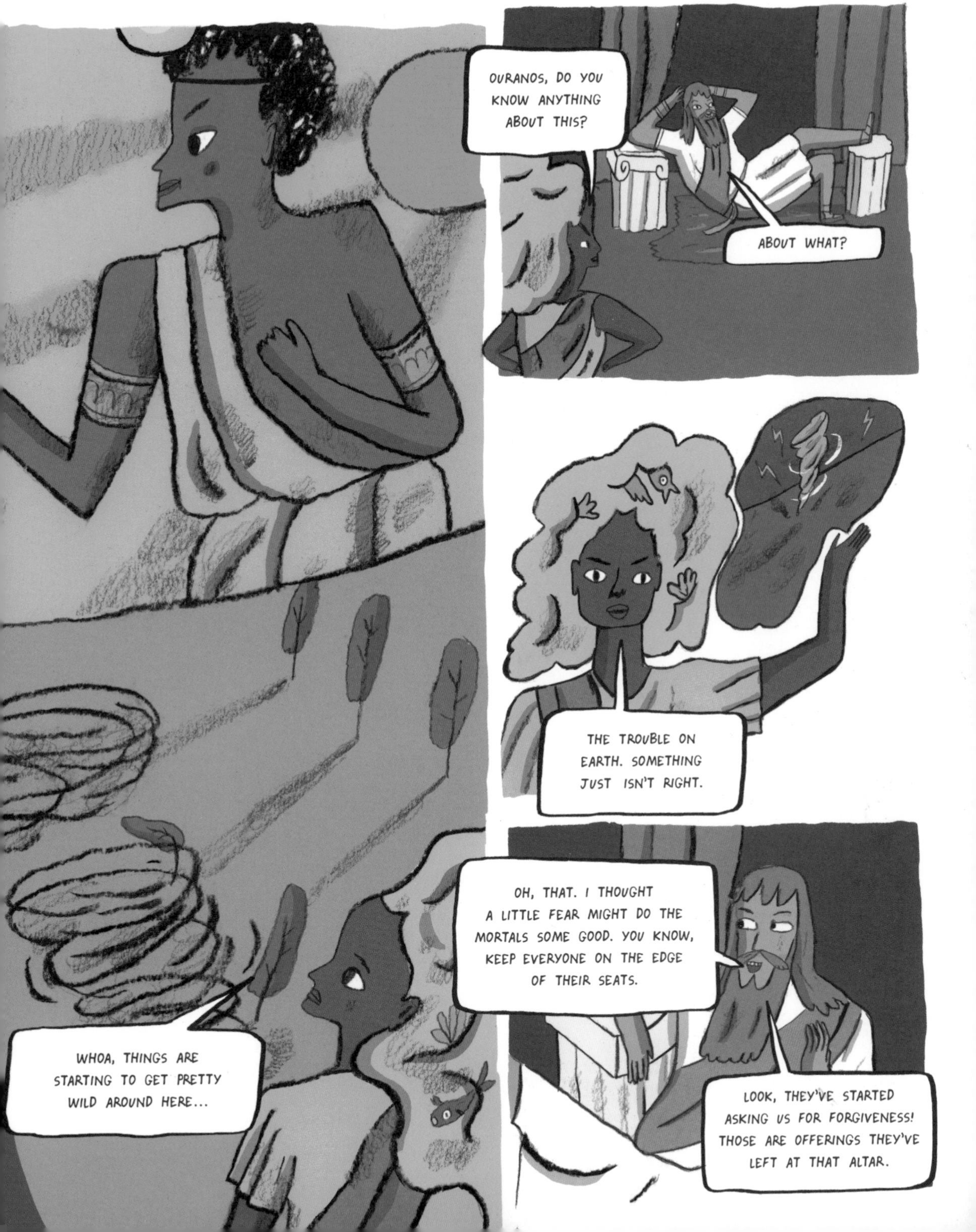

OURANOS, DO YOU KNOW ANYTHING ABOUT THIS?
ABOUT WHAT?
THE TROUBLE ON EARTH. SOMETHING JUST ISN'T RIGHT.
OH, THAT. I THOUGHT A LITTLE FEAR MIGHT DO THE MORTALS SOME GOOD. YOU KNOW, KEEP EVERYONE ON THE EDGE OF THEIR SEATS.
LOOK, THEY'VE STARTED ASKING US FOR FORGIVENESS! THOSE ARE OFFERINGS THEY'VE LEFT AT THAT ALTAR.
WHOA, THINGS ARE STARTING TO GET PRETTY WILD AROUND HERE...

GAIA WAS FURIOUS. SHE'D BUILT THIS WORLD AND SEEN IT GROW WITH GOODNESS AND WITH LOVE. IF SHE COULD ONLY REASON WITH OURANOS, PERHAPS HE WOULD UNDERSTAND. BUT HE WOULDN'T LISTEN TO HER! HE JUST DIDN'T CARE. AND THE MORE SHE ARGUED WITH HIM, THE MORE HIS MOOD SOURED, HIS FACE TWISTING IN RAGE. HE GOT ANGRIER AND ANGRIER.

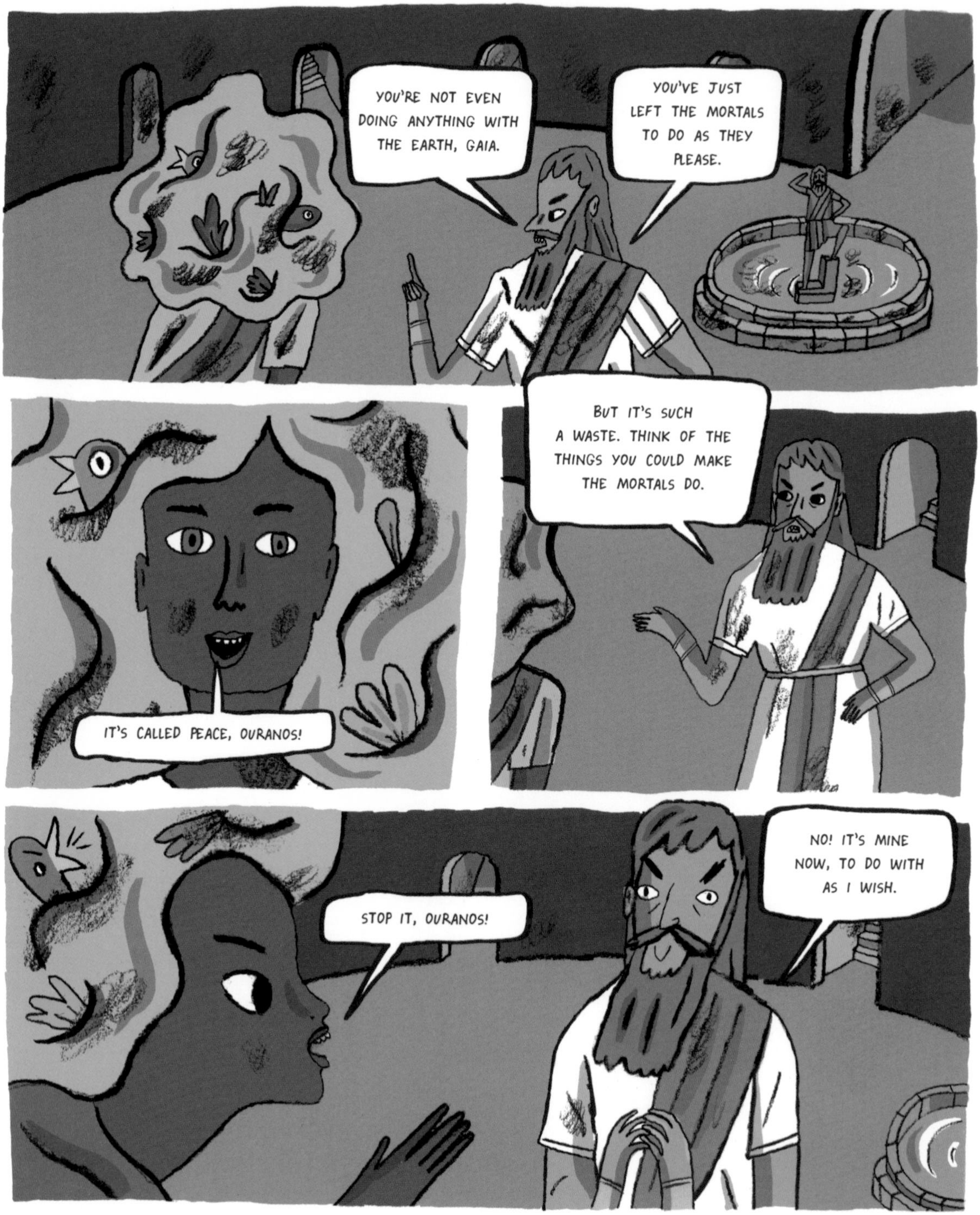
YOU'RE NOT EVEN DOING ANYTHING WITH THE EARTH, GAIA.
YOU'VE JUST LEFT THE MORTALS TO DO AS THEY PLEASE.
IT'S CALLED PEACE, OURANOS!
BUT IT'S SUCH A WASTE. THINK OF THE THINGS YOU COULD MAKE THE MORTALS DO.
STOP IT, OURANOS!
NO! IT'S MINE NOW, TO DO WITH AS I WISH.

PART II

Ouranos and Cronus

ENRAGED, OURANOS TURNED HIS POWER ON GAIA. HE TIED HER IN BONDS OF THUNDER AND LIGHTNING, TRAPPING HER IN THE STRENGTH OF HER OWN CREATIONS. GLEEFUL, AND IN CHARGE AT LAST, HE SENT FLOODS ACROSS THE EARTH AND SET THE HEAVENS ABLAZE. THE OTHER TITANS BOWED DOWN BEFORE HIM, LEAVING GAIA DEFENSELESS AND ALONE.

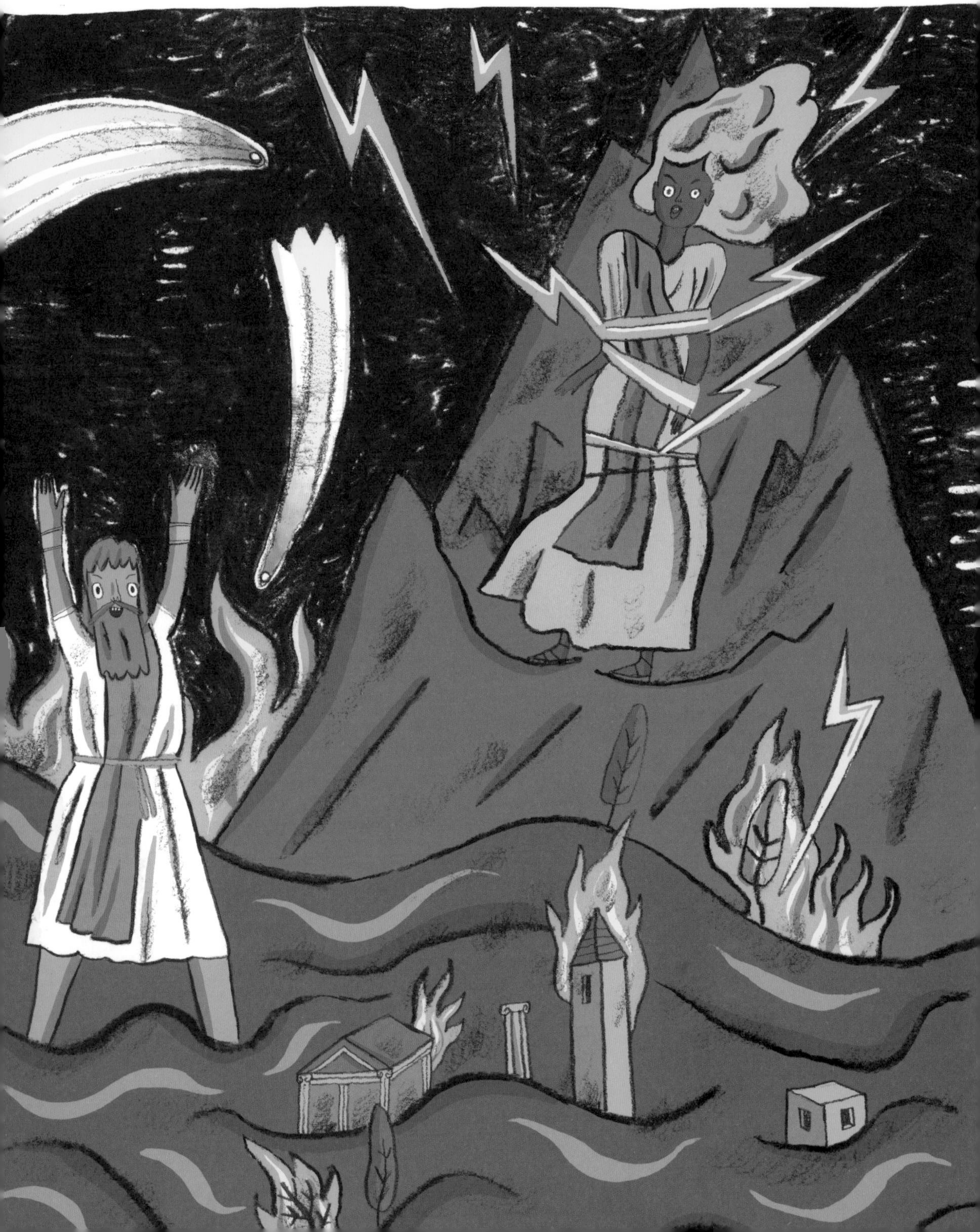

GAIA WAS LOCKED IN A DARK PRISON, SUSPENDED ABOVE THE HEAVENS, WITH ONLY THE CRACKLE OF LIGHTNING TO SEE BY. SHE WAS IN PAIN, AND POWERLESS TO STOP OURANOS. HE ALLOWED HER NO FREEDOM, EXCEPT VISITS FROM HER CHILDREN. BUT THEY WERE TOO AFRAID OF THEIR FATHER TO HELP HER.

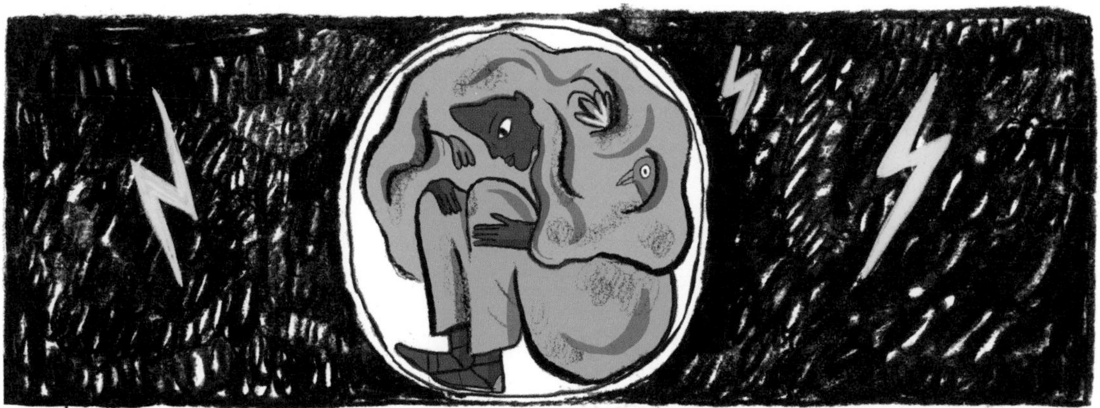

EXCEPT FOR CRONUS, HER YOUNGEST SON. HE WAS BOLD, LIKE HIS FATHER. CRONUS WASN'T JUST FEARLESS—HE WAS CUNNING TOO. TOGETHER, HE AND GAIA HATCHED A PLAN.

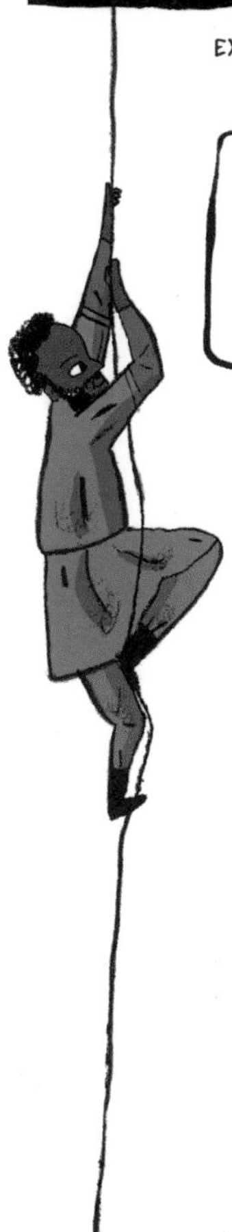

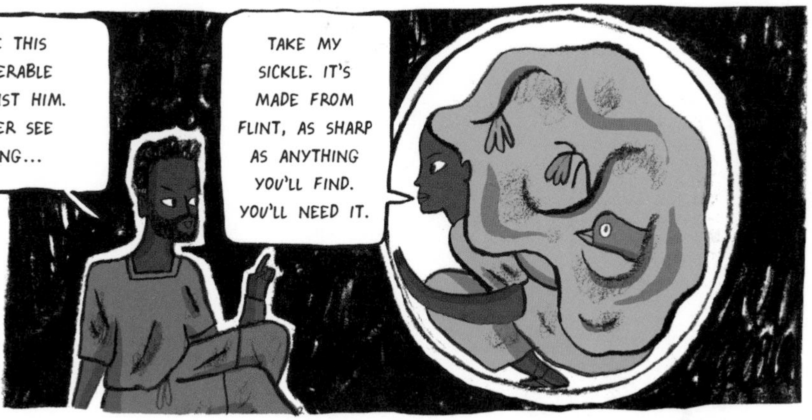
WE'LL USE THIS DARK, MISERABLE PLACE AGAINST HIM. HE'LL NEVER SEE ME COMING...
TAKE MY SICKLE. IT'S MADE FROM FLINT, AS SHARP AS ANYTHING YOU'LL FIND. YOU'LL NEED IT.

SO CRONUS LAY IN WAIT FOR HIS FATHER. OURANOS CAME TO SEE GAIA IN THE DARKEST HOUR OF THE NIGHT. IN THE GLOOM, CRONUS SNUCK UP ON HIS FATHER AND ATTACKED HIM WITH THE SICKLE.

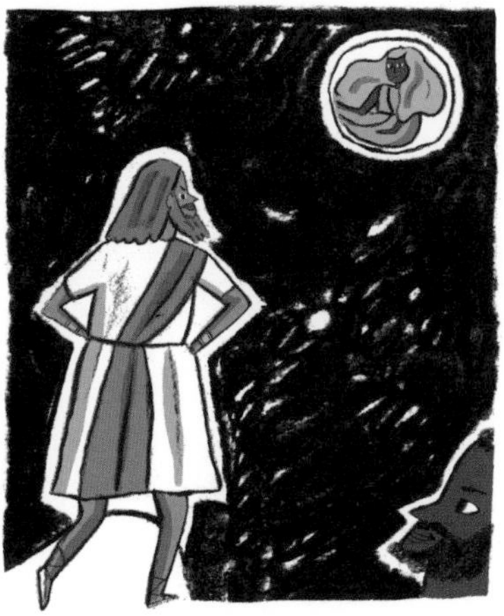

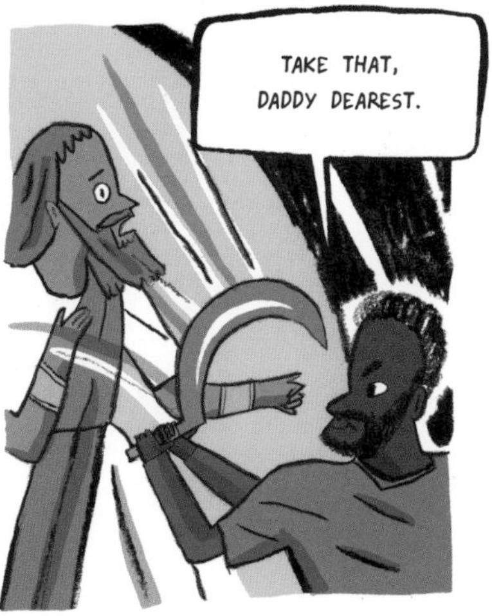
TAKE THAT, DADDY DEAREST.

CRONUS THEN RACED TO SET GAIA FREE, BREAKING THE CRACKLING BONDS THAT TIED HER. GAIA LIMPED INTO THE LIGHT AND SAW THE SUNSHINE AGAIN. SHE WAS SURROUNDED BY HER CHILDREN AND GRANDCHILDREN AND ALL THE TITANS TOO.

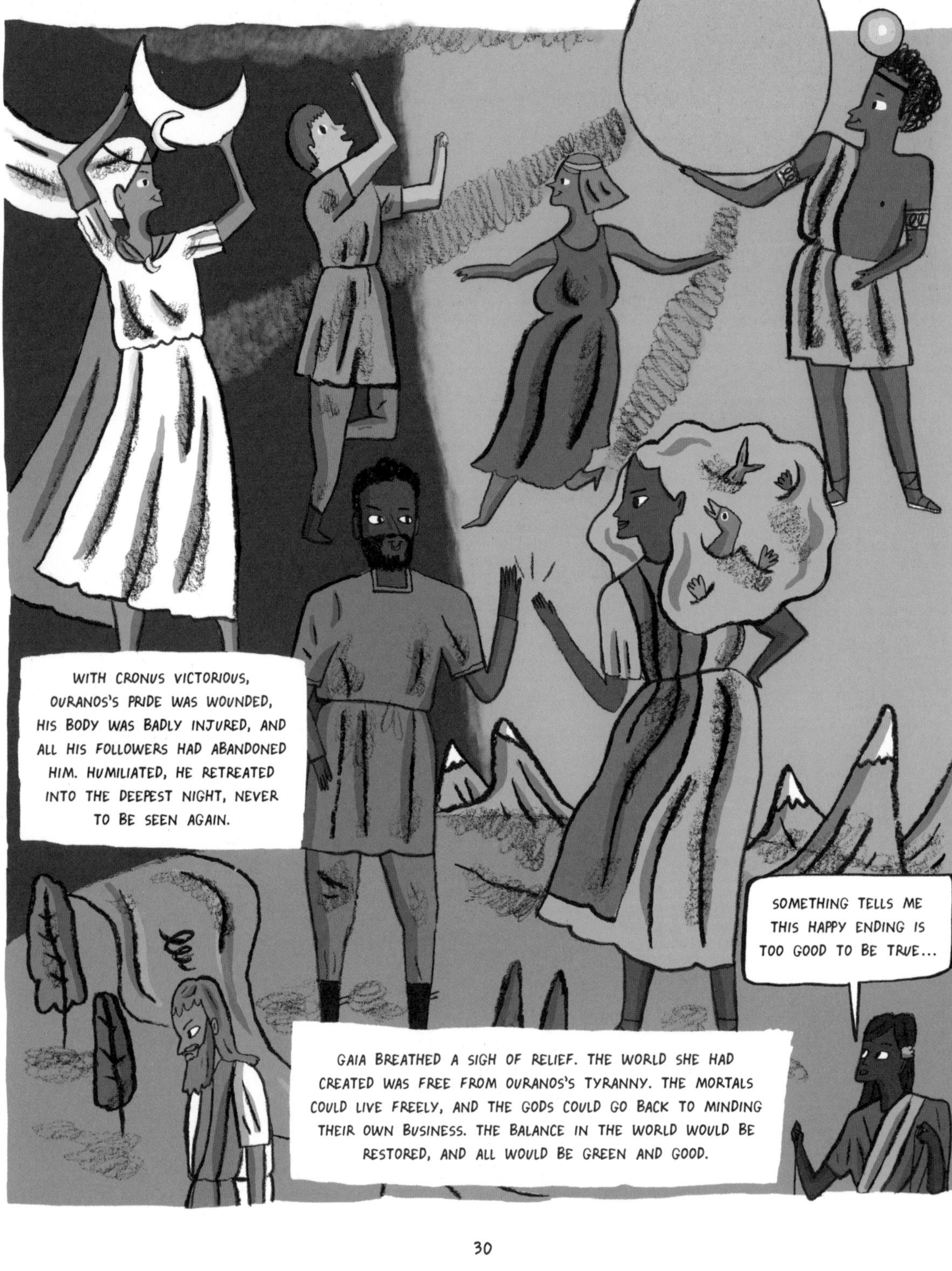
WITH CRONUS VICTORIOUS, OURANOS'S PRIDE WAS WOUNDED, HIS BODY WAS BADLY INJURED, AND ALL HIS FOLLOWERS HAD ABANDONED HIM. HUMILIATED, HE RETREATED INTO THE DEEPEST NIGHT, NEVER TO BE SEEN AGAIN.
SOMETHING TELLS ME THIS HAPPY ENDING IS TOO GOOD TO BE TRUE...
GAIA BREATHED A SIGH OF RELIEF. THE WORLD SHE HAD CREATED WAS FREE FROM OURANOS'S TYRANNY. THE MORTALS COULD LIVE FREELY, AND THE GODS COULD GO BACK TO MINDING THEIR OWN BUSINESS. THE BALANCE IN THE WORLD WOULD BE RESTORED, AND ALL WOULD BE GREEN AND GOOD.

EVERYONE APPLAUDED CRONUS FOR WHAT HE HAD DONE, AND HE PUFFED UP WITH PRIDE. BUT GAIA SAW THE GLINT IN HIS EYE, AND SHE KNEW THAT SOMETHING HAD CHANGED IN HIM. THE STORY WASN'T OVER.

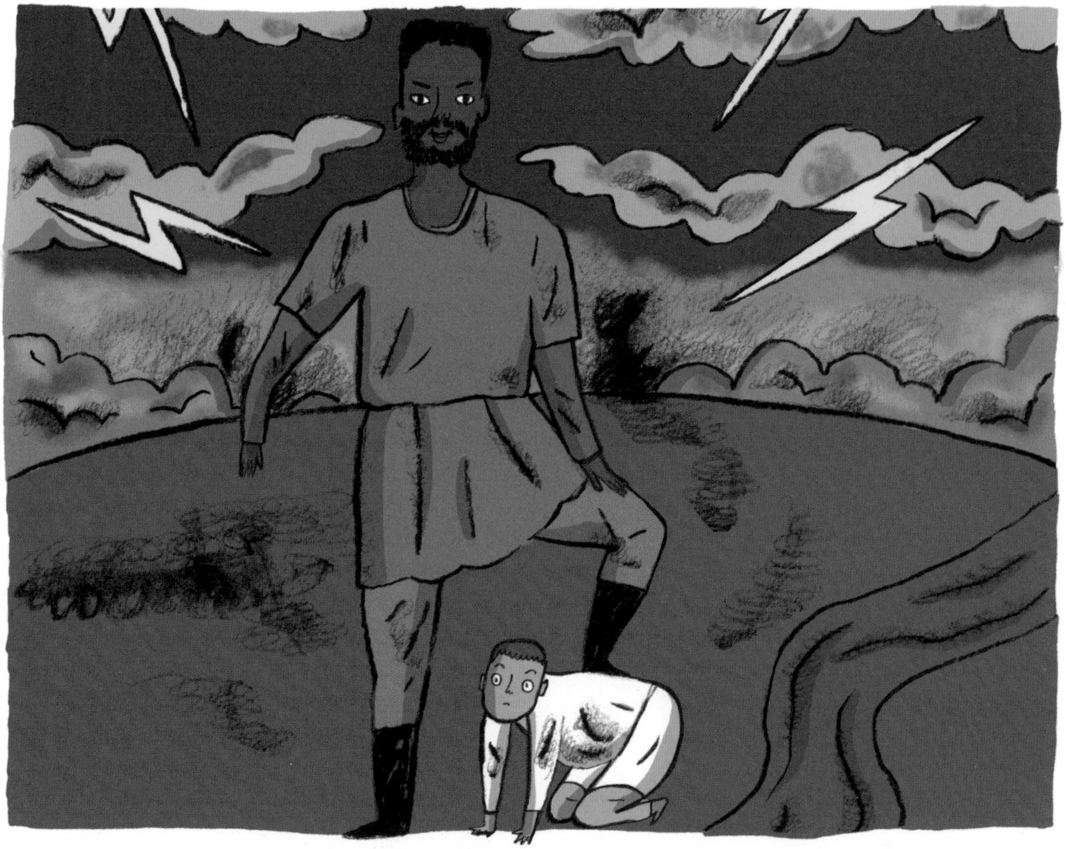

WHILE GAIA HAD BEEN LOCKED AWAY, OURANOS HAD RAISED CRONUS. HE'D TAUGHT HIS SON TO BE JUST LIKE HIM. SO CRONUS LOOKED DOWN ON EARTH JUST AS OURANOS HAD, WITH GREED AND DISDAIN. HE BELIEVED HE HAD EARNED THE RIGHT TO RULE OVER THE TITANS—AND WHY STOP THERE? WHY NOT THE EARTH AND THE MORTALS TOO? THE DRUMBEAT OF CHAOS SOUNDED OUT ONCE AGAIN. AND CRONUS BECAME JUST AS MUCH OF A TYRANT AS HIS FATHER BEFORE HIM. HIS WIFE, RHEA, STOOD NERVOUSLY BY HIS SIDE.

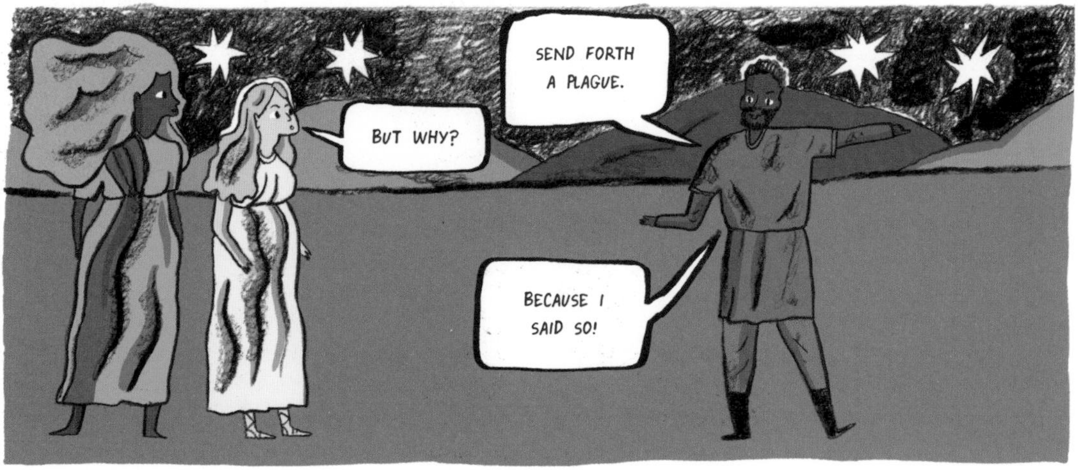
BUT WHY?
SEND FORTH A PLAGUE.
BECAUSE I SAID SO!

BUT AS TIME PASSED, CRONUS BECAME PARANOID, DOUBTING EVERYONE AROUND HIM. IF HE HAD OVERTHROWN HIS FATHER, WHAT WAS STOPPING HIS OWN CHILDREN FROM DOING THE SAME TO HIM ONE DAY?

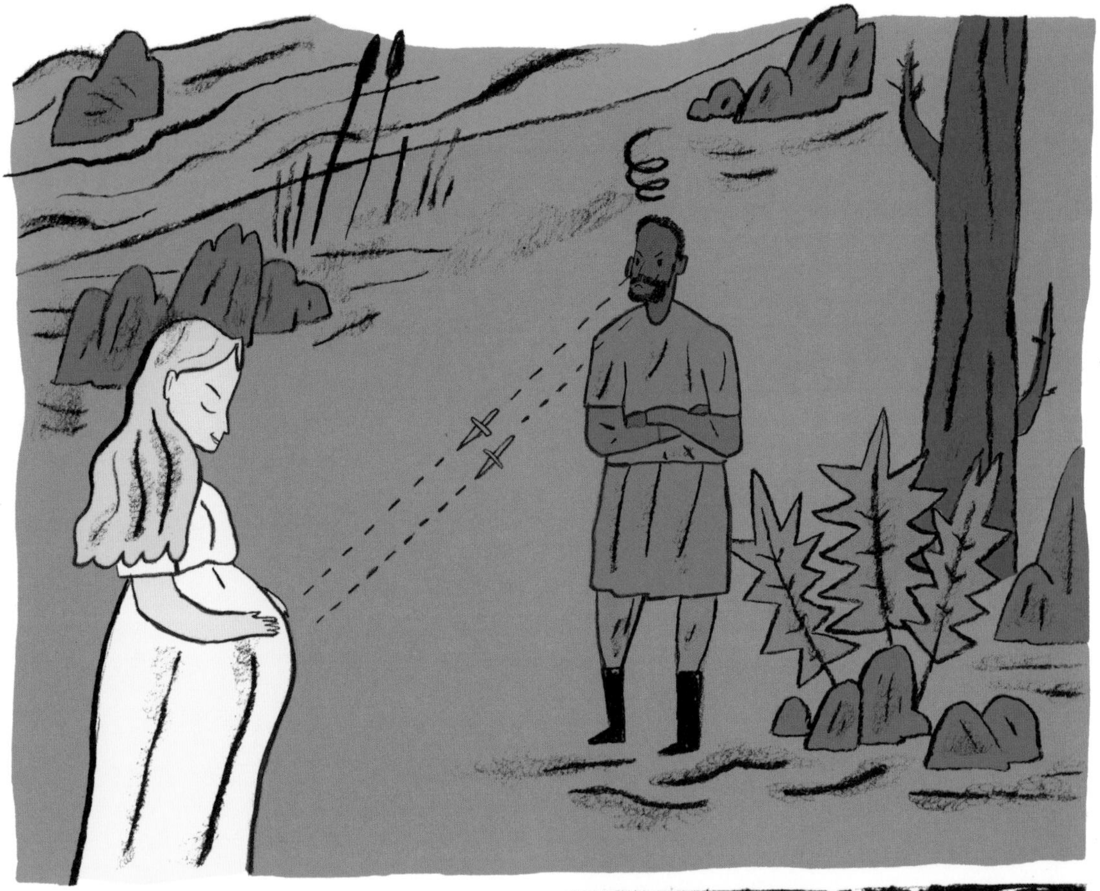

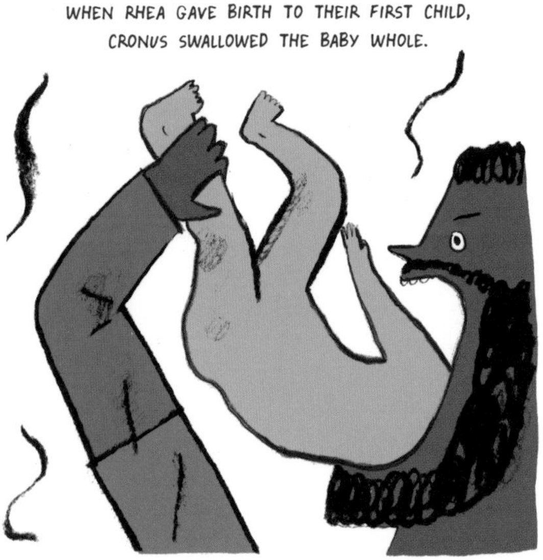
WHEN RHEA GAVE BIRTH TO THEIR FIRST CHILD, CRONUS SWALLOWED THE BABY WHOLE.

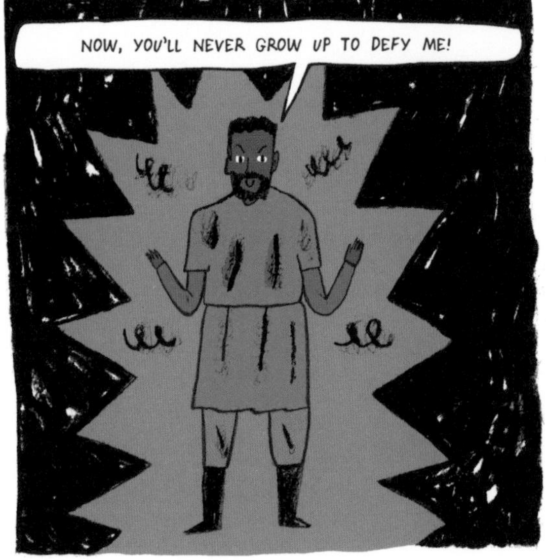
NOW, YOU'LL NEVER GROW UP TO DEFY ME!

RHEA LOST FIVE CHILDREN TO CRONUS'S APPETITES, ONE AFTER ANOTHER.

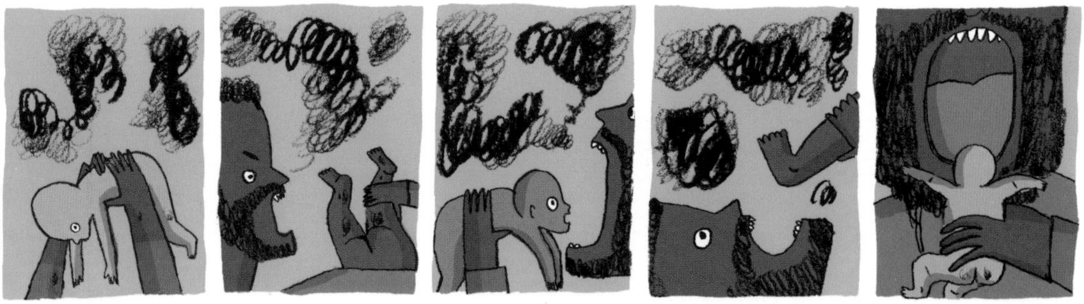

WHEN SHE WAS PREGNANT FOR A SIXTH TIME, RHEA ASKED GAIA FOR HELP. SHE COULDN'T BEAR TO LOSE ANOTHER CHILD.

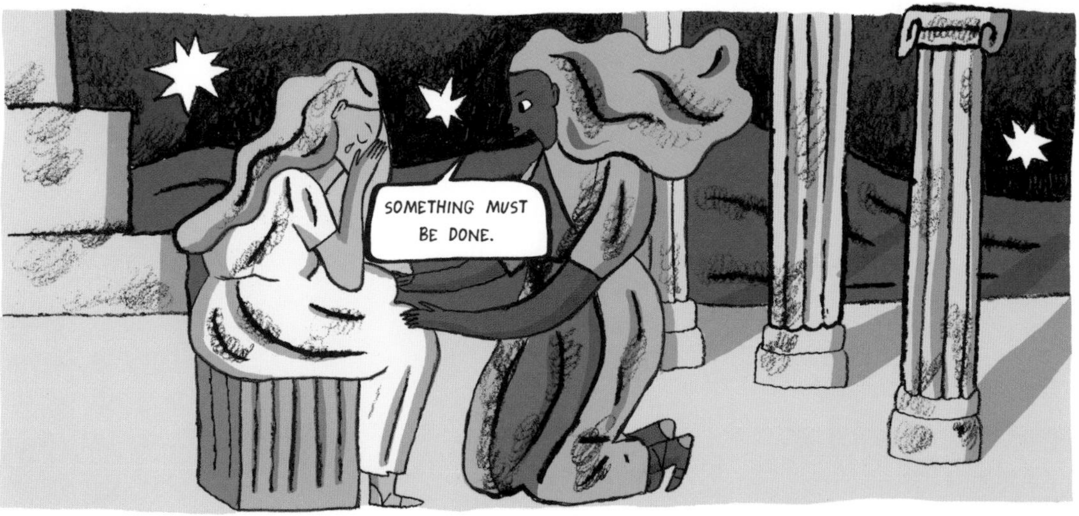
SOMETHING MUST BE DONE.

WHEN THE SIXTH BABY WAS BORN, GAIA SWADDLED UP TWO LITTLE BUNDLES. THE FIRST CONTAINED THE HAPPY LITTLE BOY, WHO GAIA QUICKLY SNUCK OUT OF THE ROOM. THE SECOND CONTAINED A ROCK. WHEN CRONUS STORMED INTO THE ROOM, HE LOOKED DOWN ON WHAT HE THOUGHT WAS HIS NEW CHILD...

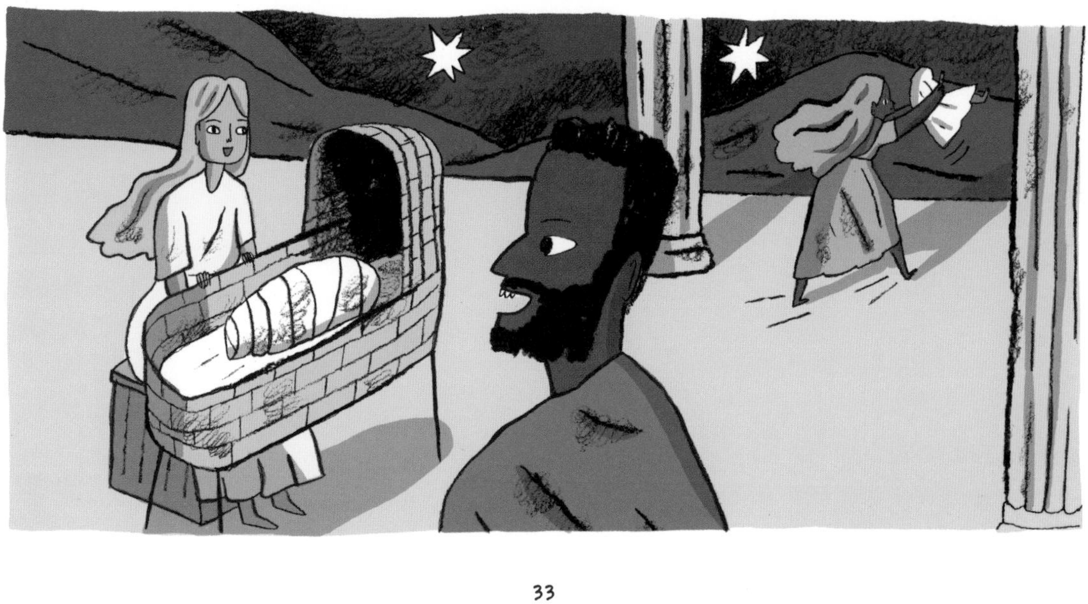

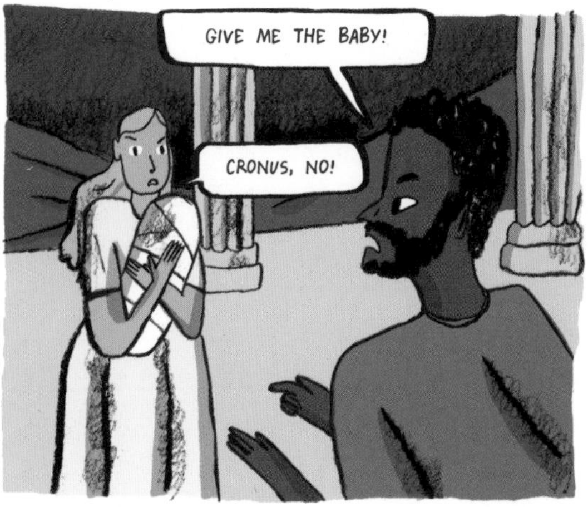
GIVE ME THE BABY!
CRONUS, NO!

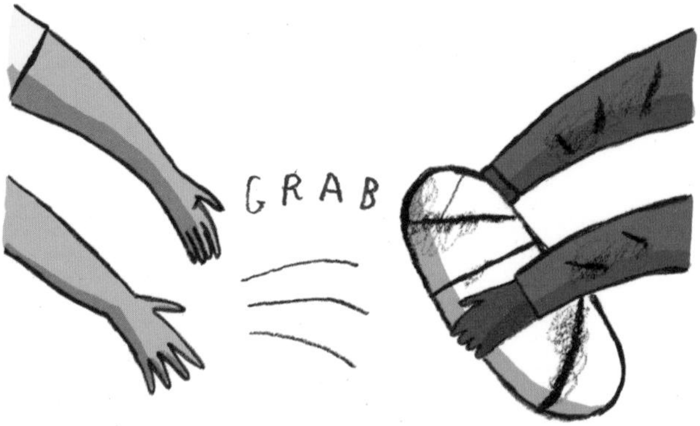
GRAB

AND HE SWALLOWED THE ROCK WHOLE.

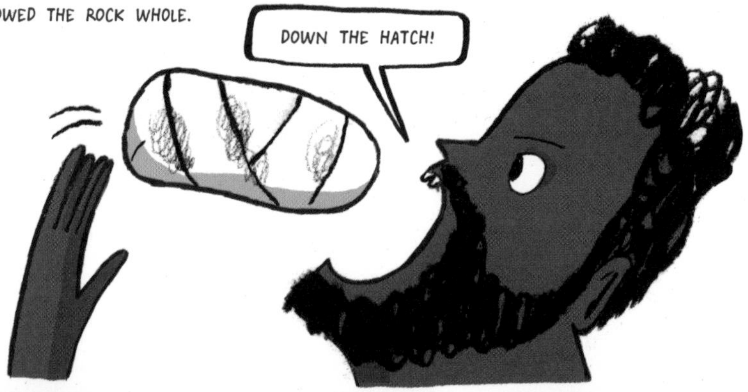
DOWN THE HATCH!

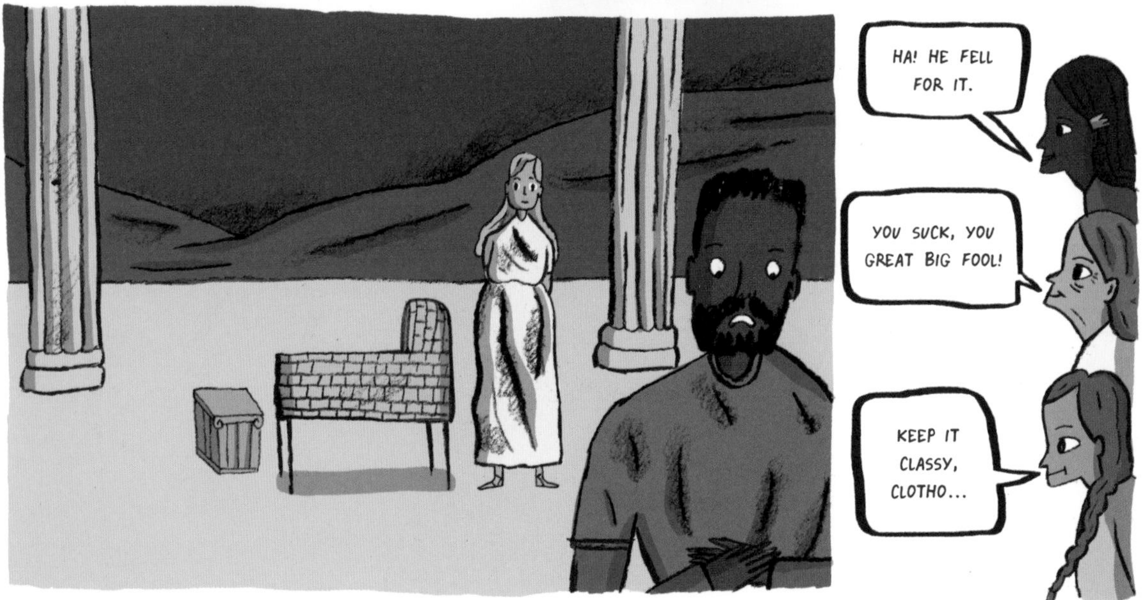
HA! HE FELL FOR IT.
YOU SUCK, YOU GREAT BIG FOOL!
KEEP IT CLASSY, CLOTHO...

AT THE TOP OF MOUNT OLYMPUS, THE HIGHEST PEAK IN GREECE, CRONUS HAD A STOMACHACHE THAT LASTED FIFTEEN LONG YEARS.

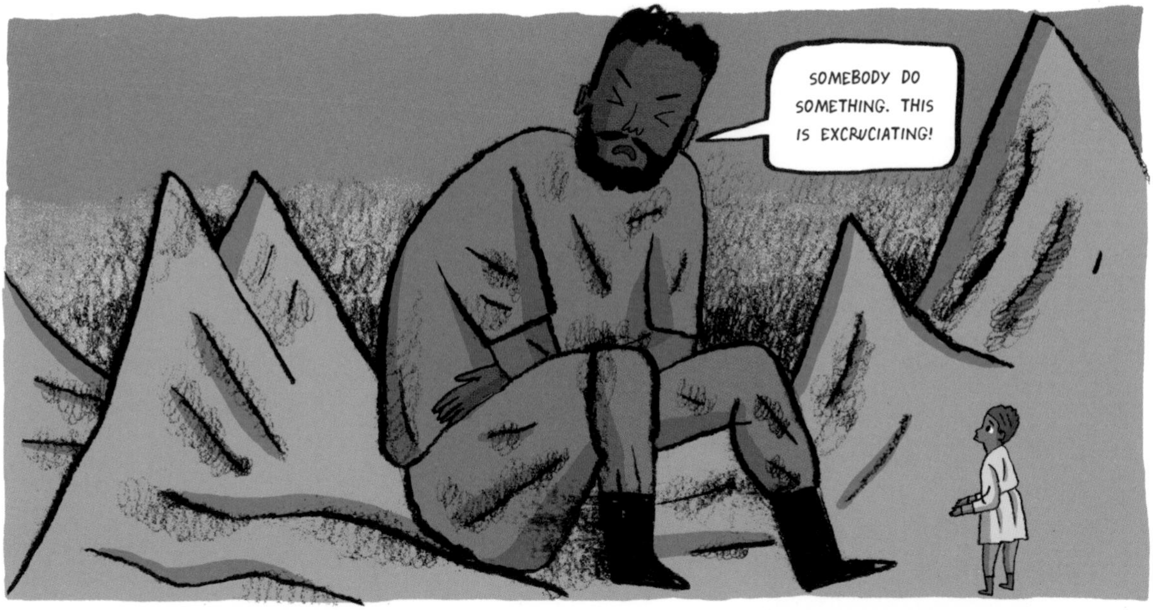
SOMEBODY DO SOMETHING. THIS IS EXCRUCIATING!

HE PUNISHED THE WORLD WITH PLAGUE, FAMINE, AND FLOODING. BUT IT MADE NO DIFFERENCE.

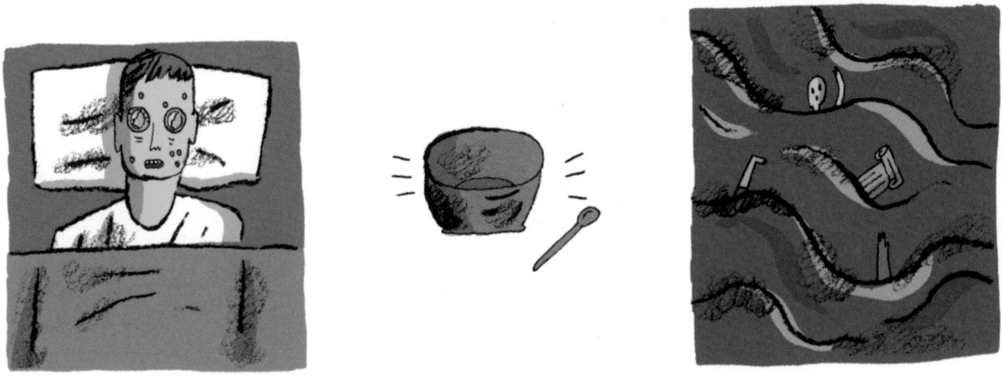

HIS STOMACH STILL TWISTED AND TURNED, TRYING TO EXPEL GAIA'S ROCK.

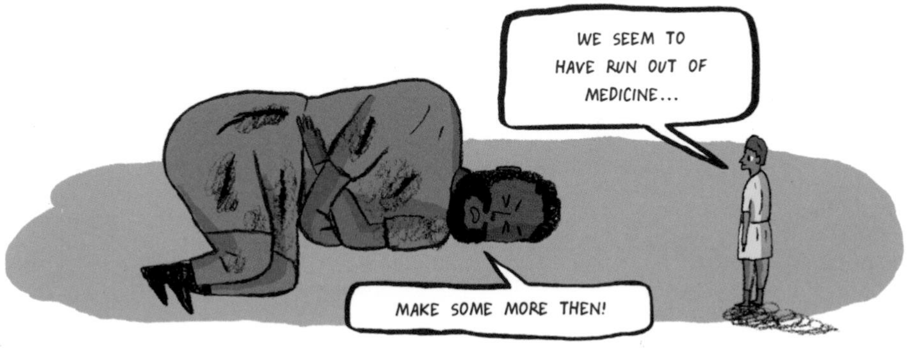
WE SEEM TO HAVE RUN OUT OF MEDICINE...
MAKE SOME MORE THEN!

PART III

Zeus

MEANWHILE, IN A LITTLE TOWN DOWN ON EARTH, GAIA AND RHEA
WERE HIDDEN AWAY AMONG THE MORTALS WITH THE CHILD, WHO THEY'D NAMED ZEUS. THE BABY GREW UP INTO A TODDLER, THEN A BOY, AND SOON HE WAS NEARLY A MAN.

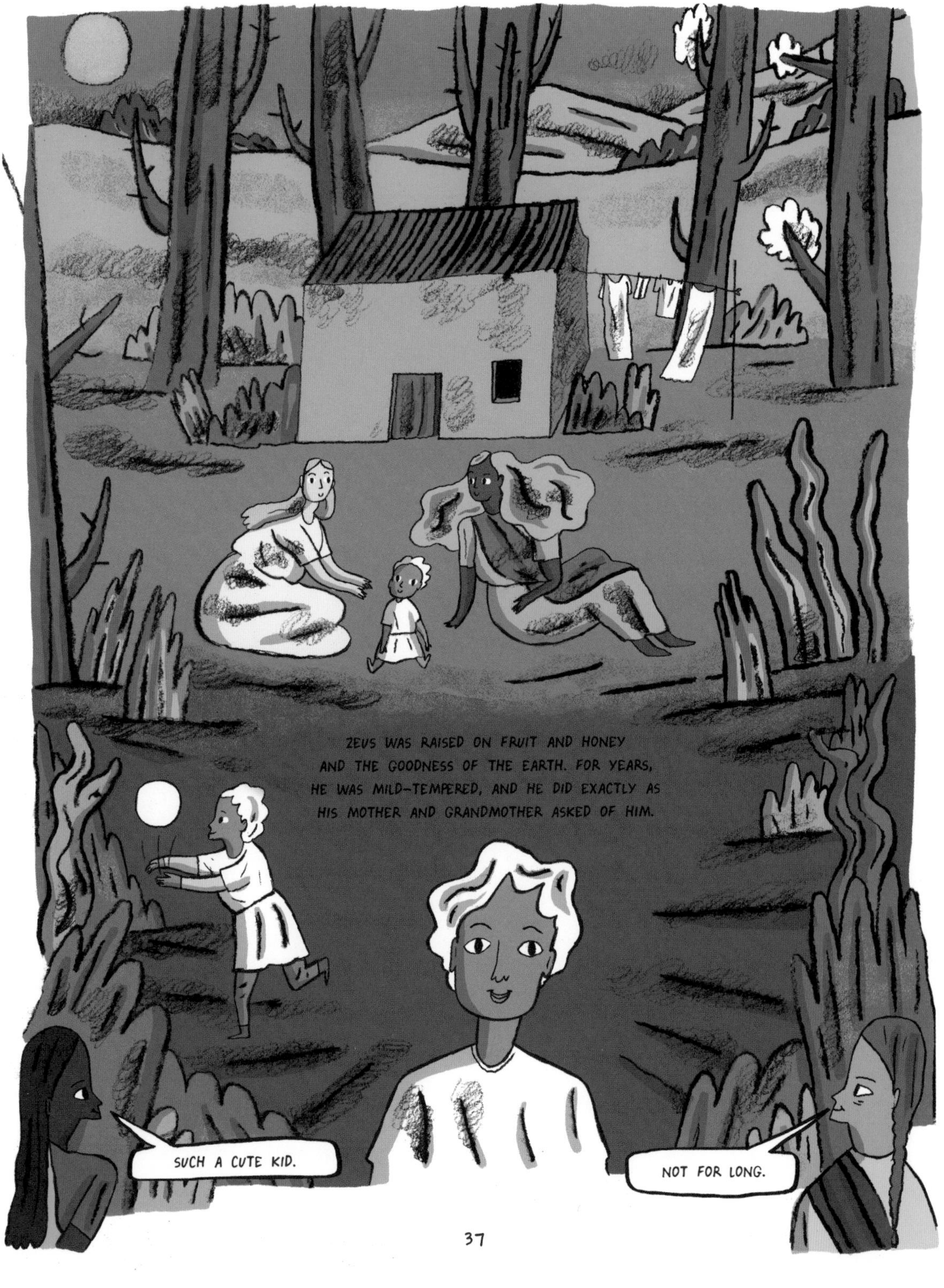

ZEUS WAS RAISED ON FRUIT AND HONEY AND THE GOODNESS OF THE EARTH. FOR YEARS, HE WAS MILD-TEMPERED, AND HE DID EXACTLY AS HIS MOTHER AND GRANDMOTHER ASKED OF HIM.
SUCH A CUTE KID.
NOT FOR LONG.

BUT WHEN ZEUS TURNED FIFTEEN, SOMETHING CHANGED. HE'D ALWAYS BEEN EXTRAORDINARILY FAST AND BEAT EVERY OTHER KID IN THE TOWN RACES, BUT NOW, HE LAUGHED IN THEIR FACES WHEN HE WON.

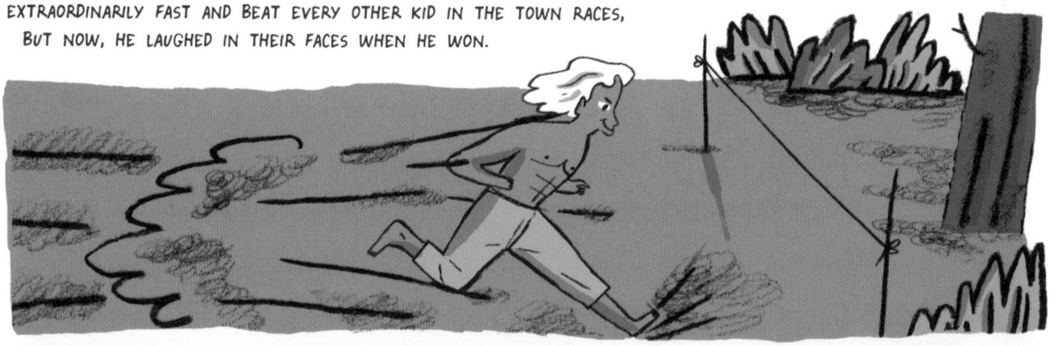

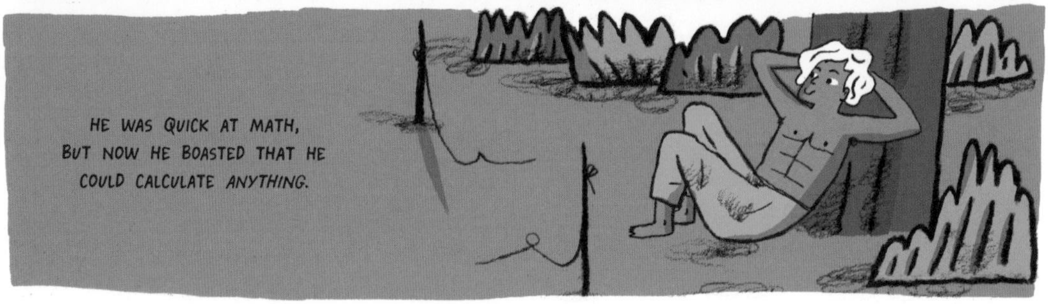
HE WAS QUICK AT MATH, BUT NOW HE BOASTED THAT HE COULD CALCULATE *ANYTHING*.

HE BECAME MORE AND MORE CONVINCED OF HIS OWN BRILLIANCE. WHEN ZEUS DISCOVERED HIS REFLECTION IN THE STILL WATERS OF THE RIVER, HE WENT BACK DAY AFTER DAY TO ADMIRE HIMSELF. HE WAS RESTLESS AND WOULDN'T DO AS HE WAS TOLD.

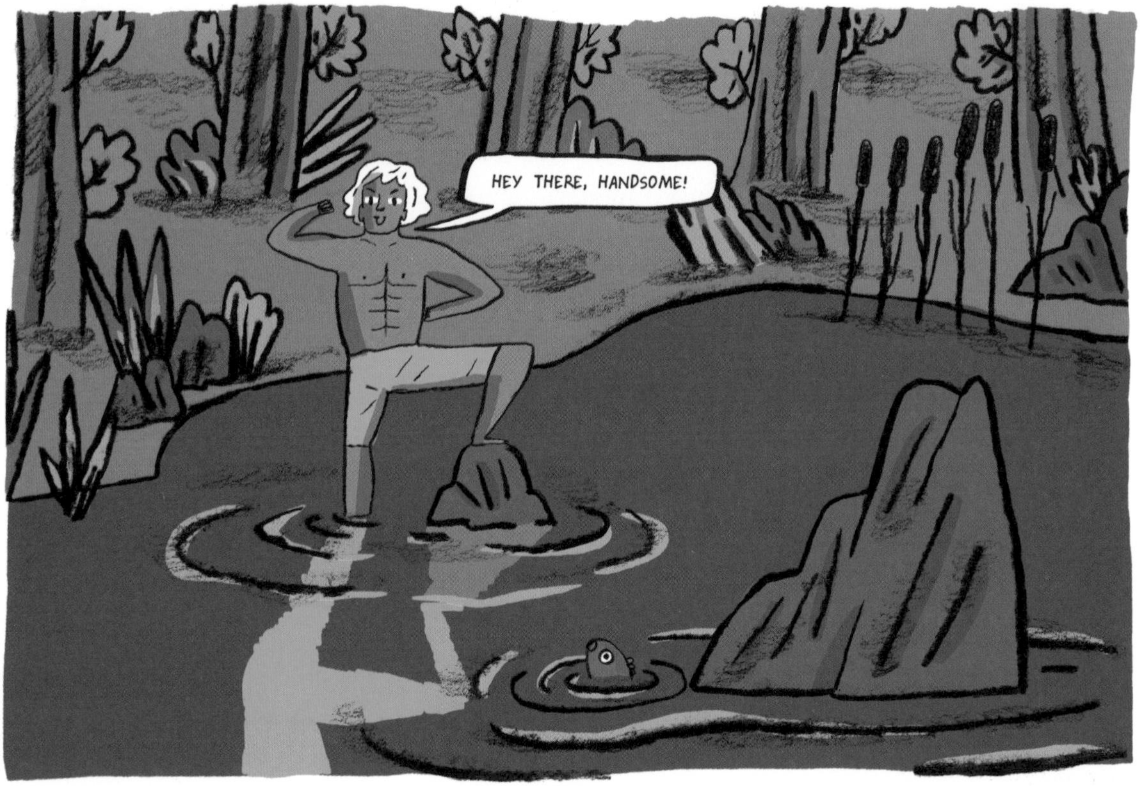
HEY THERE, HANDSOME!

GAIA WATCHED THE BOY CLOSELY. SHE RECOGNIZED THE GLINT IN HIS EYE AND THE WAY HE TAPPED HIS FINGERS ON THE TABLE IMPATIENTLY. IT HAD BEEN YEARS SINCE SHE'D HEARD THE SOUND, BUT SHE RECOGNIZED THE RHYTHM: THE DRUMBEAT OF CHAOS.

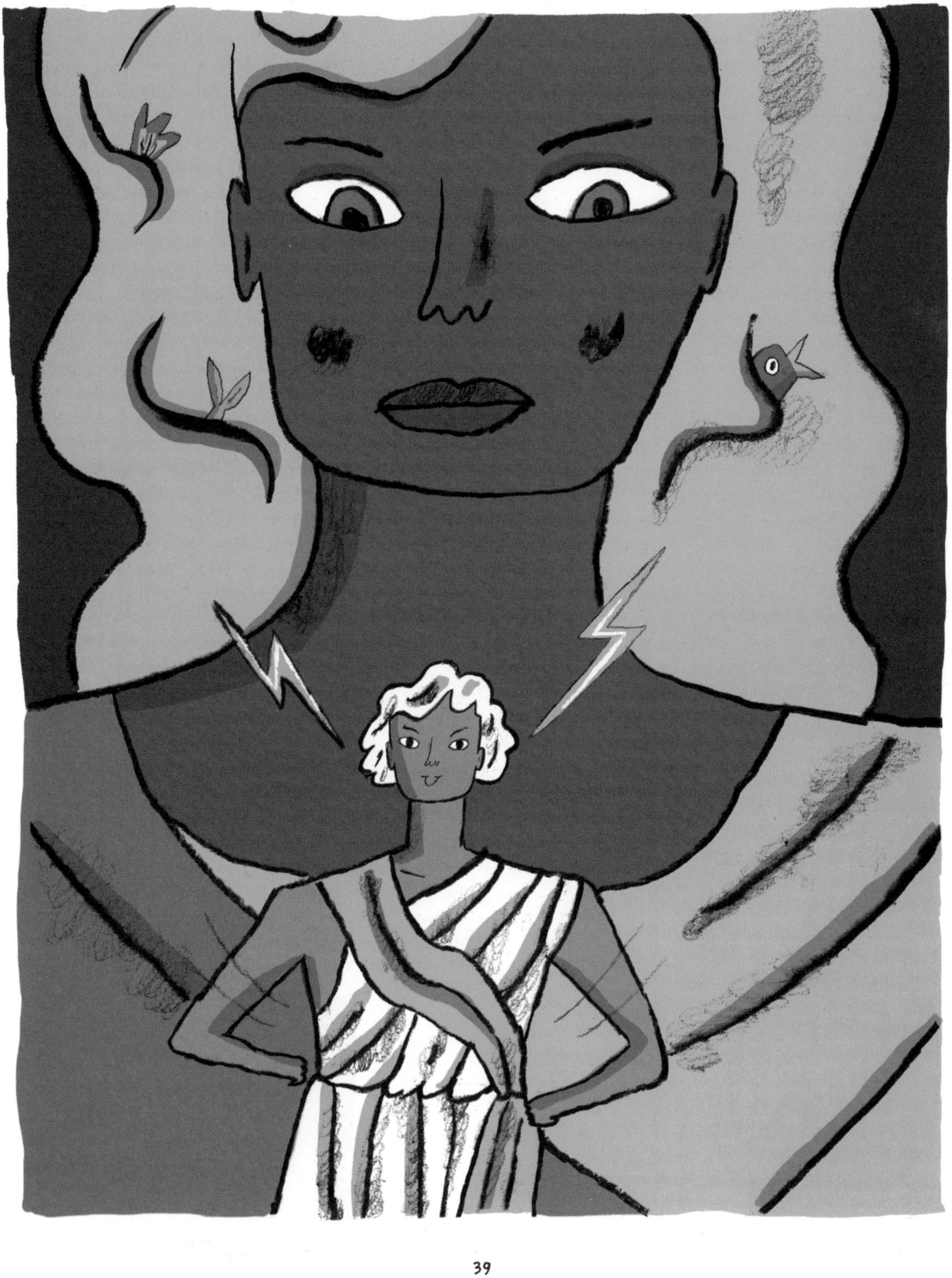

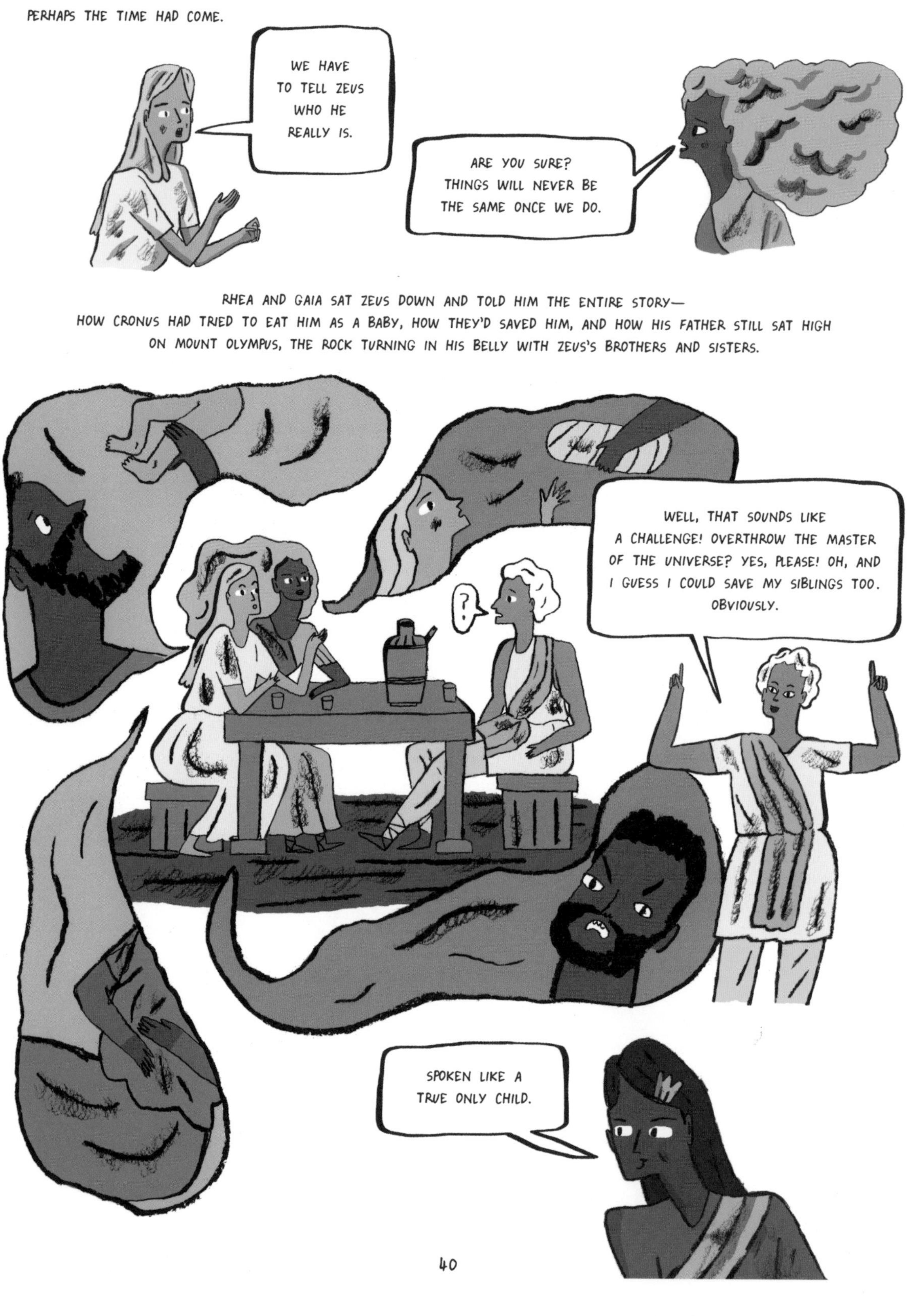
PERHAPS THE TIME HAD COME.
WE HAVE TO TELL ZEUS WHO HE REALLY IS.
ARE YOU SURE? THINGS WILL NEVER BE THE SAME ONCE WE DO.
RHEA AND GAIA SAT ZEUS DOWN AND TOLD HIM THE ENTIRE STORY— HOW CRONUS HAD TRIED TO EAT HIM AS A BABY, HOW THEY'D SAVED HIM, AND HOW HIS FATHER STILL SAT HIGH ON MOUNT OLYMPUS, THE ROCK TURNING IN HIS BELLY WITH ZEUS'S BROTHERS AND SISTERS.
?
WELL, THAT SOUNDS LIKE A CHALLENGE! OVERTHROW THE MASTER OF THE UNIVERSE? YES, PLEASE! OH, AND I GUESS I COULD SAVE MY SIBLINGS TOO. OBVIOUSLY.
SPOKEN LIKE A TRUE ONLY CHILD.

ZEUS PACKED A BAG AND SET OUT FOR MOUNT OLYMPUS. HE CROSSED HILLS AND PLAINS, TRAVERSED FORESTS AND GLADES, AND WHEN HE REACHED THE FOOT OF THE MOUNTAIN, HE SWORE HE WOULDN'T RETURN UNTIL HIS FATHER WAS DEFEATED.

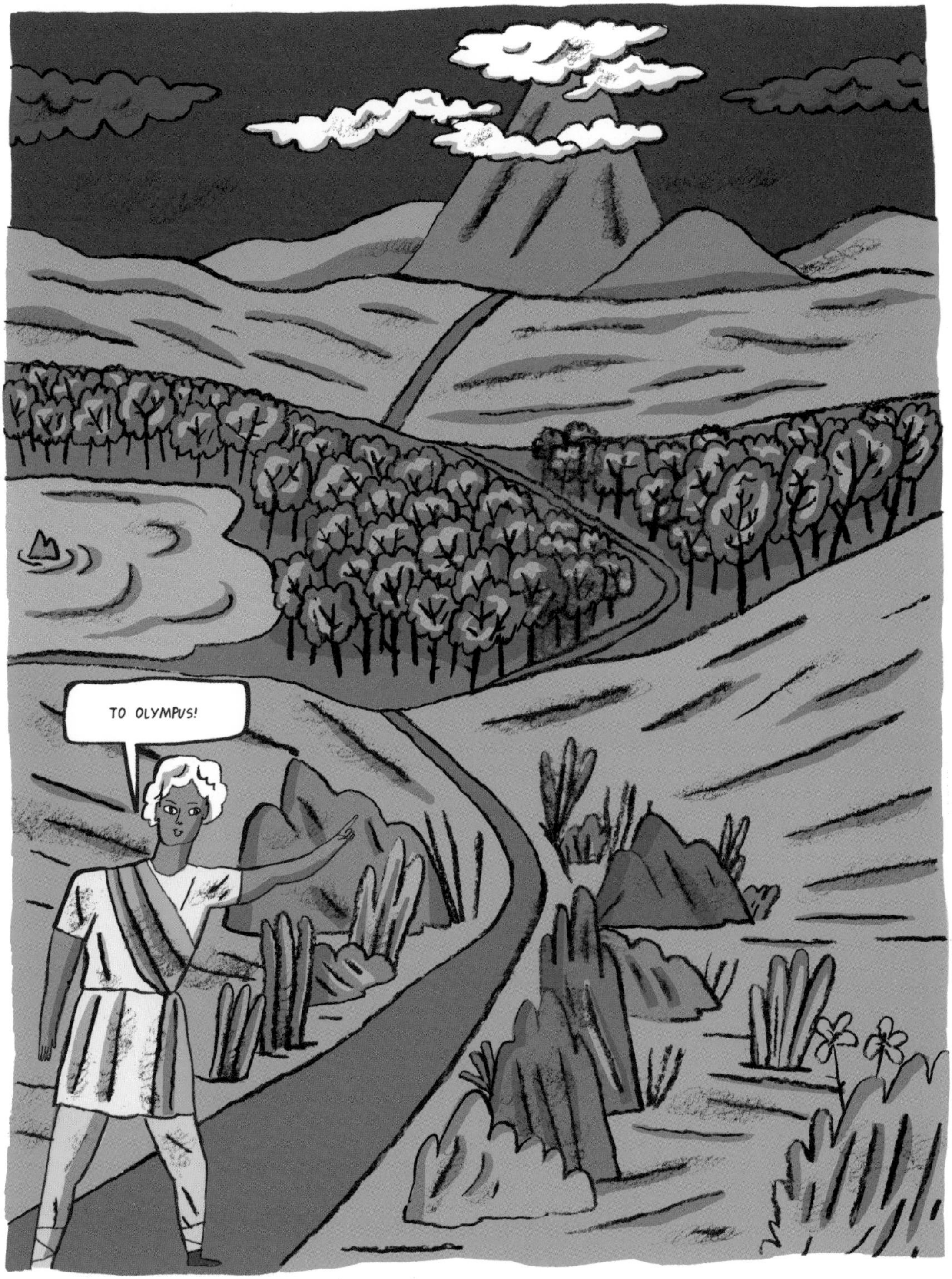
TO OLYMPUS!

ZEUS ARRIVED BREATHLESS AND WEARING A CUNNING DISGUISE.

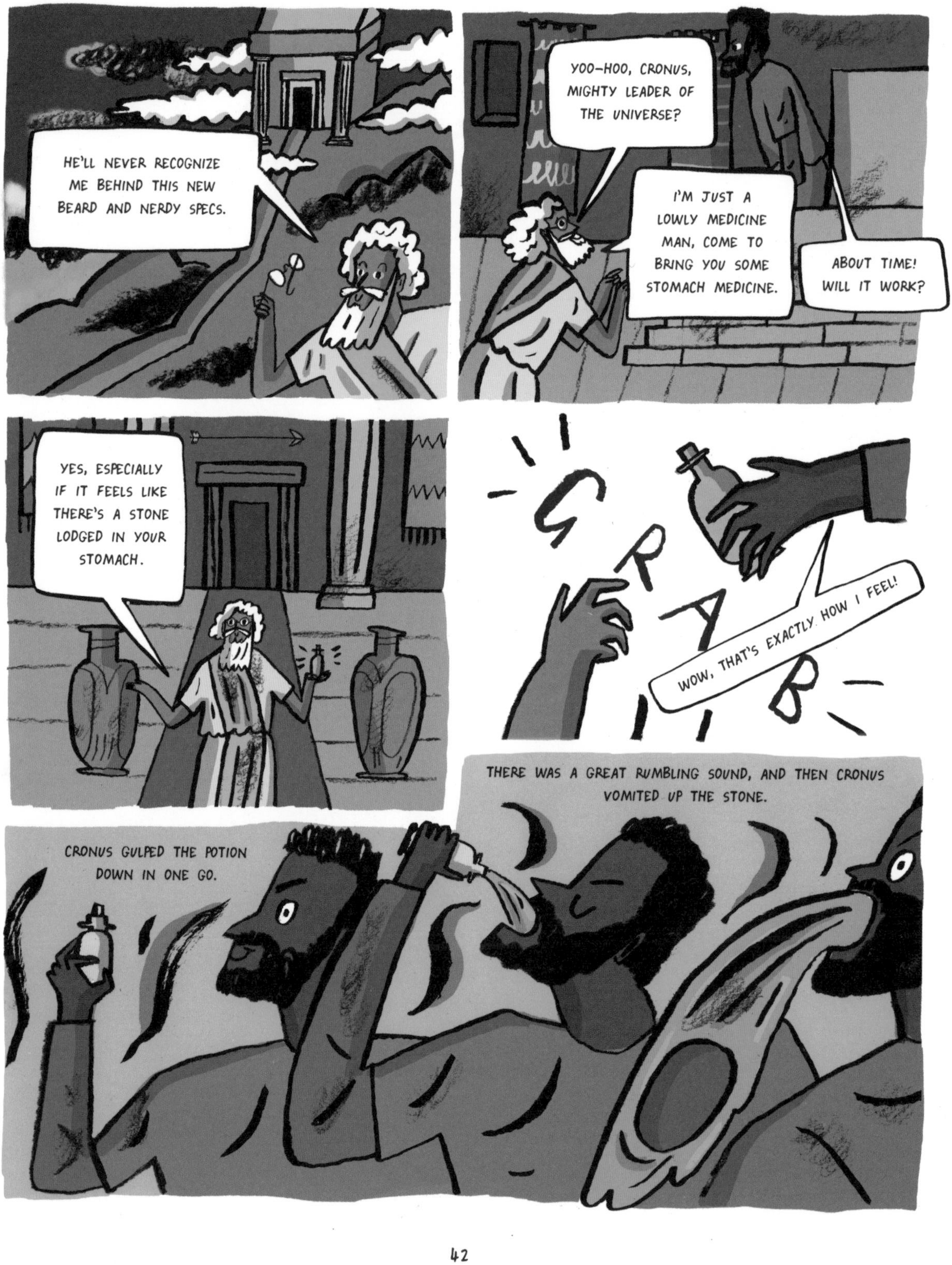

HE'LL NEVER RECOGNIZE ME BEHIND THIS NEW BEARD AND NERDY SPECS.
YOO-HOO, CRONUS, MIGHTY LEADER OF THE UNIVERSE?
I'M JUST A LOWLY MEDICINE MAN, COME TO BRING YOU SOME STOMACH MEDICINE.
ABOUT TIME! WILL IT WORK?
YES, ESPECIALLY IF IT FEELS LIKE THERE'S A STONE LODGED IN YOUR STOMACH.
GRAB
WOW, THAT'S EXACTLY HOW I FEEL!
THERE WAS A GREAT RUMBLING SOUND, AND THEN CRONUS VOMITED UP THE STONE.
CRONUS GULPED THE POTION DOWN IN ONE GO.

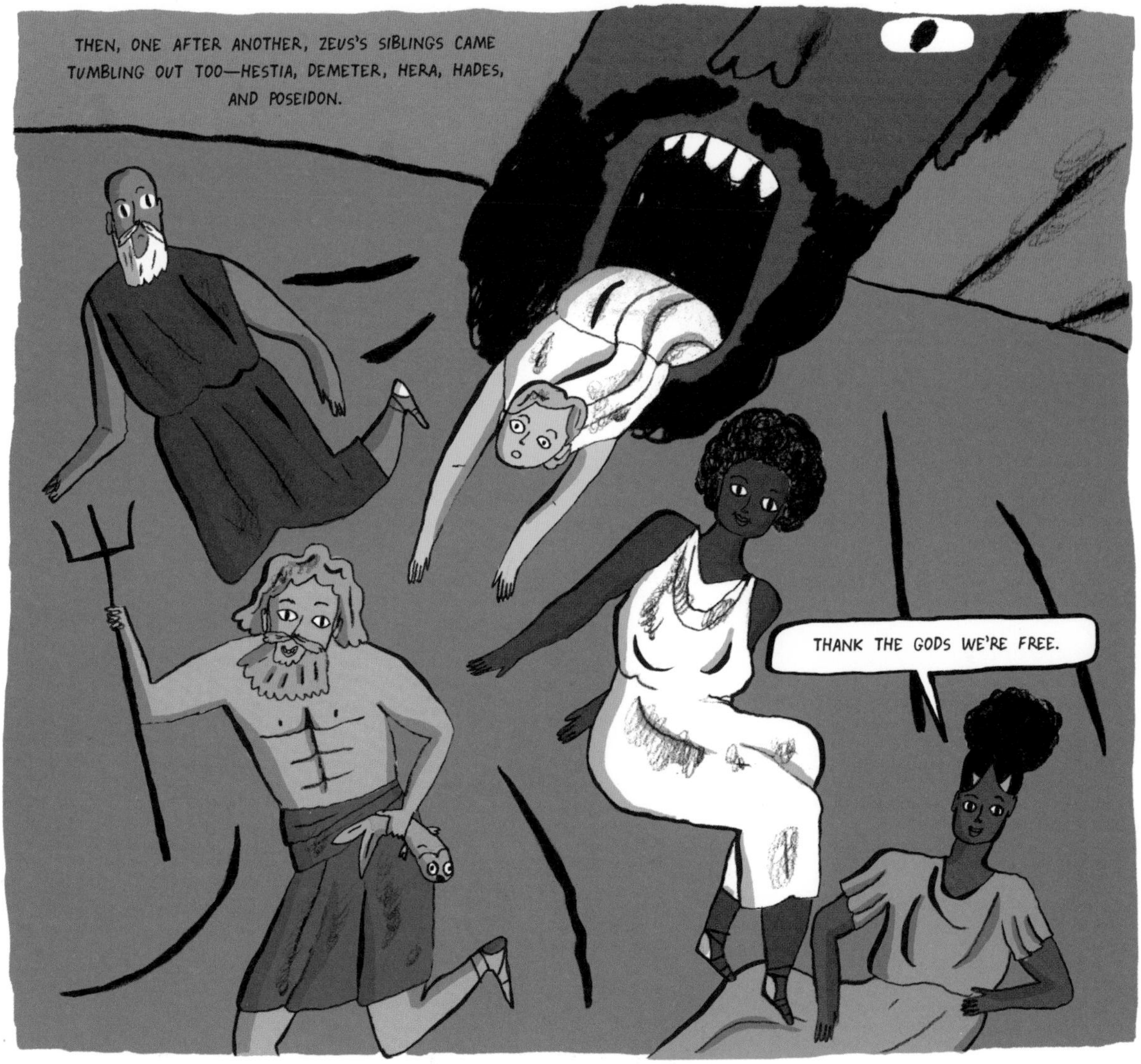
THEN, ONE AFTER ANOTHER, ZEUS'S SIBLINGS CAME TUMBLING OUT TOO—HESTIA, DEMETER, HERA, HADES, AND POSEIDON.
THANK THE GODS WE'RE FREE.

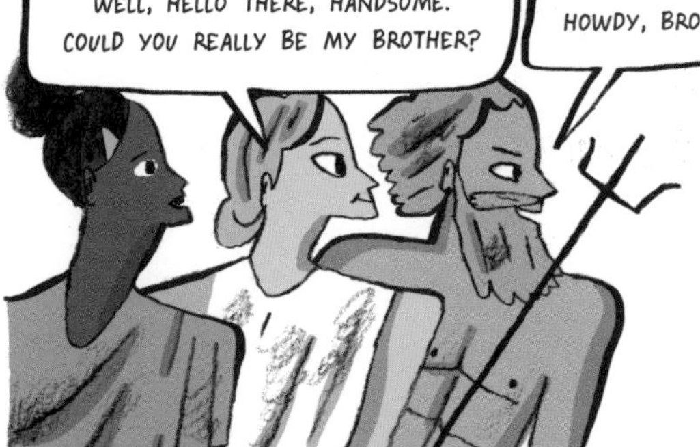
WELL, HELLO THERE, HANDSOME. COULD YOU REALLY BE MY BROTHER?
HOWDY, BRO.

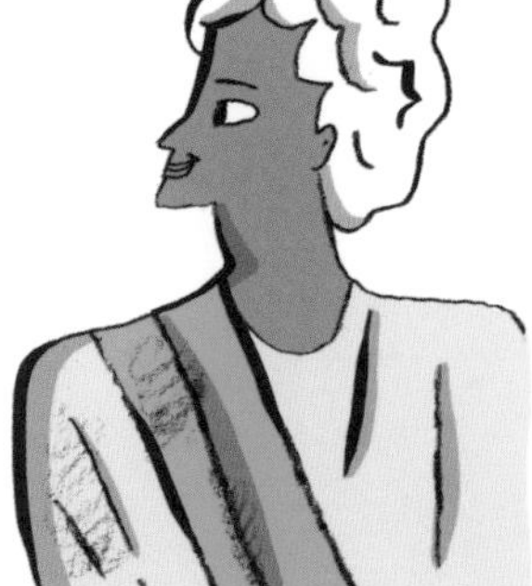

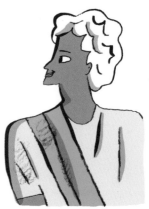

PART IV

The Olympians

ZEUS AND HIS SIBLINGS WERE THE NEW KIDS IN TOWN. THEY CALLED THEMSELVES THE OLYMPIANS, AND THEY INTENDED TO WAGE WAR AGAINST THE OLD GODS, THE TITANS. CRONUS SAW THAT HIS GREATEST FEAR HAD COME TRUE, SO HE FLED BEFORE HIS CHILDREN COULD TURN ON HIM.

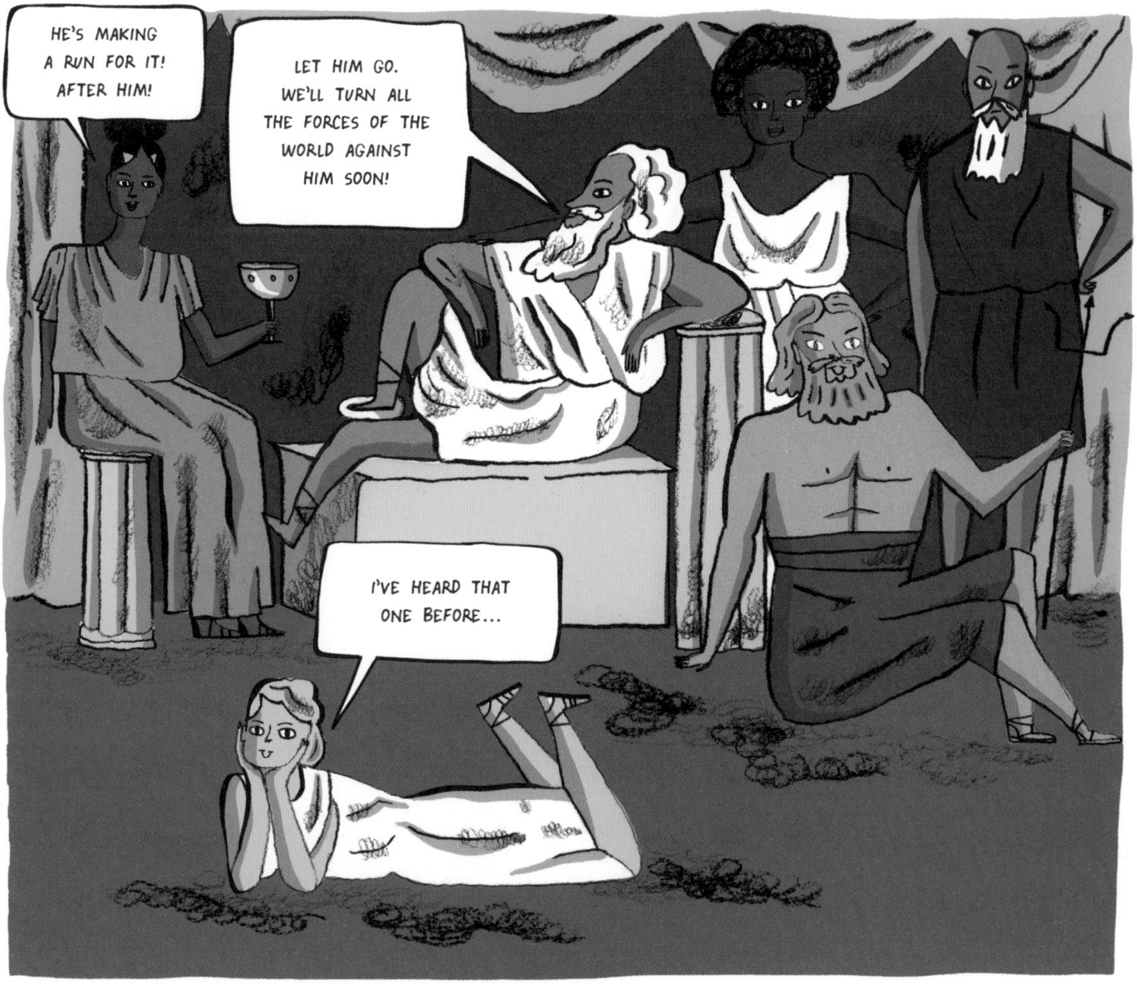
HE'S MAKING A RUN FOR IT! AFTER HIM!
LET HIM GO. WE'LL TURN ALL THE FORCES OF THE WORLD AGAINST HIM SOON!
I'VE HEARD THAT ONE BEFORE...

CRONUS HAD SULKED AWAY LIKE HIS FATHER BEFORE HIM. BUT, UNLIKE HIS FATHER, HE HAD THE MIGHT OF THE TITANS ON HIS SIDE. IN THE SHADOW OF THE EARTH, CRONUS GATHERED HIS EVIL FORCES.

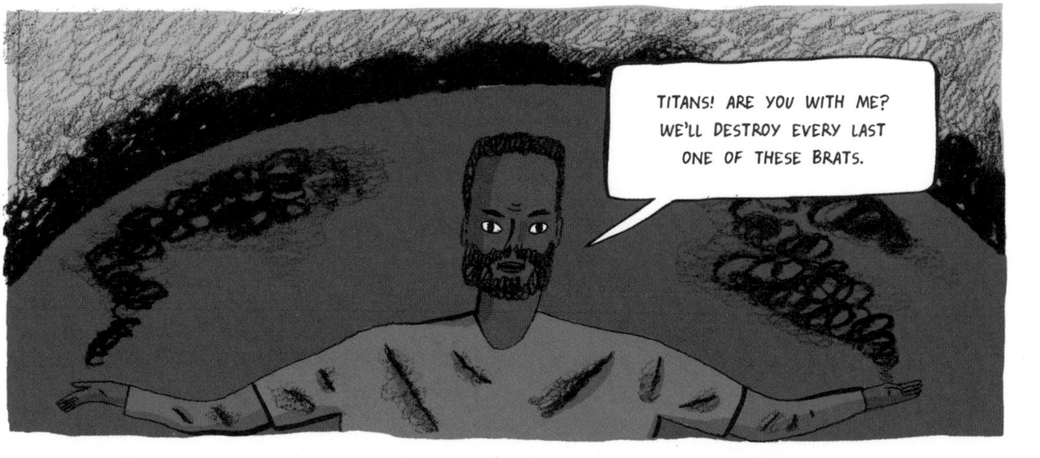
TITANS! ARE YOU WITH ME? WE'LL DESTROY EVERY LAST ONE OF THESE BRATS.

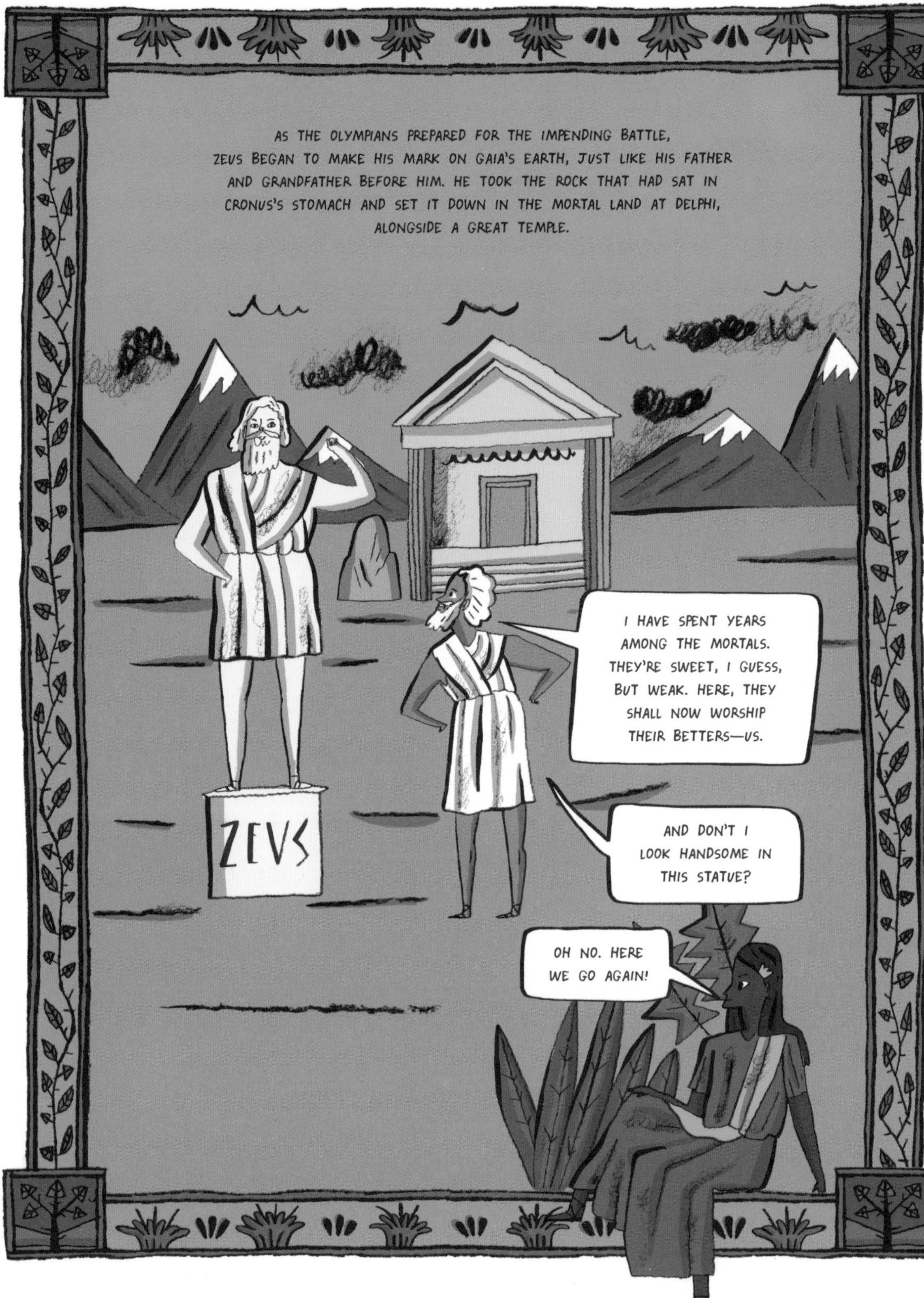
AS THE OLYMPIANS PREPARED FOR THE IMPENDING BATTLE, ZEUS BEGAN TO MAKE HIS MARK ON GAIA'S EARTH, JUST LIKE HIS FATHER AND GRANDFATHER BEFORE HIM. HE TOOK THE ROCK THAT HAD SAT IN CRONUS'S STOMACH AND SET IT DOWN IN THE MORTAL LAND AT DELPHI, ALONGSIDE A GREAT TEMPLE.
ZEUS
I HAVE SPENT YEARS AMONG THE MORTALS. THEY'RE SWEET, I GUESS, BUT WEAK. HERE, THEY SHALL NOW WORSHIP THEIR BETTERS—US.
AND DON'T I LOOK HANDSOME IN THIS STATUE?
OH NO. HERE WE GO AGAIN!

FOR ZEUS AND HIS SIBLINGS, A WAR WAS AN EXCITING OPPORTUNITY FOR THEM TO TEST THEIR POWERS. POSEIDON WAS THE SLY GOD OF THE SEA, WHILE HADES GUARDED THE GREAT GLOOM OF THE UNDERWORLD.

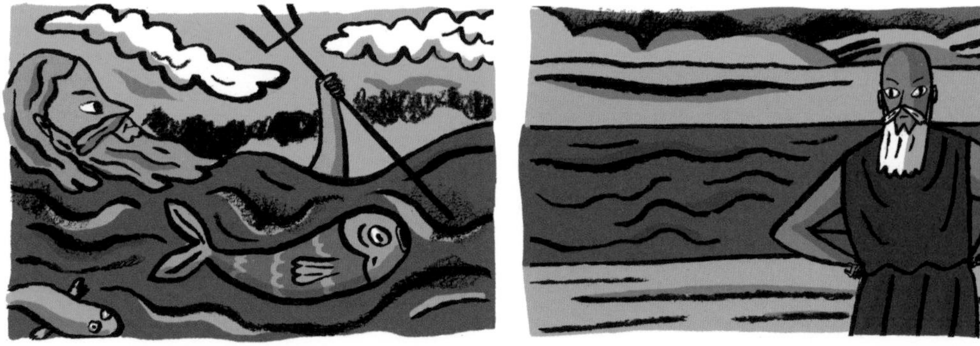

DEMETER TOOK AFTER GAIA AND CARED FOR THE FIELDS AND FRUIT OF THE EARTH, WHILE HERA WATCHED OVER THE WOMEN OF THE WORLD, AND HESTIA WAS THE GREAT PROTECTOR OF THE HOME.

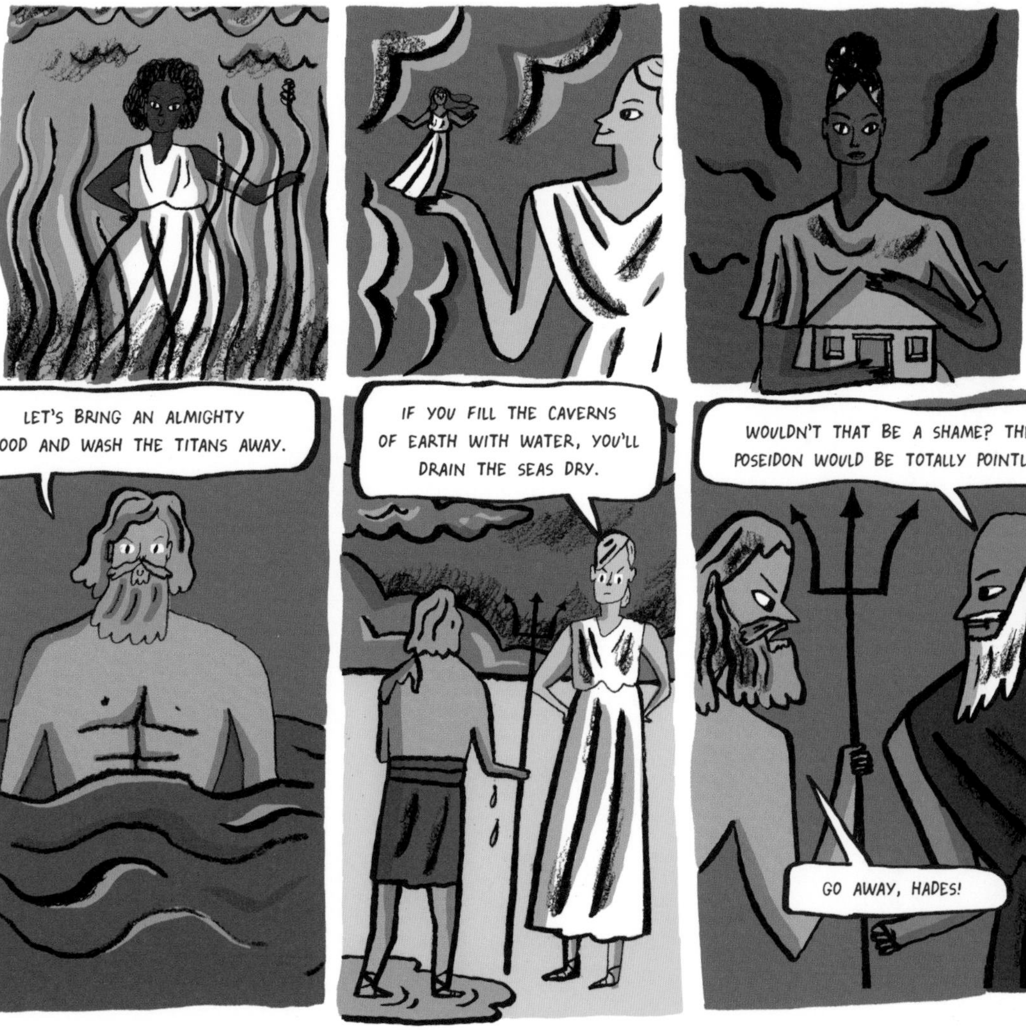
LET'S BRING AN ALMIGHTY FLOOD AND WASH THE TITANS AWAY.
IF YOU FILL THE CAVERNS OF EARTH WITH WATER, YOU'LL DRAIN THE SEAS DRY.
WOULDN'T THAT BE A SHAME? THEN POSEIDON WOULD BE TOTALLY POINTLESS.
GO AWAY, HADES!

GAIA LISTENED TO THEIR SCHEMES TO TURN THE WORLD UPSIDE DOWN AND WENT TO ZEUS, PLEADING WITH HIM TO STOP THE WAR. GAIA HATED TO SEE THE TITANS AND THE OLYMPIANS TURNING ON EACH OTHER—THEY WERE ALL HER CHILDREN; SHE'D CREATED EACH AND EVERY ONE OF THEM.

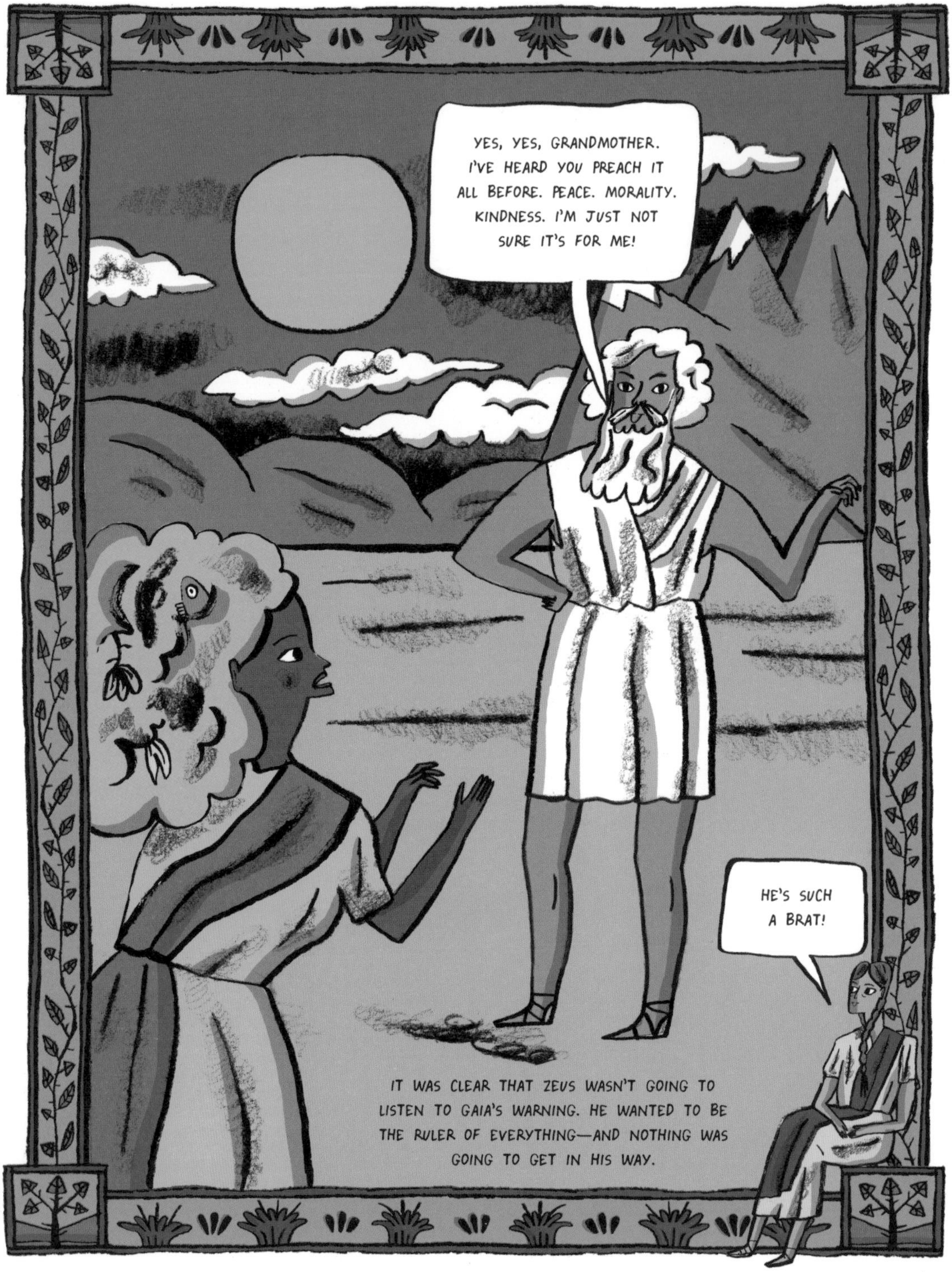
YES, YES, GRANDMOTHER. I'VE HEARD YOU PREACH IT ALL BEFORE. PEACE. MORALITY. KINDNESS. I'M JUST NOT SURE IT'S FOR ME!
HE'S SUCH A BRAT!
IT WAS CLEAR THAT ZEUS WASN'T GOING TO LISTEN TO GAIA'S WARNING. HE WANTED TO BE THE RULER OF EVERYTHING—AND NOTHING WAS GOING TO GET IN HIS WAY.

THE WAR BETWEEN THE TITANS AND THE OLYMPIANS RAGED FOR TEN LONG YEARS. ALL WAS DARKNESS AND TERROR, AND THE MORTALS WERE CAUGHT IN THE MIDDLE OF IT. THEIR CITIES BURNED, AND THE PEOPLE FLED, BY LAND OR SEA, ON FOOT OR IN BOATS, ALL DESPERATE TO ESCAPE. THE FORESTS SMOLDERED, THE SEAS CHURNED, AND THE ANIMALS WERE THROWN FROM THEIR HABITATS.

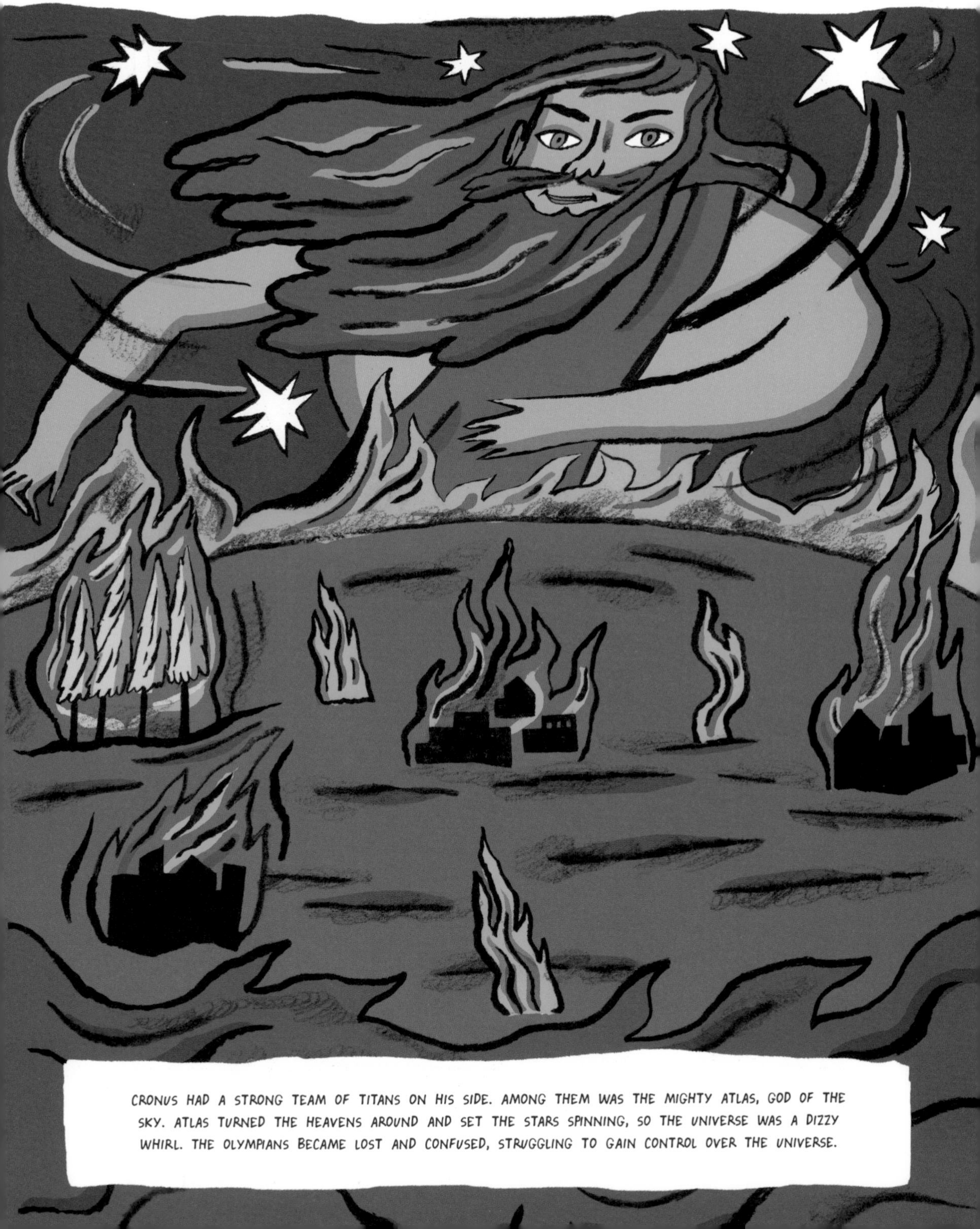

CRONUS HAD A STRONG TEAM OF TITANS ON HIS SIDE. AMONG THEM WAS THE MIGHTY ATLAS, GOD OF THE SKY. ATLAS TURNED THE HEAVENS AROUND AND SET THE STARS SPINNING, SO THE UNIVERSE WAS A DIZZY WHIRL. THE OLYMPIANS BECAME LOST AND CONFUSED, STRUGGLING TO GAIN CONTROL OVER THE UNIVERSE.

ZEUS NEEDED SOMETHING THAT COULD STOP ATLAS'S POWER, SOMETHING THAT COULD CONQUER THE SKIES. HE WENT TO SEE THE CYCLOPSES, FEARSOME ONE-EYED CREATURES THAT GAIA HAD CREATED IN THE FIRST DAYS OF THE WORLD WHEN EVERYTHING WAS A STRANGE EXPERIMENT. BECAUSE OF THEIR TERRIFYING APPEARANCE, THE CYCLOPSES LIVED HIDDEN AWAY, BUT GAIA HAD GIVEN THEM EXTRAORDINARY POWERS, AND ZEUS WANTED TO HARNESS THAT.

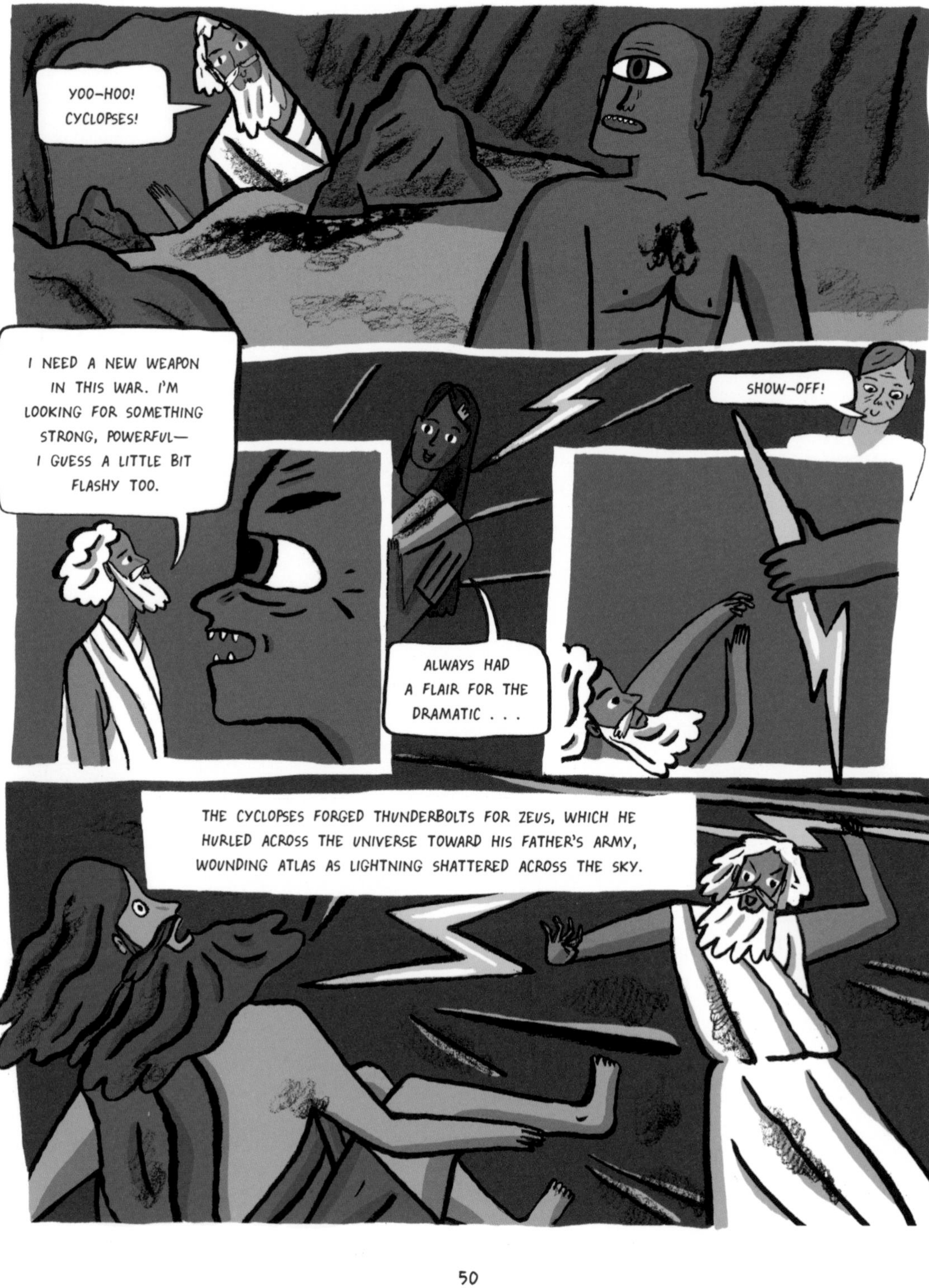
YOO-HOO! CYCLOPSES!
I NEED A NEW WEAPON IN THIS WAR. I'M LOOKING FOR SOMETHING STRONG, POWERFUL— I GUESS A LITTLE BIT FLASHY TOO.
ALWAYS HAD A FLAIR FOR THE DRAMATIC . . .
SHOW-OFF!
THE CYCLOPSES FORGED THUNDERBOLTS FOR ZEUS, WHICH HE HURLED ACROSS THE UNIVERSE TOWARD HIS FATHER'S ARMY, WOUNDING ATLAS AS LIGHTNING SHATTERED ACROSS THE SKY.

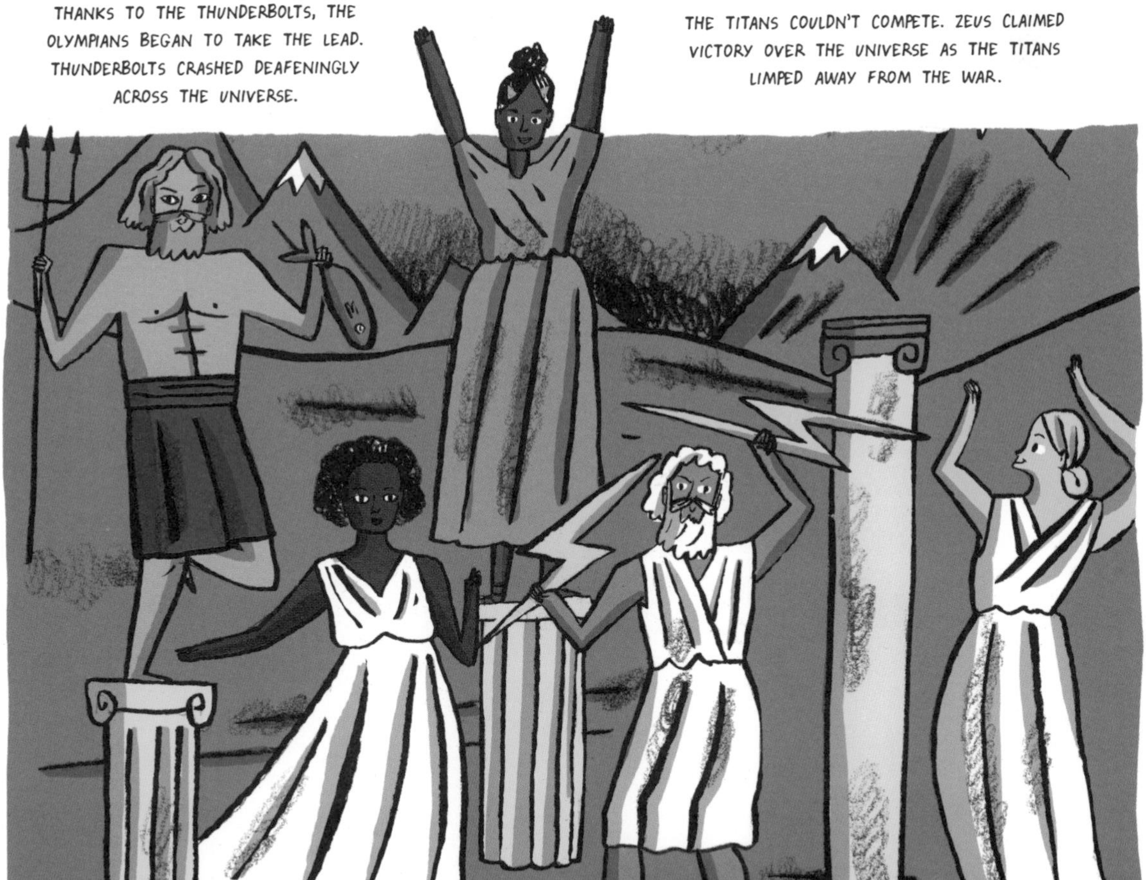
THANKS TO THE THUNDERBOLTS, THE OLYMPIANS BEGAN TO TAKE THE LEAD. THUNDERBOLTS CRASHED DEAFENINGLY ACROSS THE UNIVERSE.
THE TITANS COULDN'T COMPETE. ZEUS CLAIMED VICTORY OVER THE UNIVERSE AS THE TITANS LIMPED AWAY FROM THE WAR.

THE OLYMPIANS HAD DEFEATED THE TITANS OF OLD, AND ZEUS LOCKED HIS FATHER, CRONUS, AWAY IN THE DEPTHS OF THE EARTH. AS FOR THE OTHER TITANS WHO HAD SUPPORTED CRONUS, ZEUS LOCKED THEM IN THE DARKNESS TOO. ALL EXCEPT FOR ATLAS...

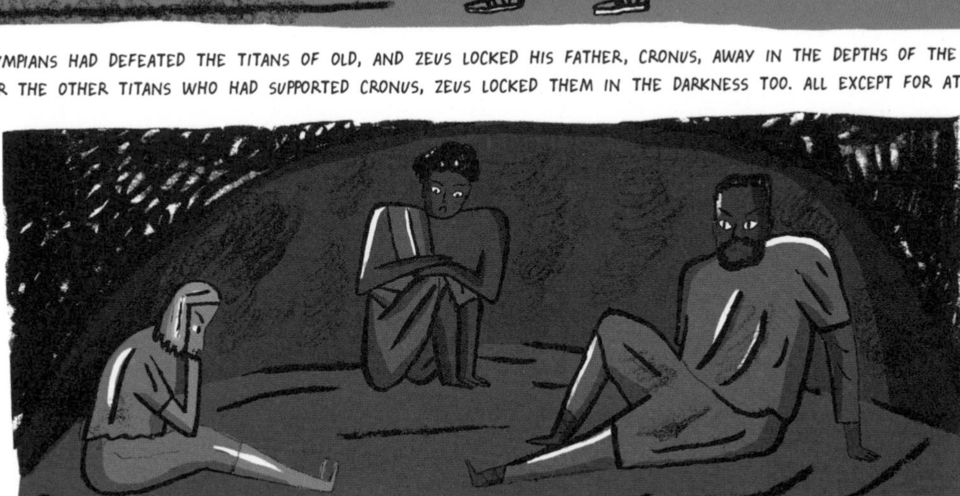

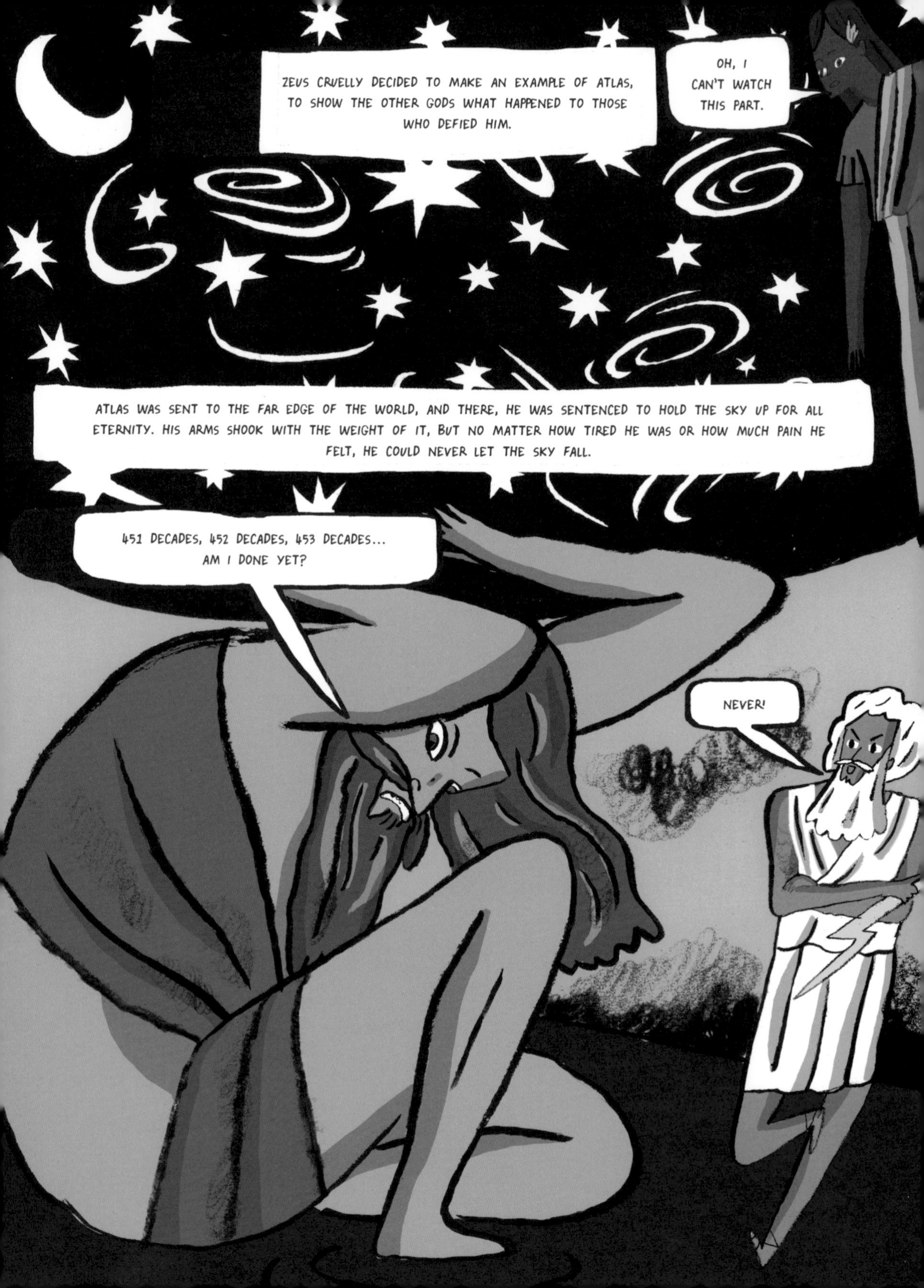

ZEUS CRUELLY DECIDED TO MAKE AN EXAMPLE OF ATLAS, TO SHOW THE OTHER GODS WHAT HAPPENED TO THOSE WHO DEFIED HIM.
OH, I CAN'T WATCH THIS PART.
ATLAS WAS SENT TO THE FAR EDGE OF THE WORLD, AND THERE, HE WAS SENTENCED TO HOLD THE SKY UP FOR ALL ETERNITY. HIS ARMS SHOOK WITH THE WEIGHT OF IT, BUT NO MATTER HOW TIRED HE WAS OR HOW MUCH PAIN HE FELT, HE COULD NEVER LET THE SKY FALL.
451 DECADES, 452 DECADES, 453 DECADES... AM I DONE YET?
NEVER!

PART V

Gaia Fights Back

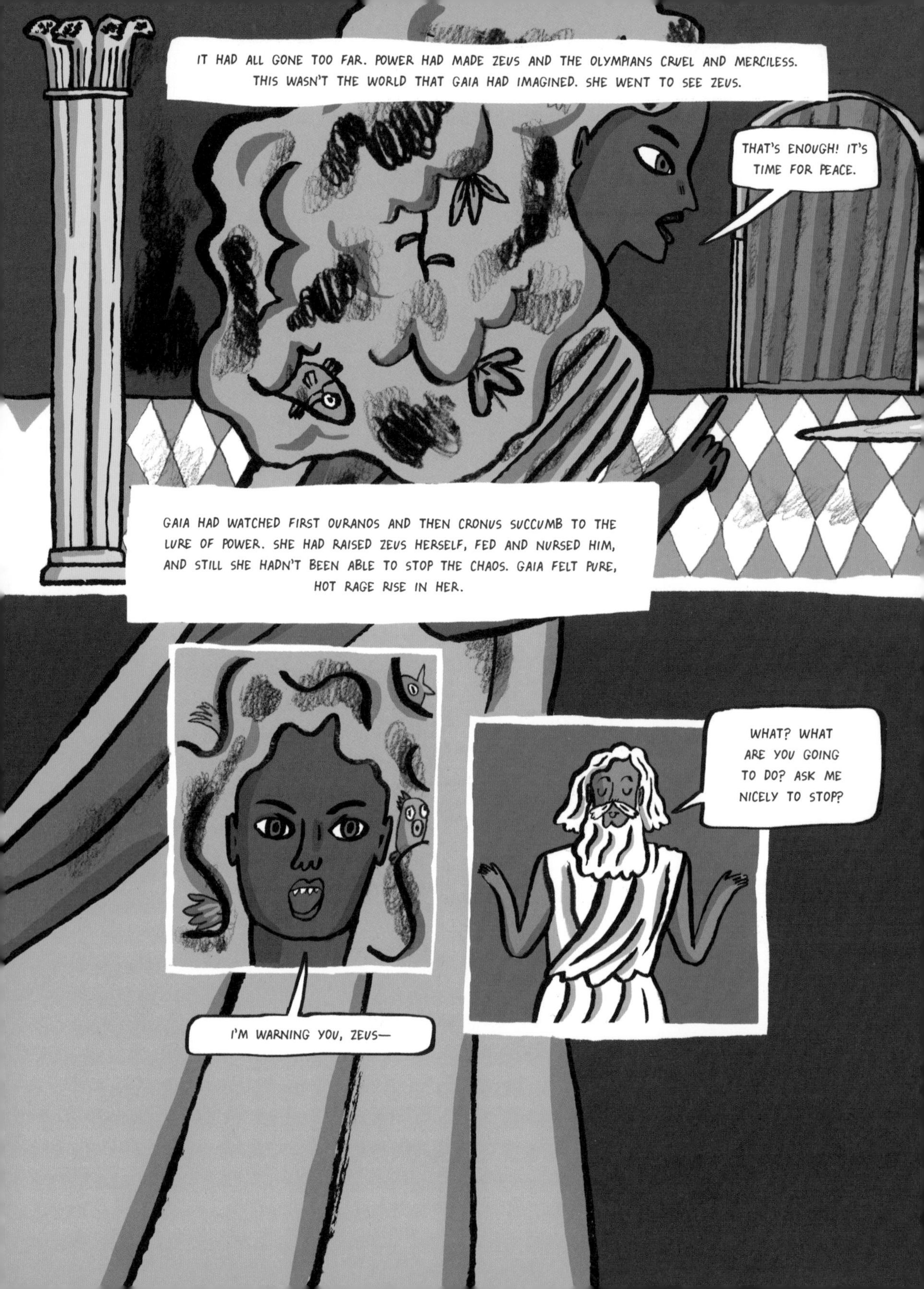
IT HAD ALL GONE TOO FAR. POWER HAD MADE ZEUS AND THE OLYMPIANS CRUEL AND MERCILESS. THIS WASN'T THE WORLD THAT GAIA HAD IMAGINED. SHE WENT TO SEE ZEUS.
THAT'S ENOUGH! IT'S TIME FOR PEACE.
GAIA HAD WATCHED FIRST OURANOS AND THEN CRONUS SUCCUMB TO THE LURE OF POWER. SHE HAD RAISED ZEUS HERSELF, FED AND NURSED HIM, AND STILL SHE HADN'T BEEN ABLE TO STOP THE CHAOS. GAIA FELT PURE, HOT RAGE RISE IN HER.
I'M WARNING YOU, ZEUS—
WHAT? WHAT ARE YOU GOING TO DO? ASK ME NICELY TO STOP?

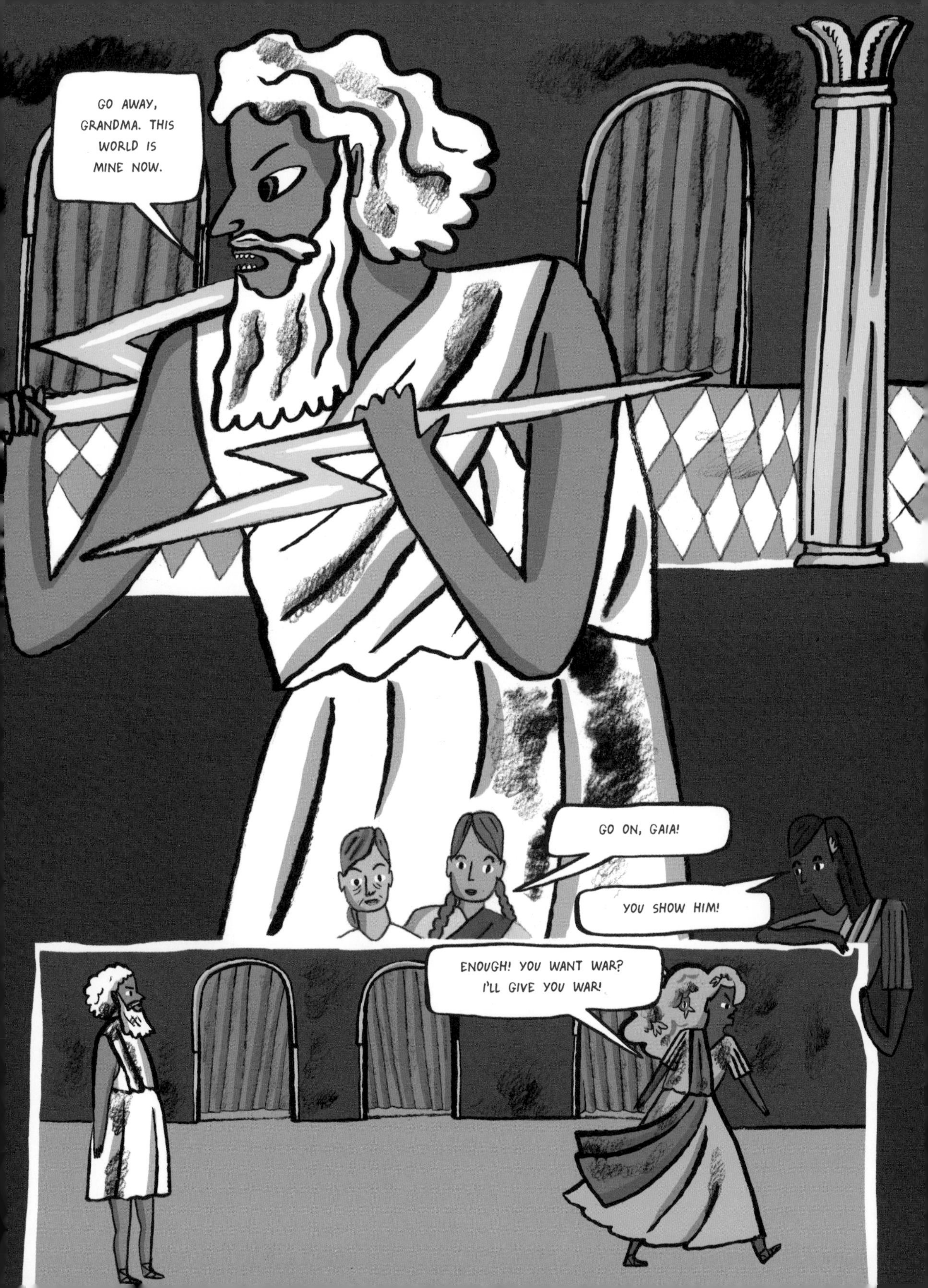
GO AWAY, GRANDMA. THIS WORLD IS MINE NOW.
GO ON, GAIA!
YOU SHOW HIM!
ENOUGH! YOU WANT WAR? I'LL GIVE YOU WAR!

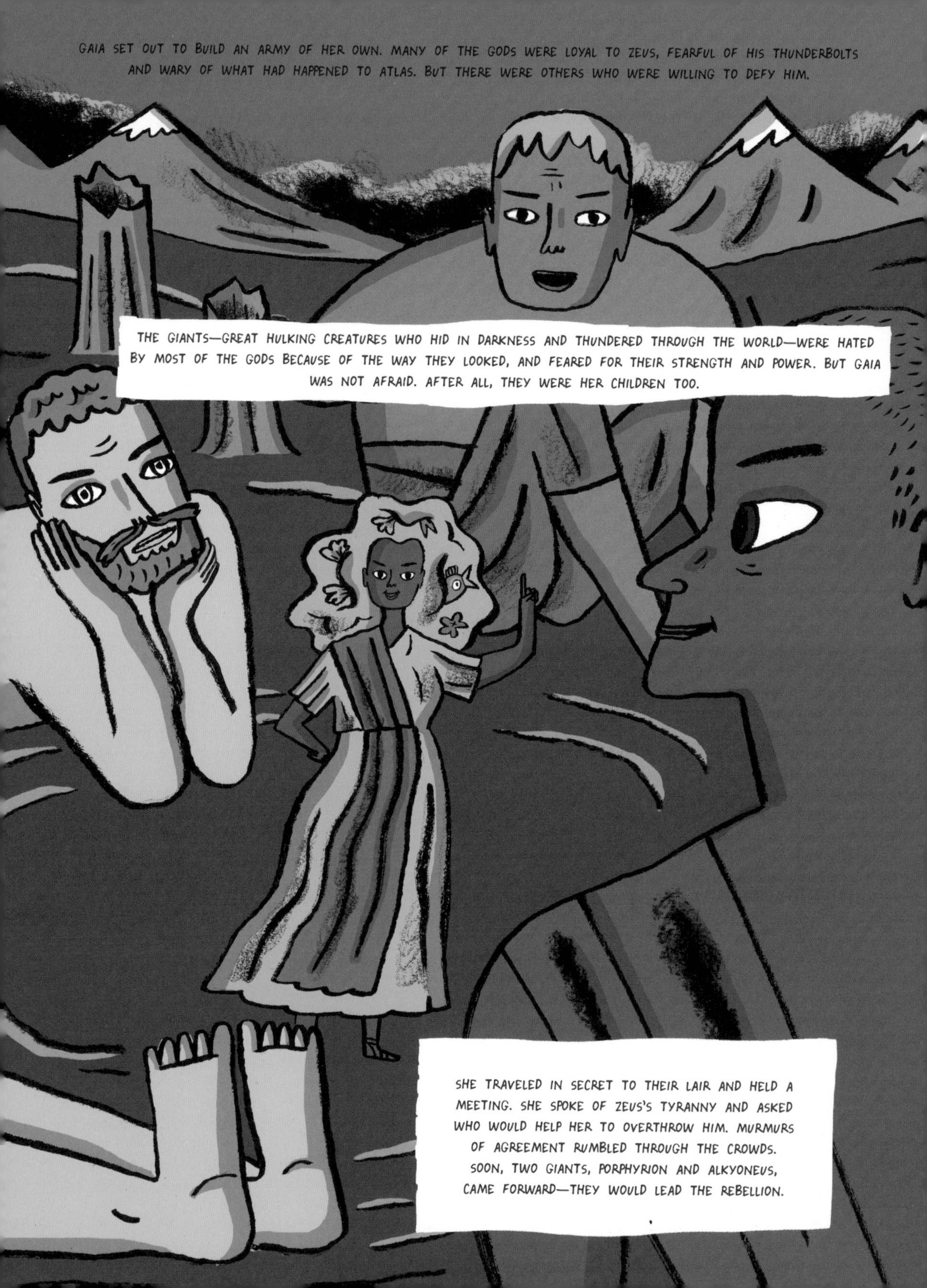
GAIA SET OUT TO BUILD AN ARMY OF HER OWN. MANY OF THE GODS WERE LOYAL TO ZEUS, FEARFUL OF HIS THUNDERBOLTS AND WARY OF WHAT HAD HAPPENED TO ATLAS. BUT THERE WERE OTHERS WHO WERE WILLING TO DEFY HIM.
THE GIANTS—GREAT HULKING CREATURES WHO HID IN DARKNESS AND THUNDERED THROUGH THE WORLD—WERE HATED BY MOST OF THE GODS BECAUSE OF THE WAY THEY LOOKED, AND FEARED FOR THEIR STRENGTH AND POWER. BUT GAIA WAS NOT AFRAID. AFTER ALL, THEY WERE HER CHILDREN TOO.
SHE TRAVELED IN SECRET TO THEIR LAIR AND HELD A MEETING. SHE SPOKE OF ZEUS'S TYRANNY AND ASKED WHO WOULD HELP HER TO OVERTHROW HIM. MURMURS OF AGREEMENT RUMBLED THROUGH THE CROWDS. SOON, TWO GIANTS, PORPHYRION AND ALKYONEUS, CAME FORWARD—THEY WOULD LEAD THE REBELLION.

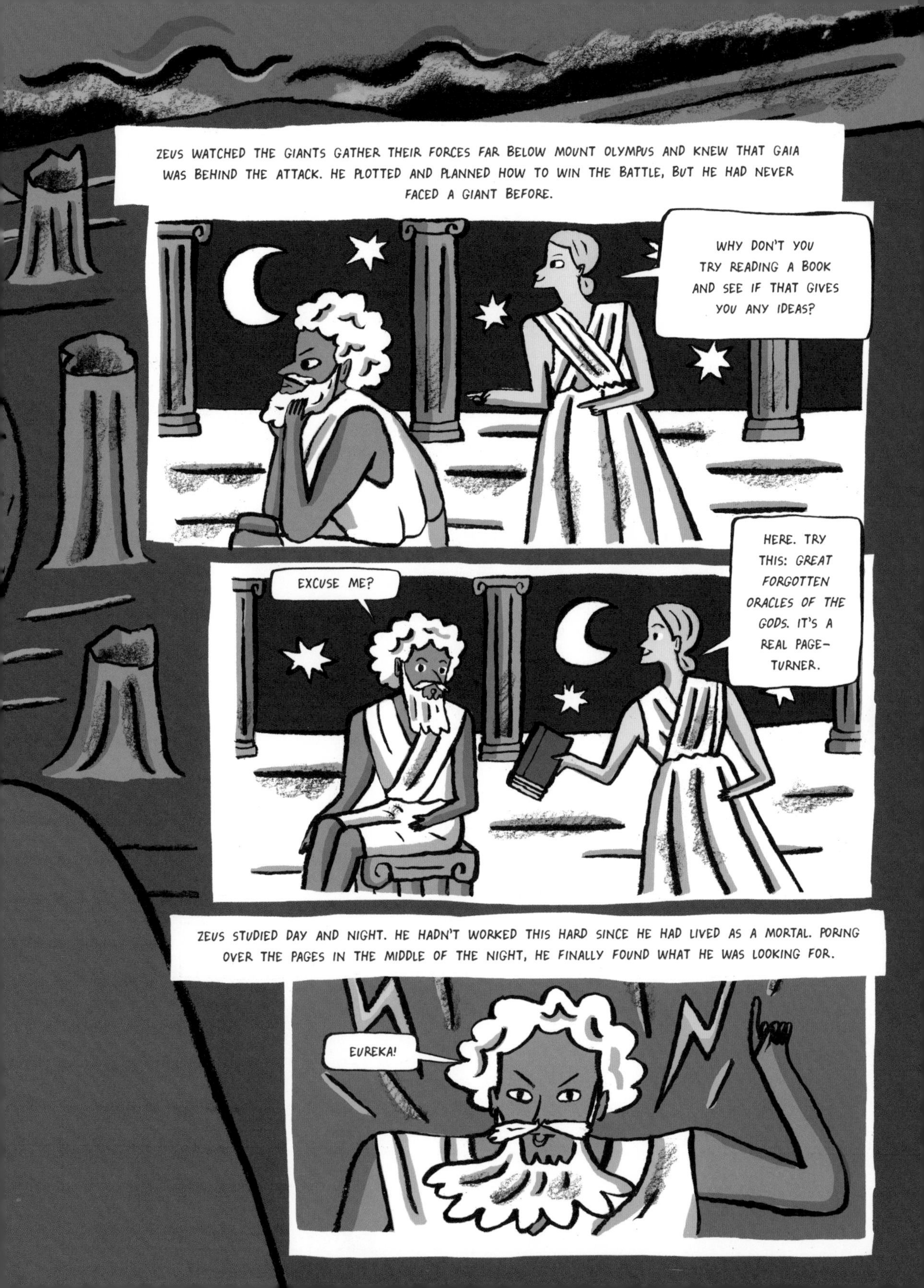
ZEUS WATCHED THE GIANTS GATHER THEIR FORCES FAR BELOW MOUNT OLYMPUS AND KNEW THAT GAIA WAS BEHIND THE ATTACK. HE PLOTTED AND PLANNED HOW TO WIN THE BATTLE, BUT HE HAD NEVER FACED A GIANT BEFORE.
WHY DON'T YOU TRY READING A BOOK AND SEE IF THAT GIVES YOU ANY IDEAS?
EXCUSE ME?
HERE. TRY THIS: *GREAT FORGOTTEN ORACLES OF THE GODS*. IT'S A REAL PAGE-TURNER.
ZEUS STUDIED DAY AND NIGHT. HE HADN'T WORKED THIS HARD SINCE HE HAD LIVED AS A MORTAL. PORING OVER THE PAGES IN THE MIDDLE OF THE NIGHT, HE FINALLY FOUND WHAT HE WAS LOOKING FOR.
EUREKA!

ZEUS SUMMONED HELIOS, SELENE, AND EOS TO MOUNT OLYMPUS AND DEMANDED THEIR LOYALTY AGAINST GAIA. THE UNEASY TRUCE BETWEEN THE SIBLINGS HAD HELD ALL THESE YEARS, BUT THAT DIDN'T MEAN THEY LIKED ONE ANOTHER.

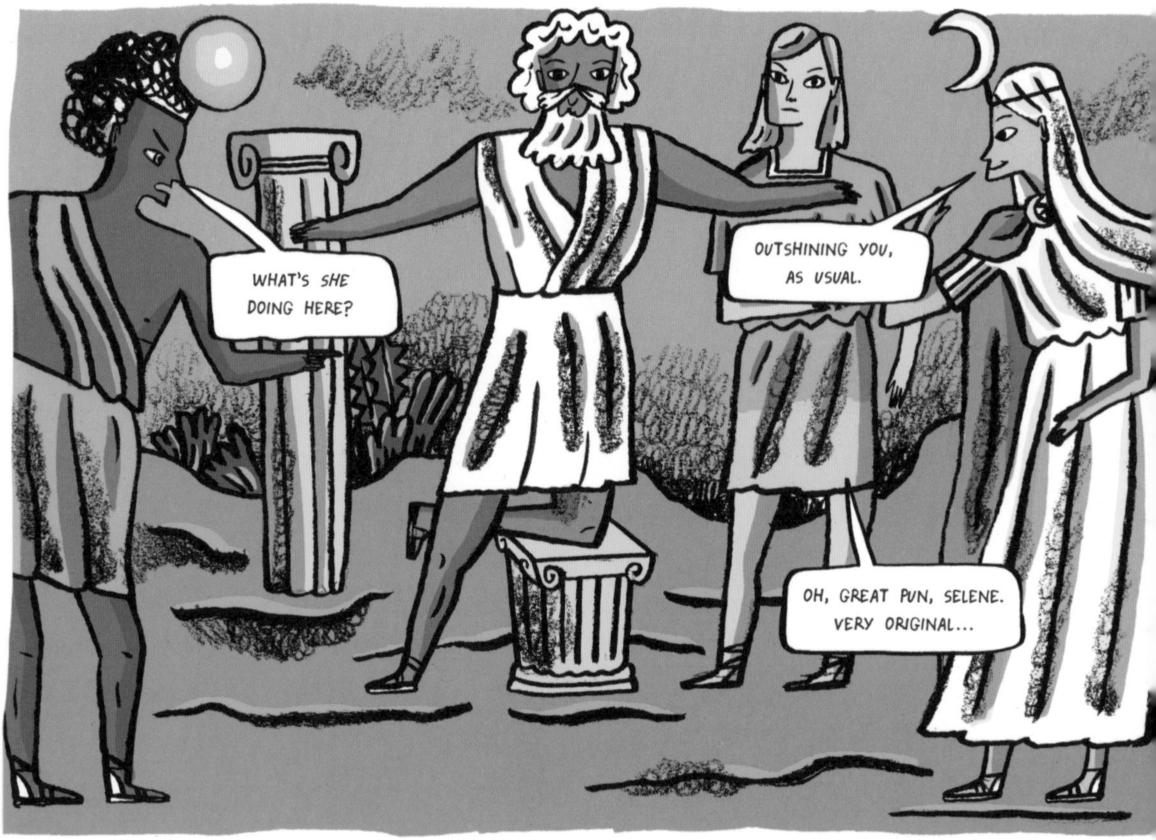
WHAT'S SHE DOING HERE?
OUTSHINING YOU, AS USUAL.
OH, GREAT PUN, SELENE. VERY ORIGINAL...

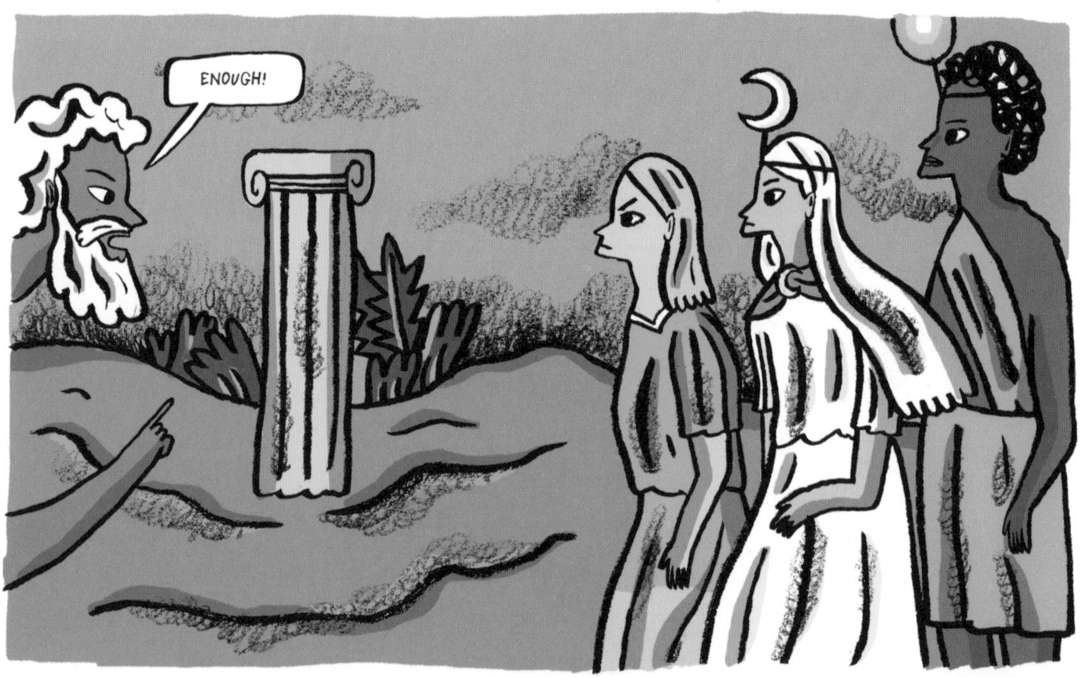
ENOUGH!

ZEUS TOLD THEM OF AN ANCIENT ORACLE WHO SAID THAT THE GODS WOULD ONLY RID THE WORLD OF GIANTS WITH THE HELP OF SOMEONE WHO WAS PART MORTAL.

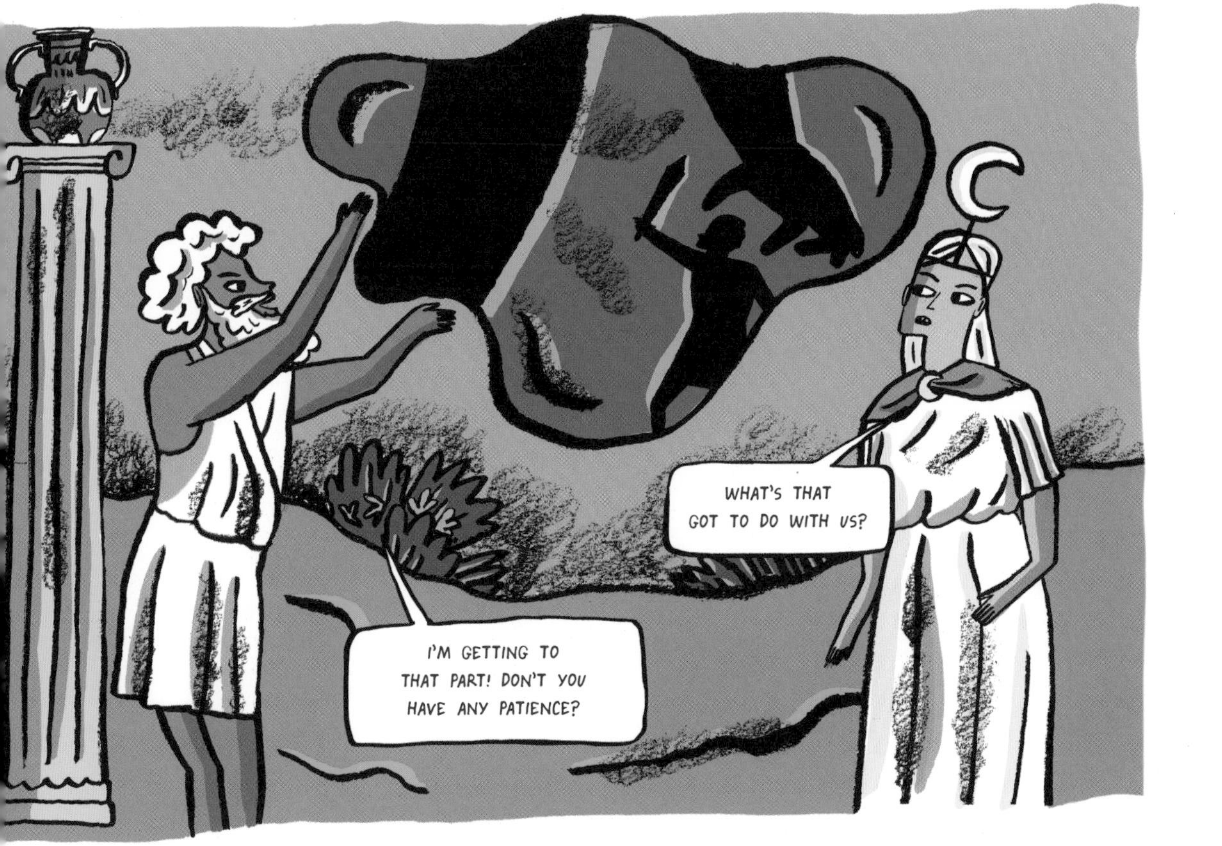
WHAT'S THAT GOT TO DO WITH US?
I'M GETTING TO THAT PART! DON'T YOU HAVE ANY PATIENCE?

GAIA HAD RAISED ZEUS AMONG THE MORTALS TO TRY TO TEACH HIM TO BE KIND AND HUMBLE. INSTEAD, HE'D LEARNED HOW TO USE THEM, AND HOW TO MANIPULATE THEIR AMBITION INTO STUPIDITY. HE'D SCOURED THE LAND TO FIND A WARRIOR WORTHY OF HIS MISSION AND COME UP WITH A PLAN.

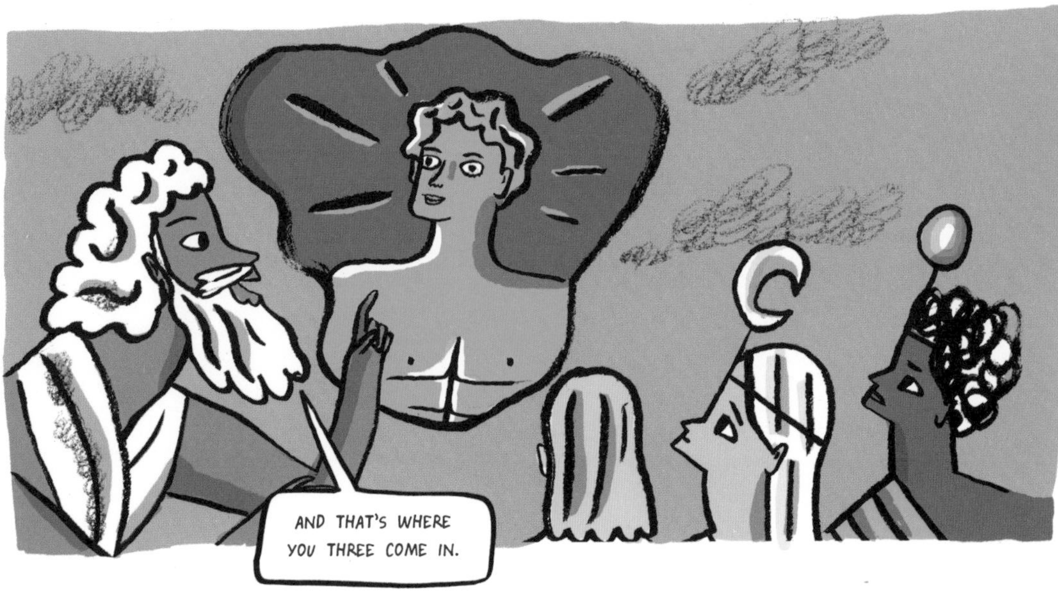
AND THAT'S WHERE YOU THREE COME IN.

THE WORLD TUMBLED INTO INKY DARKNESS.

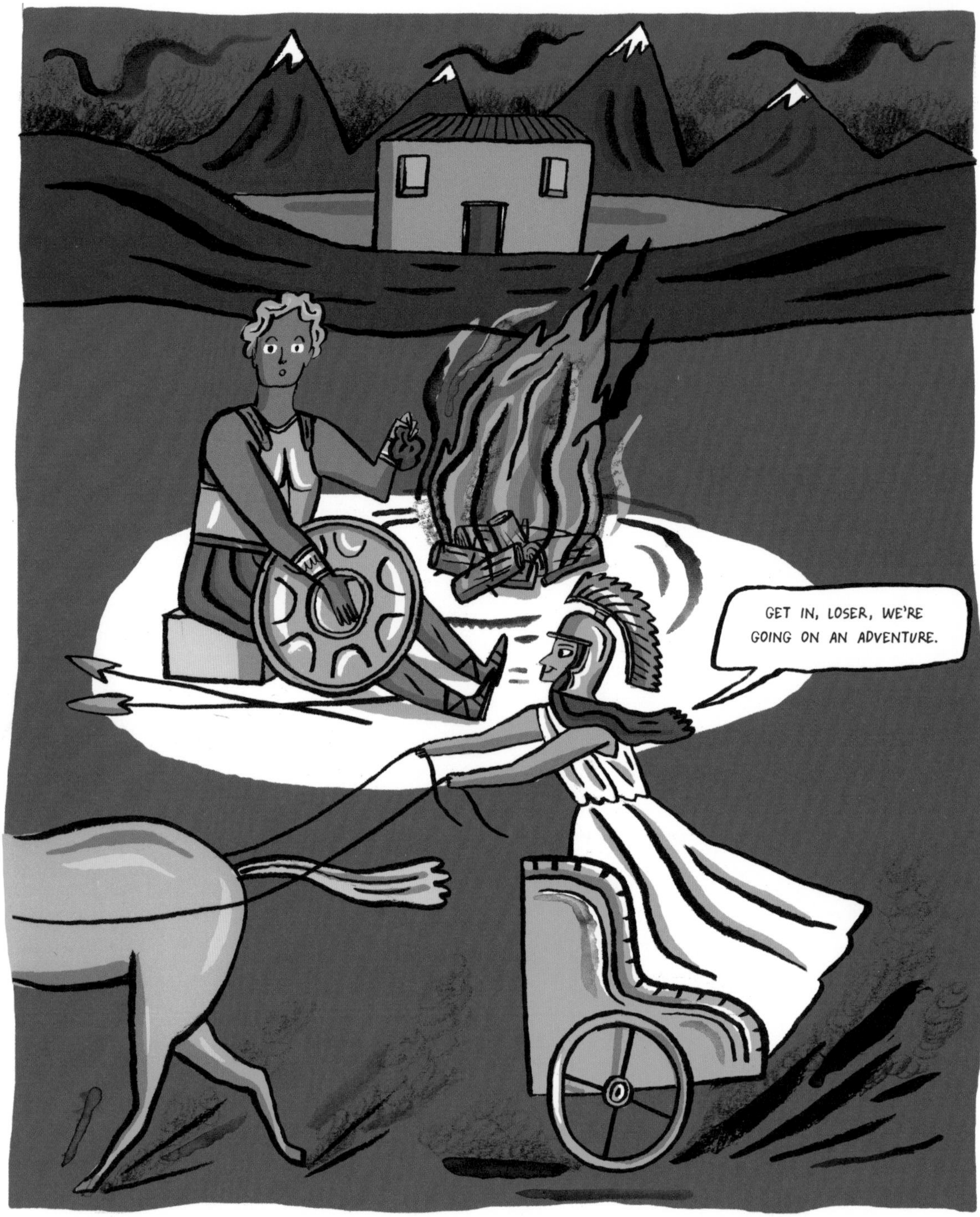
GET IN, LOSER, WE'RE GOING ON AN ADVENTURE.

THE MORTALS THOUGHT, AFTER YEARS OF WAR AND MISERY, THAT LIFE WAS COMING TO AN END. BUT ACTUALLY, IT WAS JUST THAT ZEUS HAD FORBIDDEN HELIOS, SELENE, AND EOS FROM SHINING. THE NEXT NIGHT, ZEUS SENT HIS DAUGHTER ATHENA WITH HER CHARIOT TO BRING HIS CHOSEN WARRIOR TO MOUNT OLYMPUS.

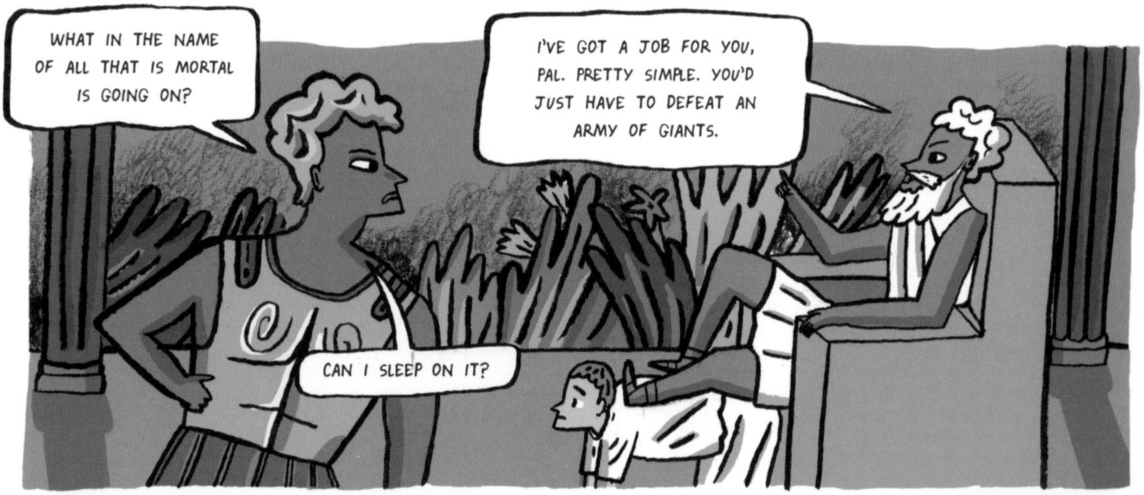
WHAT IN THE NAME OF ALL THAT IS MORTAL IS GOING ON?
I'VE GOT A JOB FOR YOU, PAL. PRETTY SIMPLE. YOU'D JUST HAVE TO DEFEAT AN ARMY OF GIANTS.
CAN I SLEEP ON IT?

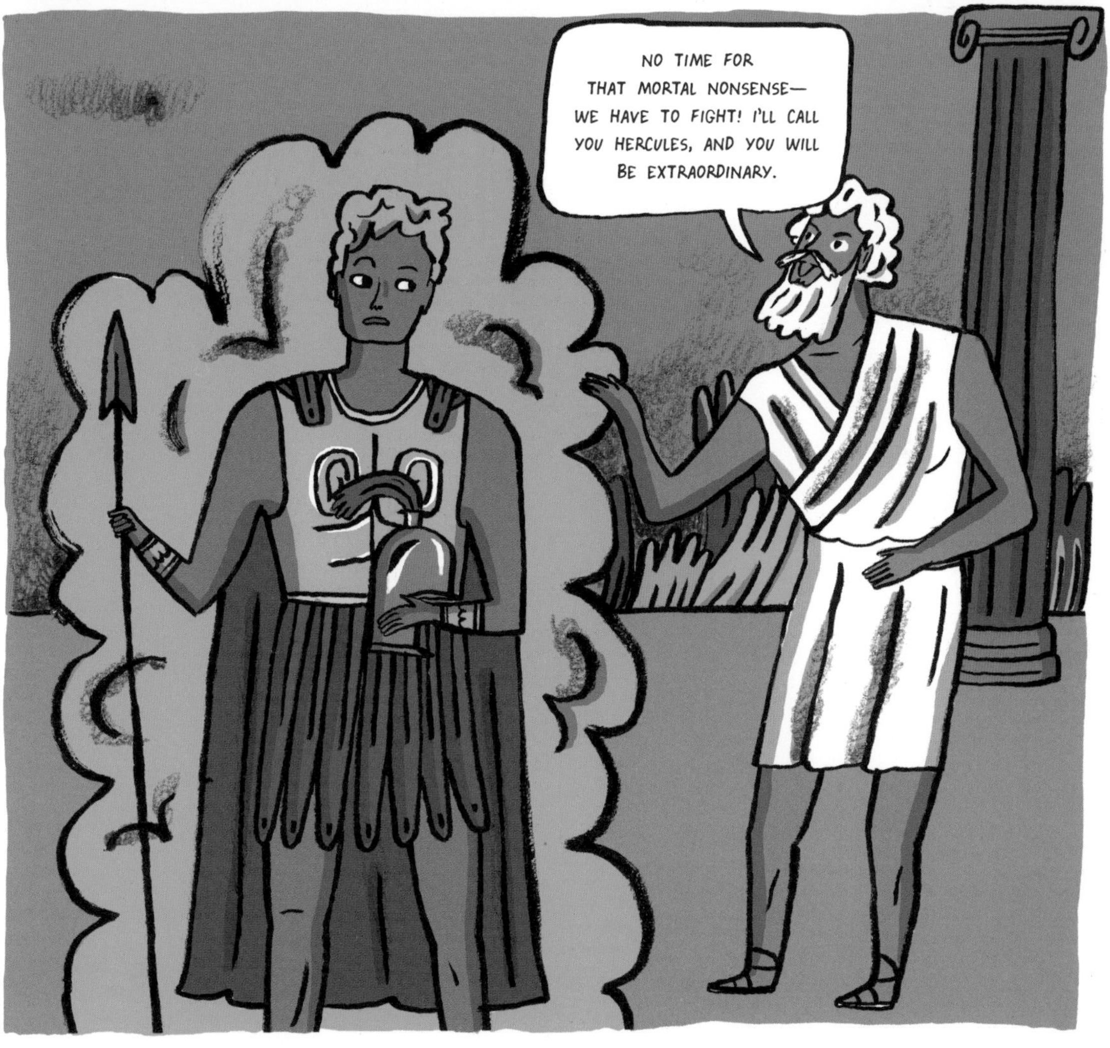
NO TIME FOR THAT MORTAL NONSENSE— WE HAVE TO FIGHT! I'LL CALL YOU HERCULES, AND YOU WILL BE EXTRAORDINARY.

AT THAT EXACT MOMENT, THERE WAS A GREAT RUMBLING, AND MOUNT OLYMPUS BEGAN TO SHAKE.

WHILE ZEUS HAD BEEN CONCOCTING HIS PLAN, PORPHYRION AND ALKYONEUS—THE LEADER OF THE GIANTS—DECIDED TO MAKE THEIR MOVE. THEY CALLED ON THE OTHER GIANTS AND BEGAN CLIMBING MOUNT OLYMPUS.

HERCULES LOOKED OVER THE EDGE OF THE CLIFF AND SAW THE MONSTROUS GIANTS COMING TOWARD HIM. BEFORE HE COULD THINK TWICE, HE DREW BACK HIS BOW AND SHOT ALKYONEUS IN THE SHOULDER.

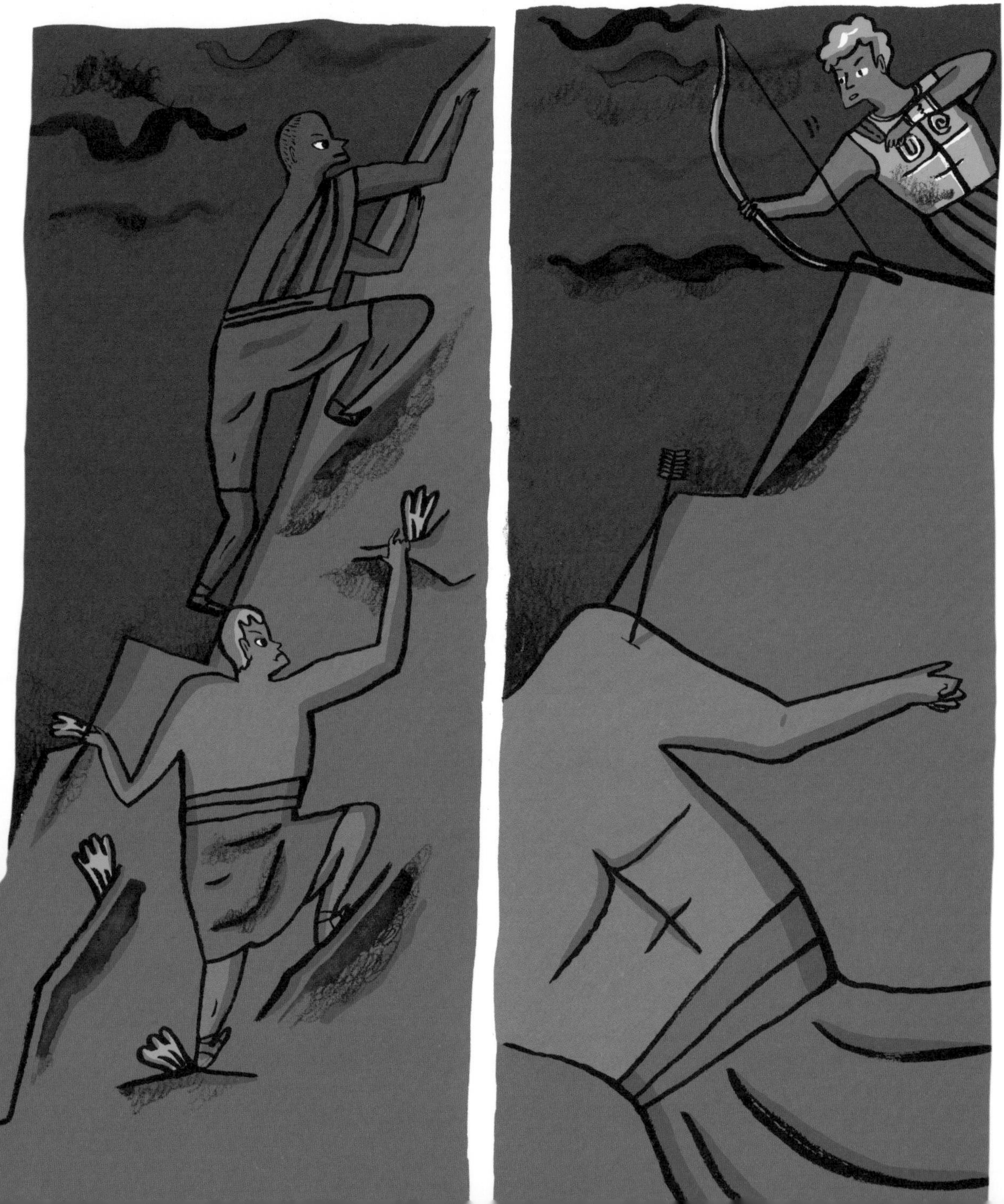

ALKYONEUS LOST HIS GRIP, TUMBLED BACK TO EARTH, AND DIED. THERE WAS A MIGHTY CRASH WHEN HE HIT THE GROUND. THE EARTH, RAVAGED FROM YEARS OF WAR, QUAKED AND SHOOK, AND A TIDAL WAVE SWEPT ACROSS THE LAND, DESTROYING EVERYTHING IN ITS PATH.

PORPHYRION WEPT FOR HIS BROTHER BUT KEPT CLIMBING. FINALLY, HE REACHED THE GREAT HEIGHTS OF OLYMPUS, WHERE THE GODS WERE WAITING, BOWS POISED. ALL THE OTHER GIANTS FOLLOWED HIM INTO THE FIGHT.

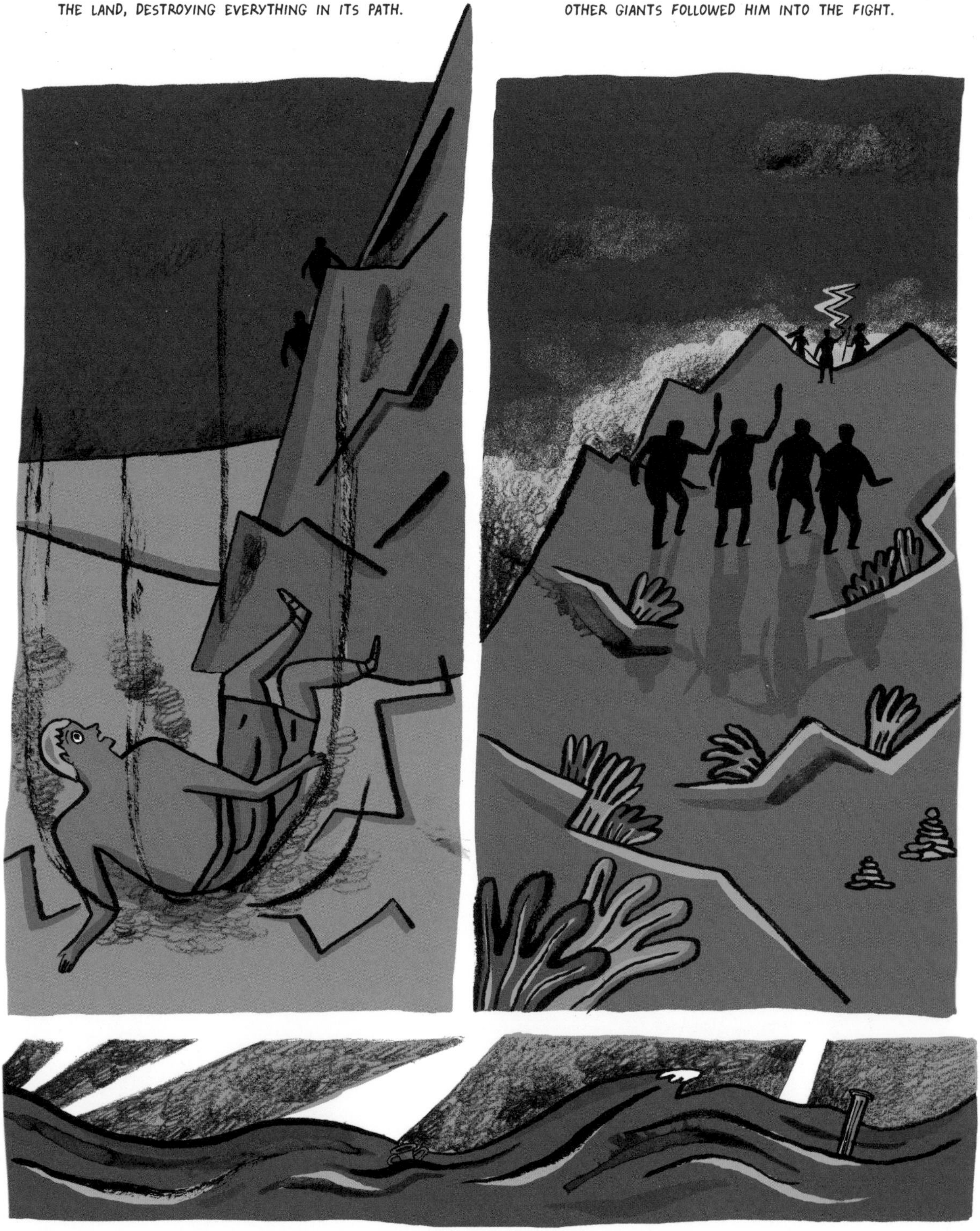

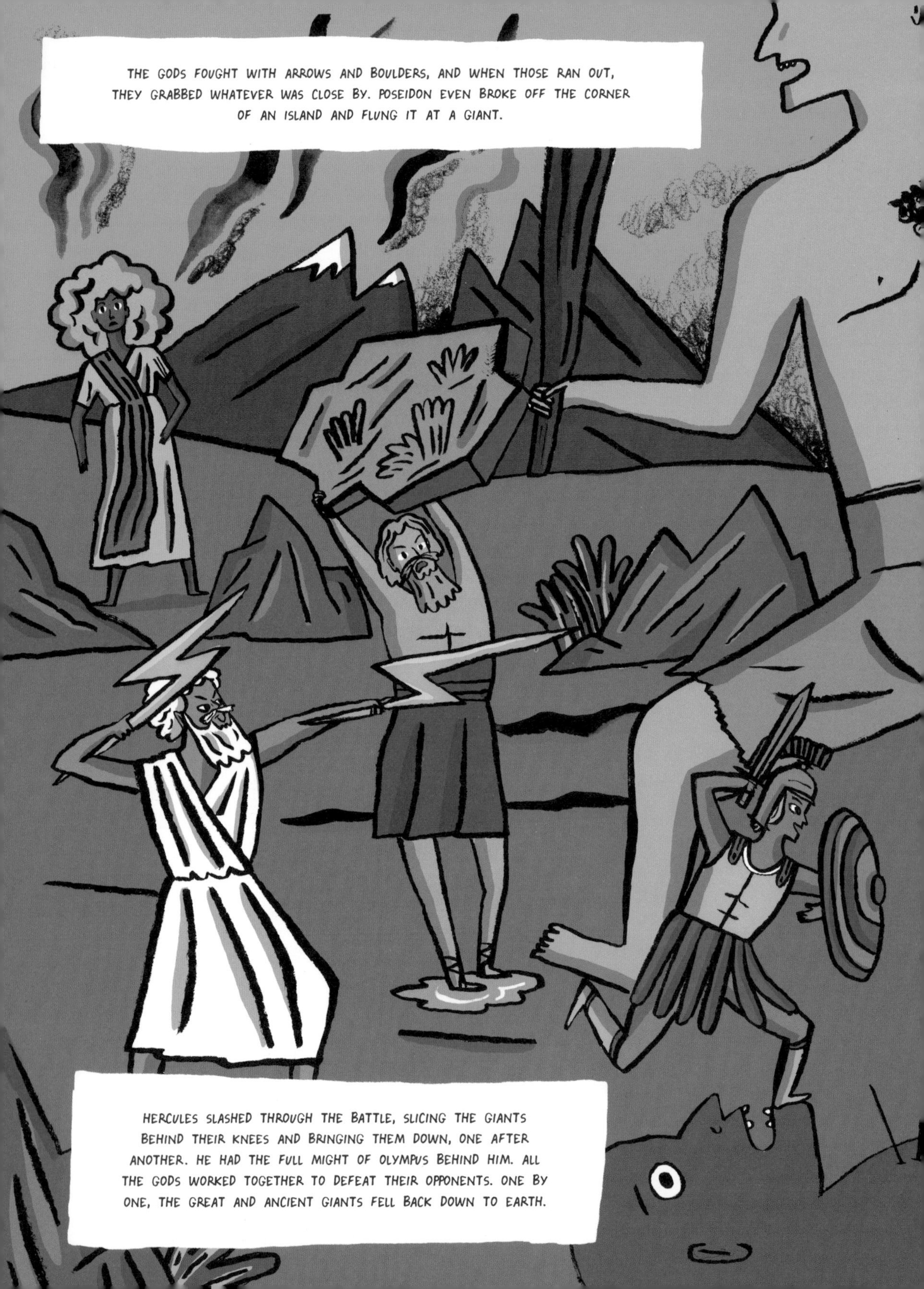
THE GODS FOUGHT WITH ARROWS AND BOULDERS, AND WHEN THOSE RAN OUT, THEY GRABBED WHATEVER WAS CLOSE BY. POSEIDON EVEN BROKE OFF THE CORNER OF AN ISLAND AND FLUNG IT AT A GIANT.
HERCULES SLASHED THROUGH THE BATTLE, SLICING THE GIANTS BEHIND THEIR KNEES AND BRINGING THEM DOWN, ONE AFTER ANOTHER. HE HAD THE FULL MIGHT OF OLYMPUS BEHIND HIM. ALL THE GODS WORKED TOGETHER TO DEFEAT THEIR OPPONENTS. ONE BY ONE, THE GREAT AND ANCIENT GIANTS FELL BACK DOWN TO EARTH.

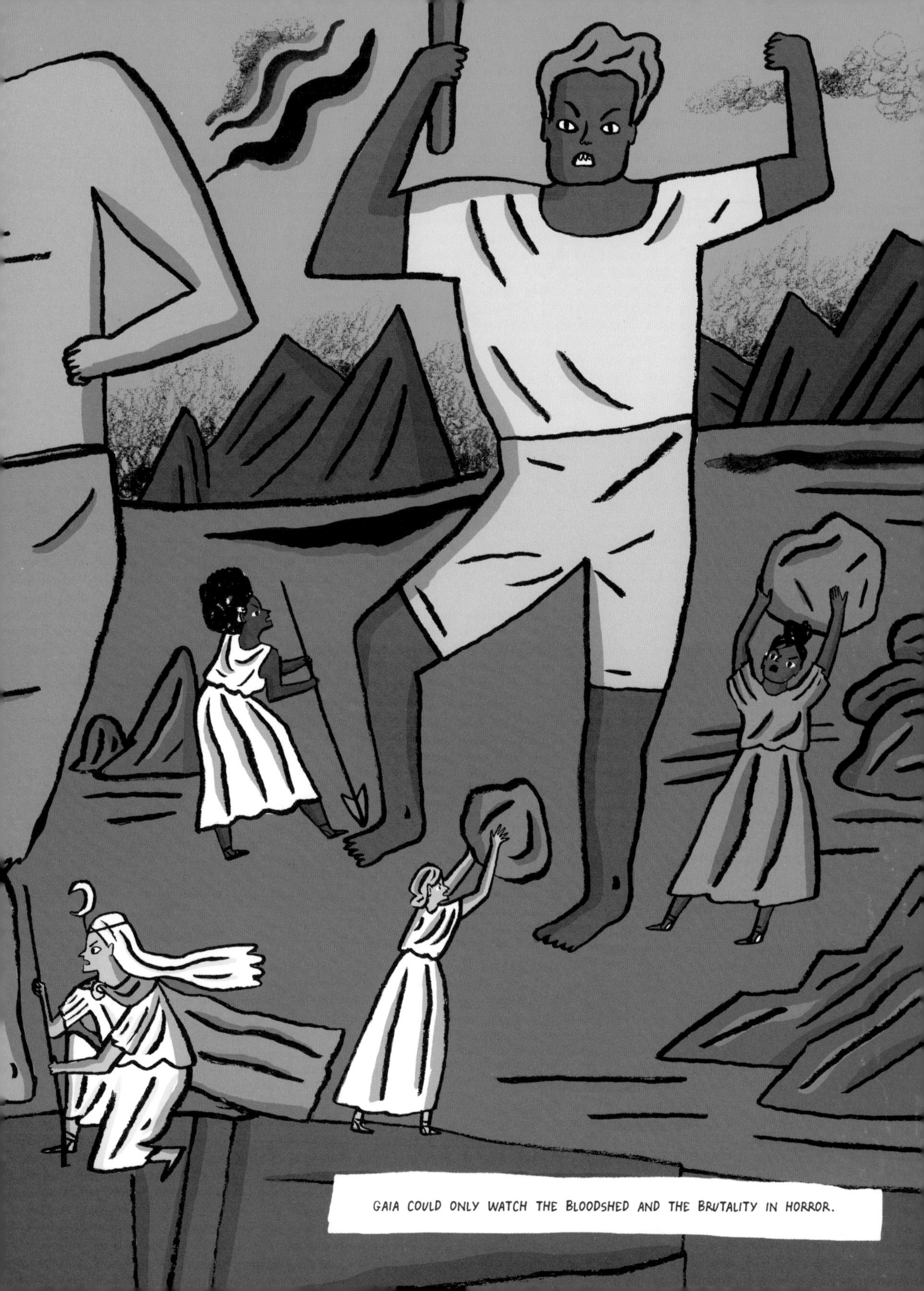
GAIA COULD ONLY WATCH THE BLOODSHED AND THE BRUTALITY IN HORROR.

WITH THE GIANTS DEFEATED, THERE WAS A GREAT CELEBRATION UP ON MOUNT OLYMPUS, AND HERCULES WAS HONORED AS A HERO. GAIA COULDN'T BEAR TO MAKE PEACE. IT WAS ALL SO UNJUST.

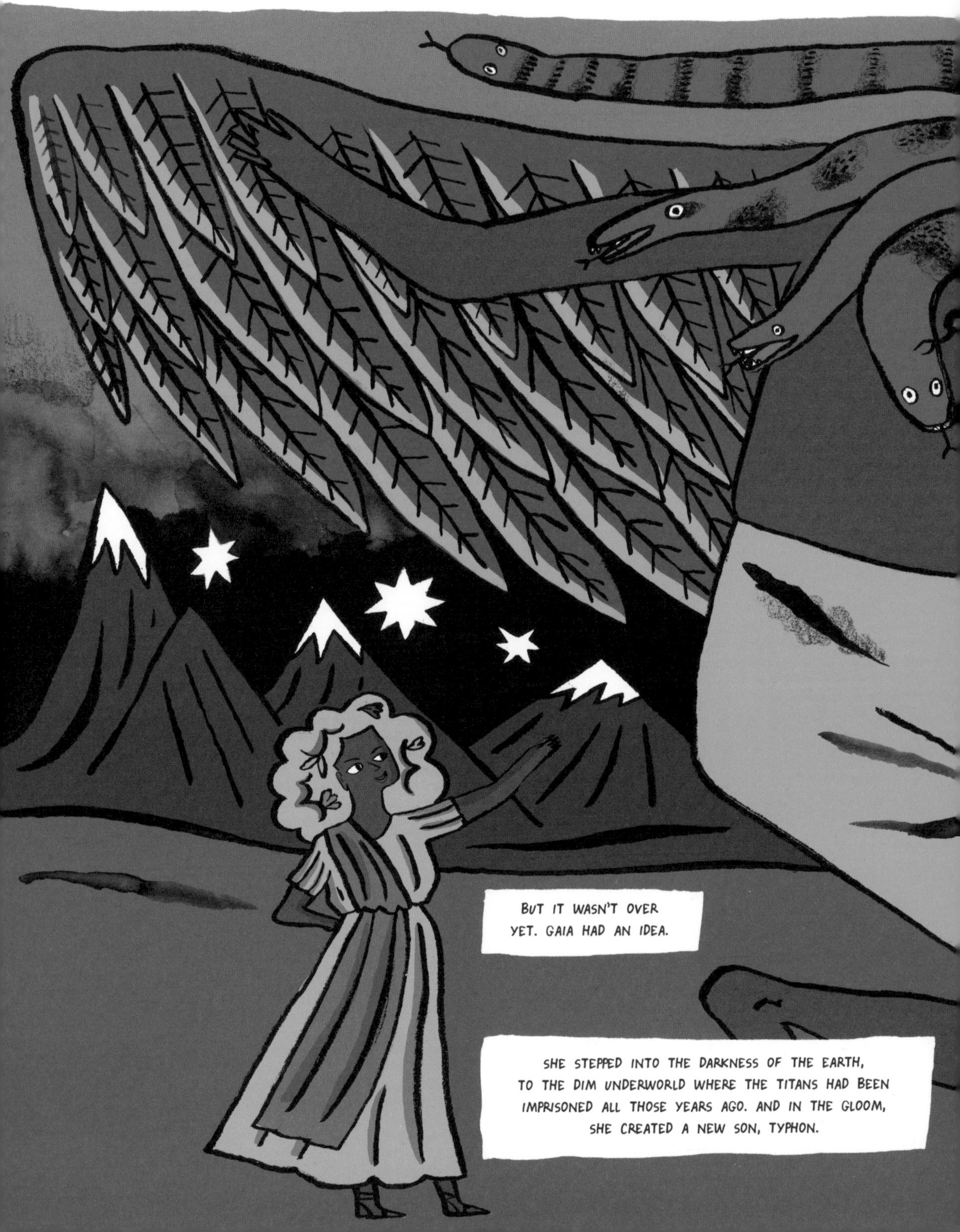

BUT IT WASN'T OVER YET. GAIA HAD AN IDEA.
SHE STEPPED INTO THE DARKNESS OF THE EARTH, TO THE DIM UNDERWORLD WHERE THE TITANS HAD BEEN IMPRISONED ALL THOSE YEARS AGO. AND IN THE GLOOM, SHE CREATED A NEW SON, TYPHON.

TYPHON WAS THE GREATEST GIANT THAT HAD EVER WALKED THE EARTH. A TERRIFYING CREATURE, HE TOWERED ABOVE THE MOUNTAINS, HIS HUNDRED SERPENT HEADS BRUSHING THE STARS. HE HAD WINGS CURLED INTO HIS BACK, AND WHEN THEY UNFURLED, THEY STRETCHED FROM THE FARTHEST WEST TO THE MOST DISTANT EAST. BUT HE WAS A HAUNTED CREATURE.

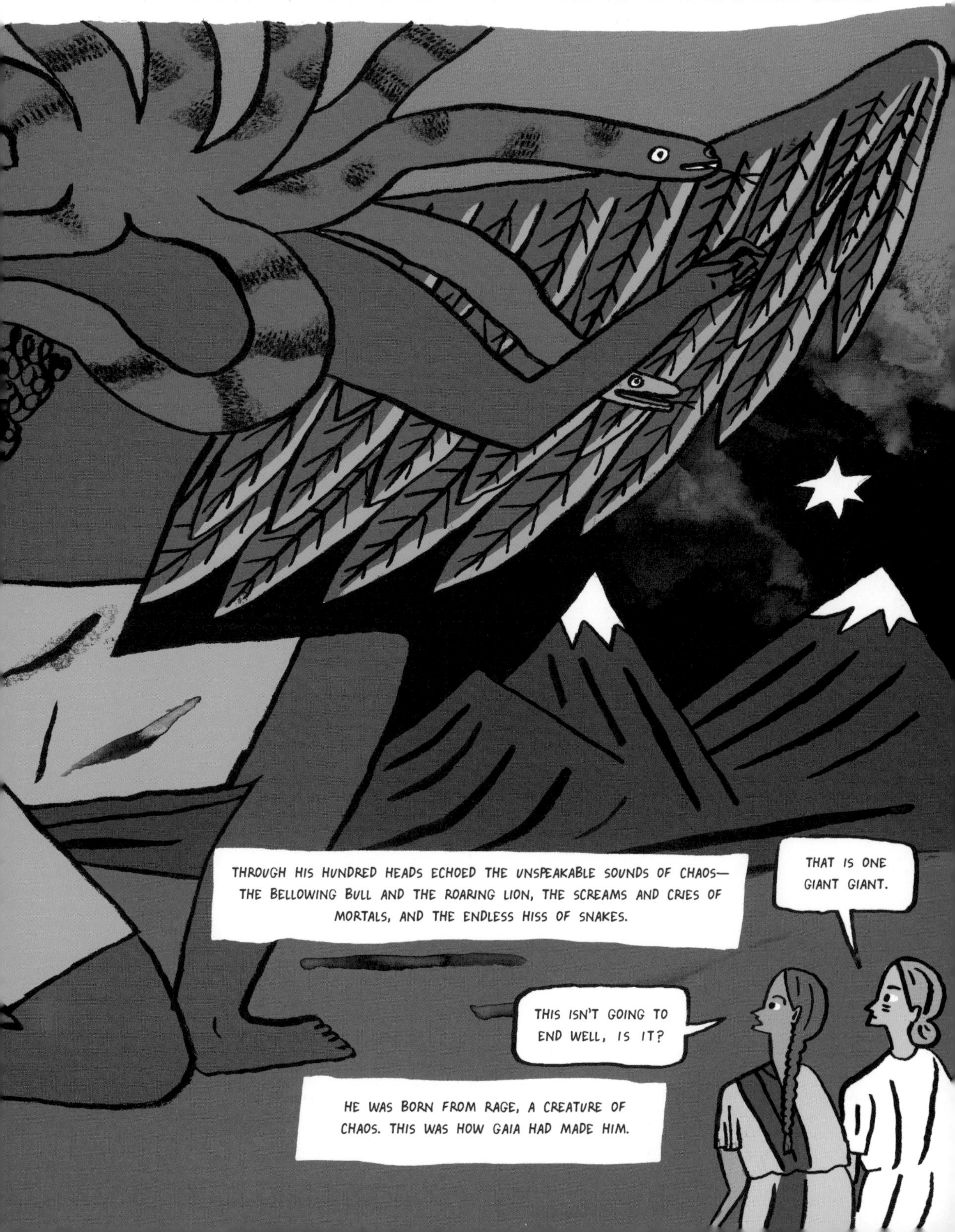
THROUGH HIS HUNDRED HEADS ECHOED THE UNSPEAKABLE SOUNDS OF CHAOS—THE BELLOWING BULL AND THE ROARING LION, THE SCREAMS AND CRIES OF MORTALS, AND THE ENDLESS HISS OF SNAKES.
THAT IS ONE GIANT GIANT.
THIS ISN'T GOING TO END WELL, IS IT?
HE WAS BORN FROM RAGE, A CREATURE OF CHAOS. THIS WAS HOW GAIA HAD MADE HIM.

THE FIRST ZEUS HEARD OF THIS NEW ENEMY WAS A DISTANT STORM OUT AT SEA. HE DIDN'T THINK MUCH OF IT, UNTIL POSEIDON ARRIVED, BREATHLESS.

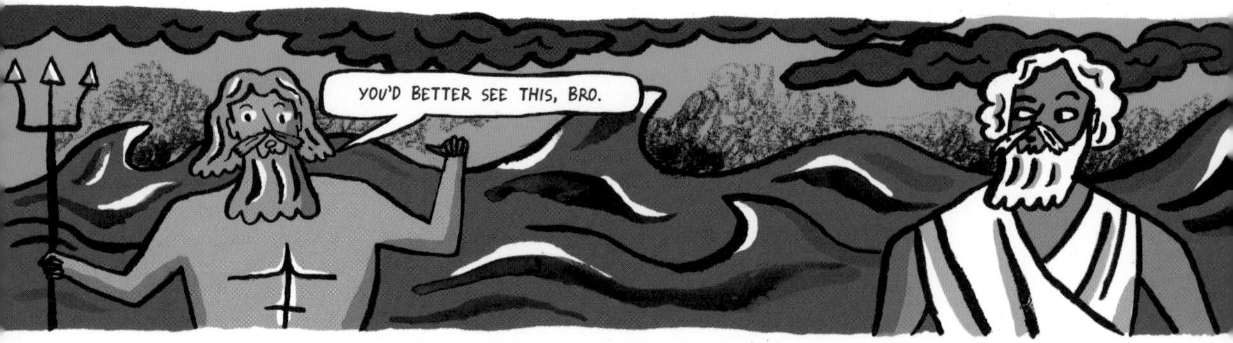
YOU'D BETTER SEE THIS, BRO.

OUT IN THE MIDDLE OF THE SEA, TYPHON WAS CREATING A HUNDRED TYPHOONS. ZEUS GRABBED HIS THUNDERBOLTS AND SET OUT TO MEET THE GIANT.

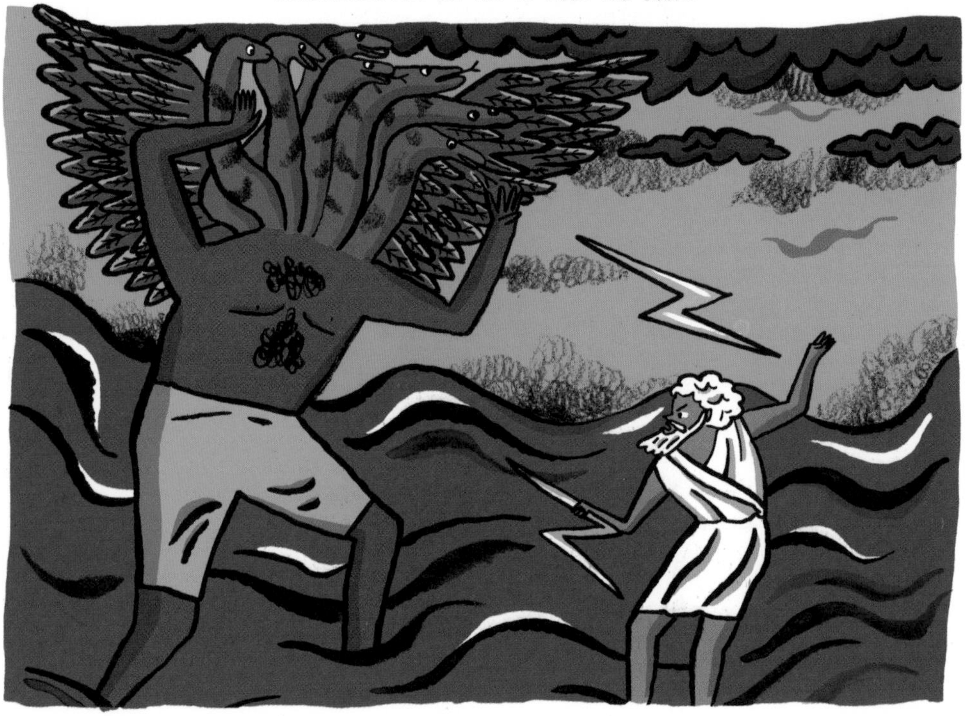

WHEN ZEUS FIRST STRUCK TYPHON WITH A THUNDERBOLT, THE CRASH ECHOED THROUGH THE WORLD, AND THE EARTH RUMBLED. THE SEA AND THE SKY SEETHED. TYPHON LAUNCHED HIMSELF AT ZEUS WITH ALL HIS STRENGTH. DARK CLOUDS CIRCLED THEM AND THE SEA, CHURNING IN A WHIRLPOOL AS THEY FOUGHT DAY AND NIGHT.

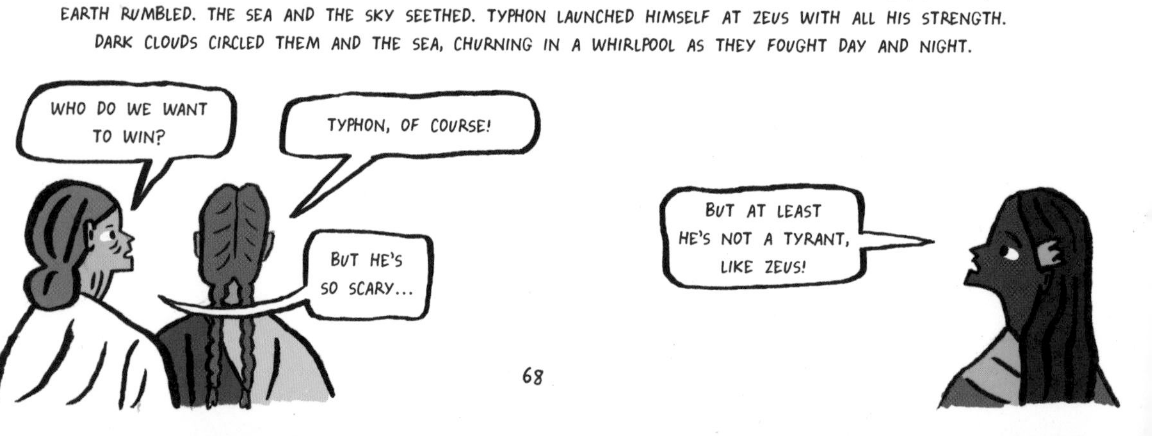
WHO DO WE WANT TO WIN?
TYPHON, OF COURSE!
BUT HE'S SO SCARY...
BUT AT LEAST HE'S NOT A TYRANT, LIKE ZEUS!

WHEN THEY WERE BOTH WOUNDED, EXHAUSTED, AND CLOSE TO COLLAPSE, ZEUS THREW HIS ONE LAST THUNDERBOLT AT THE GIANT, AND TYPHON CRASHED INTO THE SEA. ZEUS THREW TYPHON ACROSS THE SHORE, AND THE GROUND SCORCHED BENEATH HIM IN A GREAT BALL OF FIRE. AROUND THE BODY OF THE MASSIVE CREATURE, ZEUS RAISED A VOLCANO TO TRAP TYPHON IN HEAT AND FIRE FOREVER.

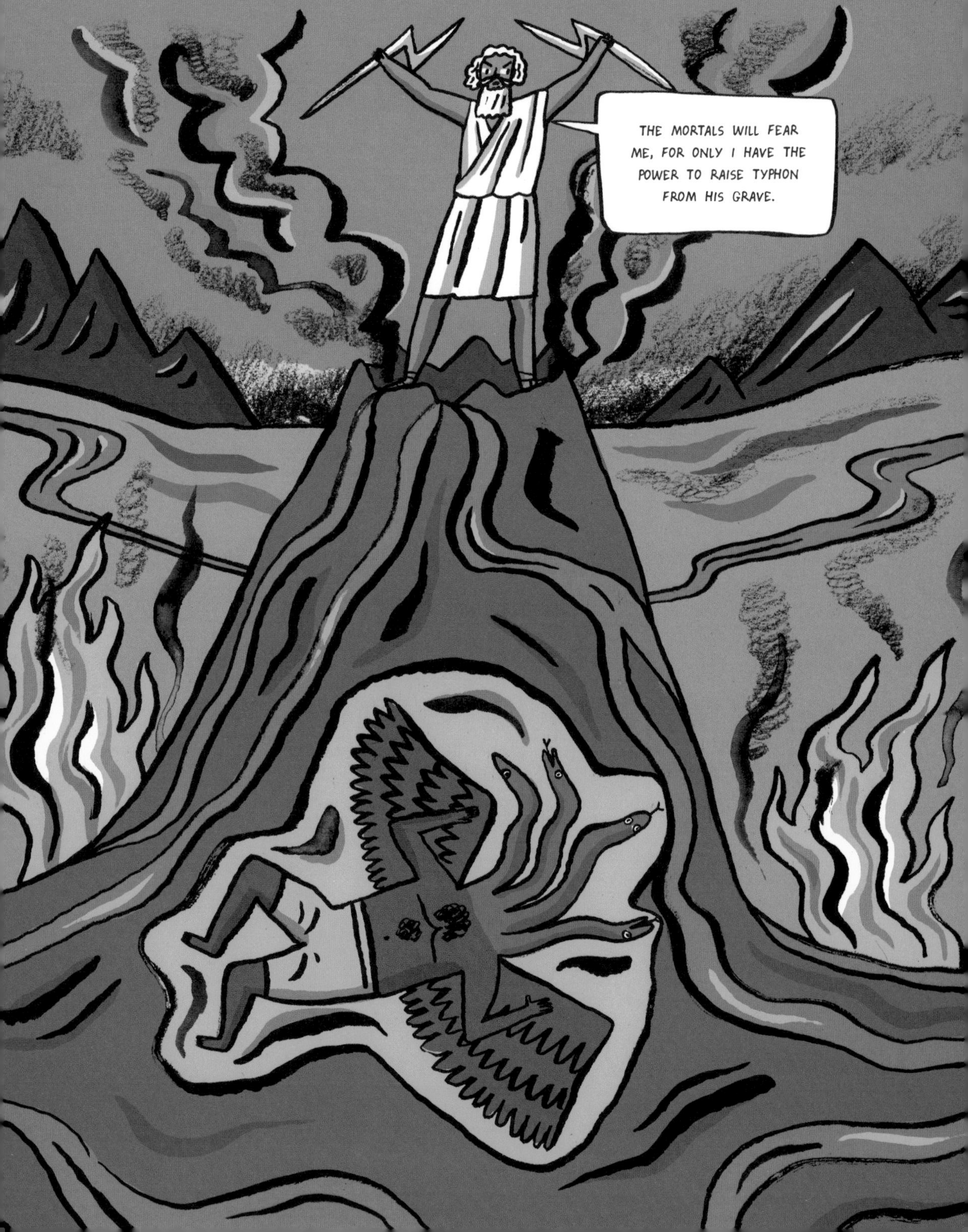
THE MORTALS WILL FEAR ME, FOR ONLY I HAVE THE POWER TO RAISE TYPHON FROM HIS GRAVE.

ZEUS RETURNED TO MOUNT OLYMPUS.

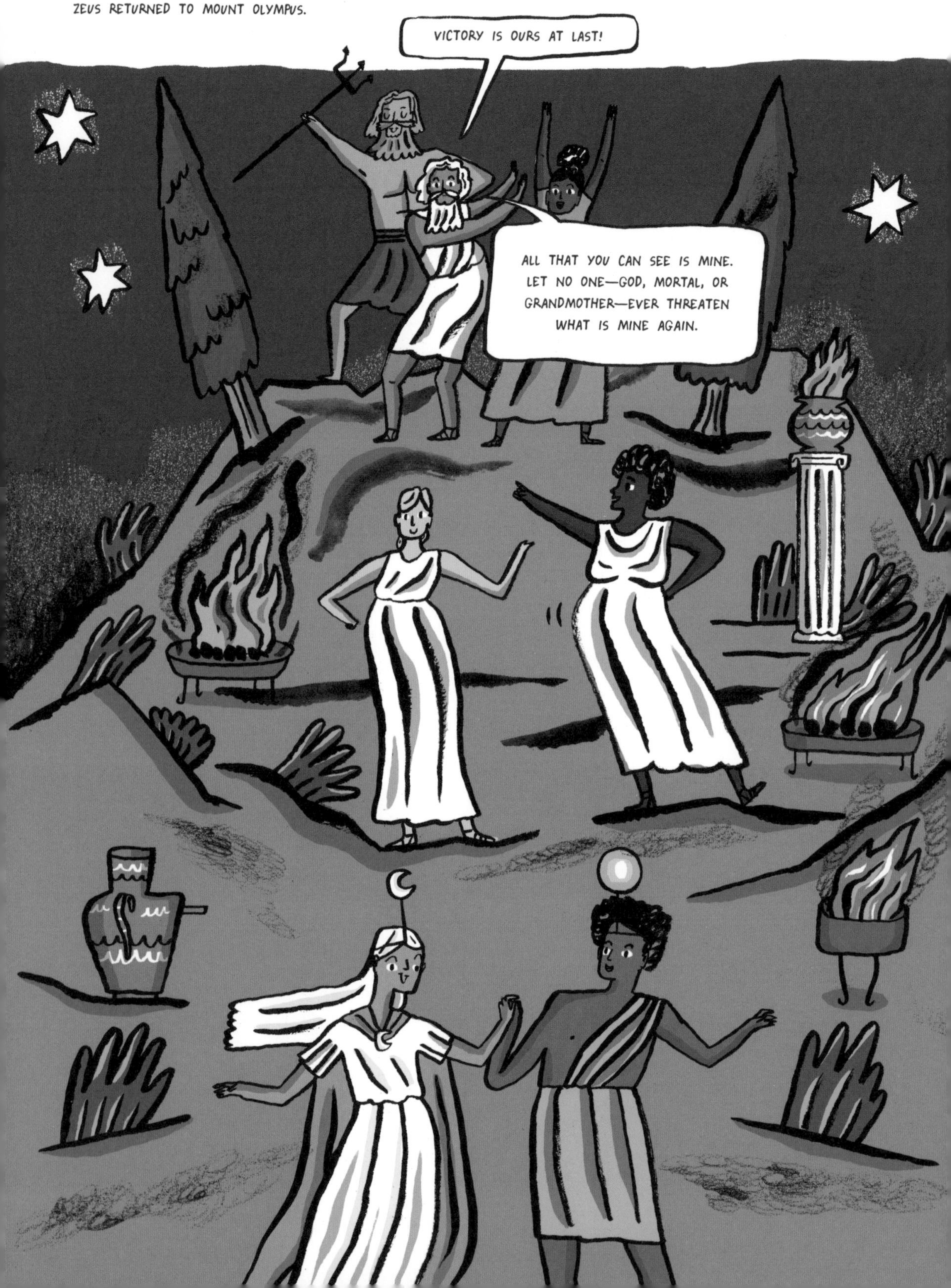
VICTORY IS OURS AT LAST!
ALL THAT YOU CAN SEE IS MINE. LET NO ONE—GOD, MORTAL, OR GRANDMOTHER—EVER THREATEN WHAT IS MINE AGAIN.

GAIA HAD WATCHED ZEUS AND TYPHON BATTLE. NOW, SHE WALKED THE EARTH WITH THE MORTALS. THE LAND WAS SCORCHED, TYPHON'S BLOOD SOAKED INTO THE BARREN GROUND, AND SHE HEARD, RUMBLING DEEP UNDER THE VOLCANO, TYPHON'S TEARS.

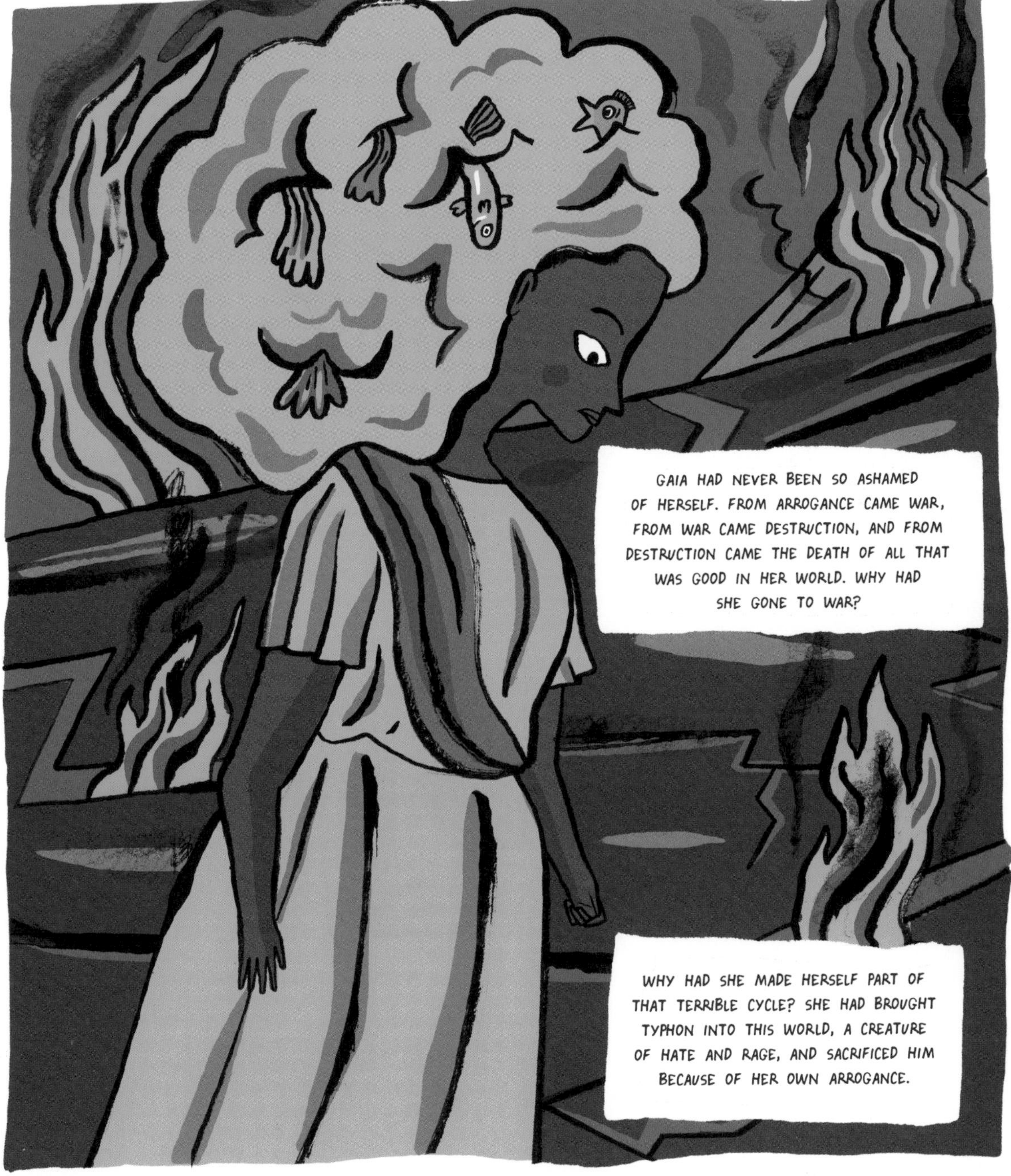
GAIA HAD NEVER BEEN SO ASHAMED OF HERSELF. FROM ARROGANCE CAME WAR, FROM WAR CAME DESTRUCTION, AND FROM DESTRUCTION CAME THE DEATH OF ALL THAT WAS GOOD IN HER WORLD. WHY HAD SHE GONE TO WAR?
WHY HAD SHE MADE HERSELF PART OF THAT TERRIBLE CYCLE? SHE HAD BROUGHT TYPHON INTO THIS WORLD, A CREATURE OF HATE AND RAGE, AND SACRIFICED HIM BECAUSE OF HER OWN ARROGANCE.

IF SHE WANTED THE WORLD TO BE GOOD AND PEACEFUL, SHE NEEDED TO FIND ANOTHER WAY. SHE WANTED THE MORTALS TO FLOURISH AND FOR THE ANIMALS, FORESTS, AND CORAL TO GROW TOO. SHE WANTED TO RESTORE BALANCE, SO NOBODY SUFFERED FOR ANOTHER'S WANTS.

PART VI

The Lives of Mortals

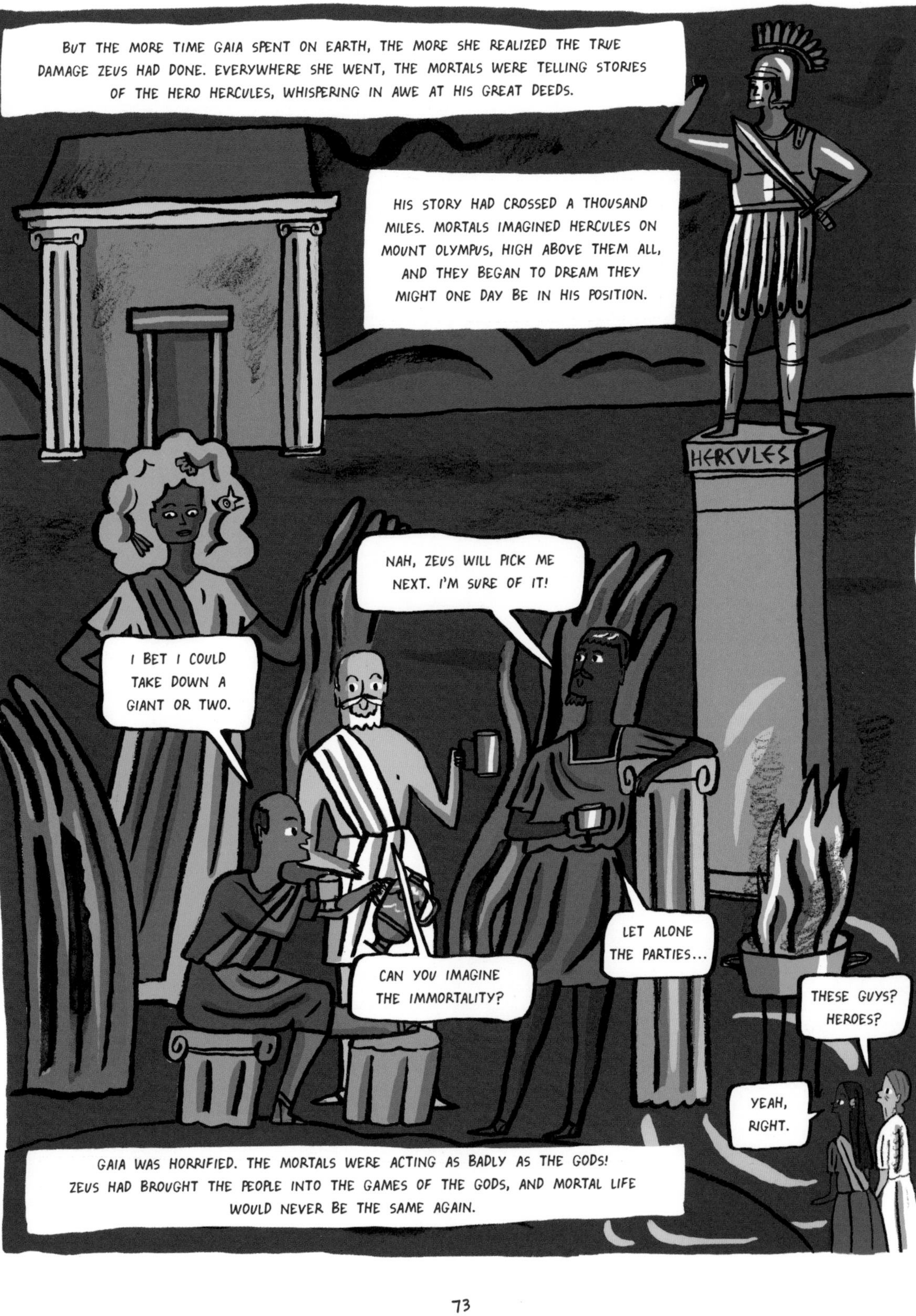
BUT THE MORE TIME GAIA SPENT ON EARTH, THE MORE SHE REALIZED THE TRUE DAMAGE ZEUS HAD DONE. EVERYWHERE SHE WENT, THE MORTALS WERE TELLING STORIES OF THE HERO HERCULES, WHISPERING IN AWE AT HIS GREAT DEEDS.
HIS STORY HAD CROSSED A THOUSAND MILES. MORTALS IMAGINED HERCULES ON MOUNT OLYMPUS, HIGH ABOVE THEM ALL, AND THEY BEGAN TO DREAM THEY MIGHT ONE DAY BE IN HIS POSITION.
HERCULES
NAH, ZEUS WILL PICK ME NEXT. I'M SURE OF IT!
I BET I COULD TAKE DOWN A GIANT OR TWO.
LET ALONE THE PARTIES...
CAN YOU IMAGINE THE IMMORTALITY?
THESE GUYS? HEROES?
YEAH, RIGHT.
GAIA WAS HORRIFIED. THE MORTALS WERE ACTING AS BADLY AS THE GODS! ZEUS HAD BROUGHT THE PEOPLE INTO THE GAMES OF THE GODS, AND MORTAL LIFE WOULD NEVER BE THE SAME AGAIN.

THE MORTALS LEFT OFFERINGS IN THE TEMPLES OF THE GODS, BEGGING TO BE CHOSEN AS THE NEXT GREAT HERO. AND SOON, ALL THE GODS OF OLYMPUS WERE MEDDLING IN THE LIVES OF THE MORTALS, USING THEM TO SETTLE THEIR OWN ARGUMENTS. THE EARTH HAD BECOME THEIR PLAYGROUND.

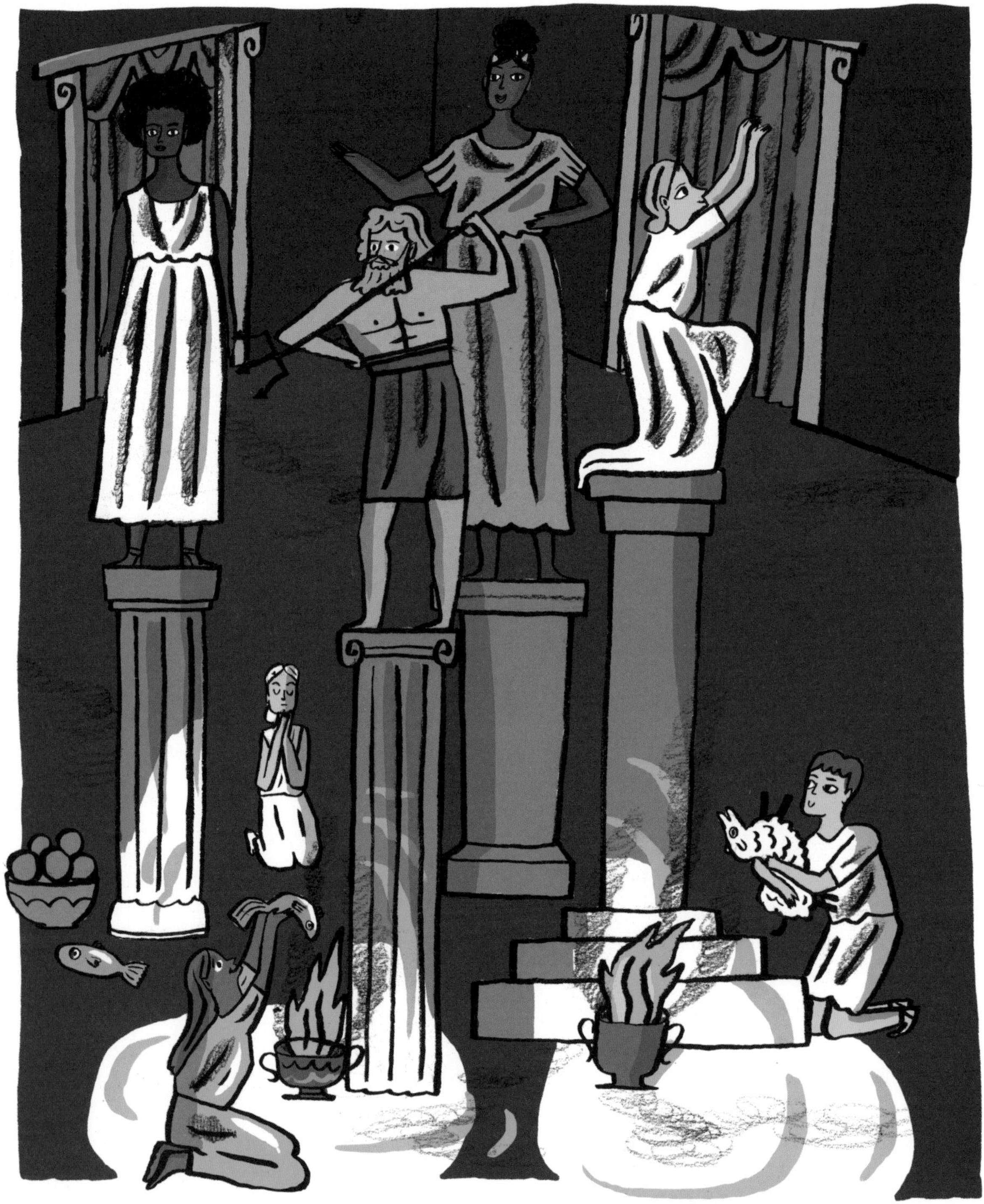

PART VII

A New World

THE GREAT BATTLE FOR TROY WAS FOUGHT IN THE SANDS OUTSIDE THE ANCIENT CITY. BUT IT WAS THE GODS ABOVE WHO STARTED THE WAR AND PITTED THE MORTALS AGAINST ONE ANOTHER.

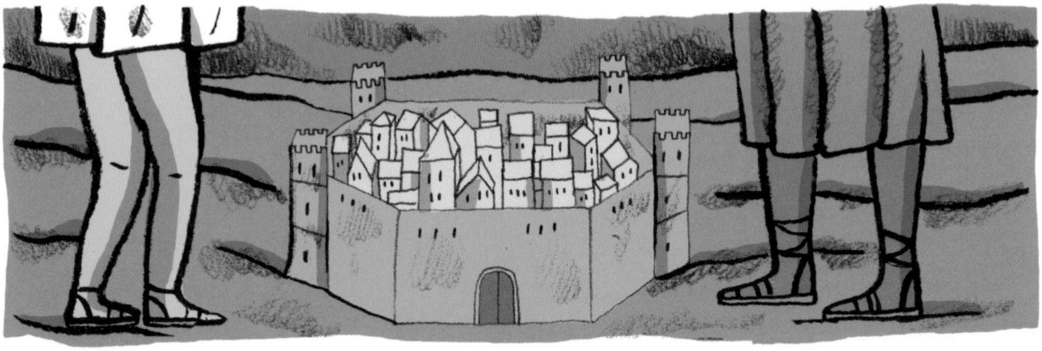

APHRODITE—THE GODDESS OF LOVE AND BEAUTY—MADE A TROJAN PRINCE NAMED PARIS FALL IN LOVE WITH THE GREATEST GREEK BEAUTY, HELEN. AND WHEN PARIS STOLE HER AWAY FROM HER HUSBAND, A THOUSAND GREEK SHIPS CHASED AFTER THEM.

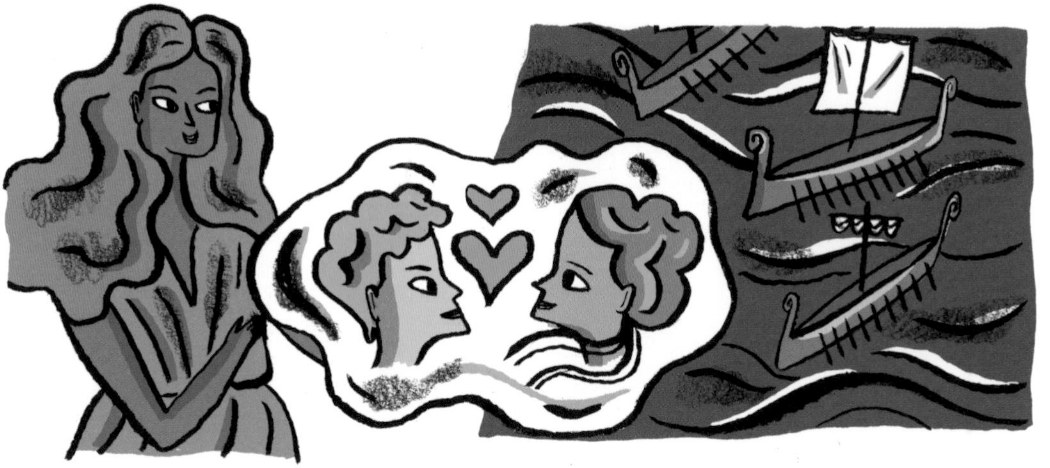

IT WAS APHRODITE'S SISTER ATHENA—GODDESS OF WISDOM AND WAR—WHO SENT THE FRIGHTENING GREEK WARRIOR ACHILLES INTO BATTLE TO RECAPTURE HELEN.

AND IT WAS THEIR BROTHER APOLLO—GOD OF PROPHECY AND POETRY—WHO SENT HECTOR, THE OTHER TROJAN PRINCE, ONTO THE BATTLEFIELD TO TRY TO DEFEAT ACHILLES.

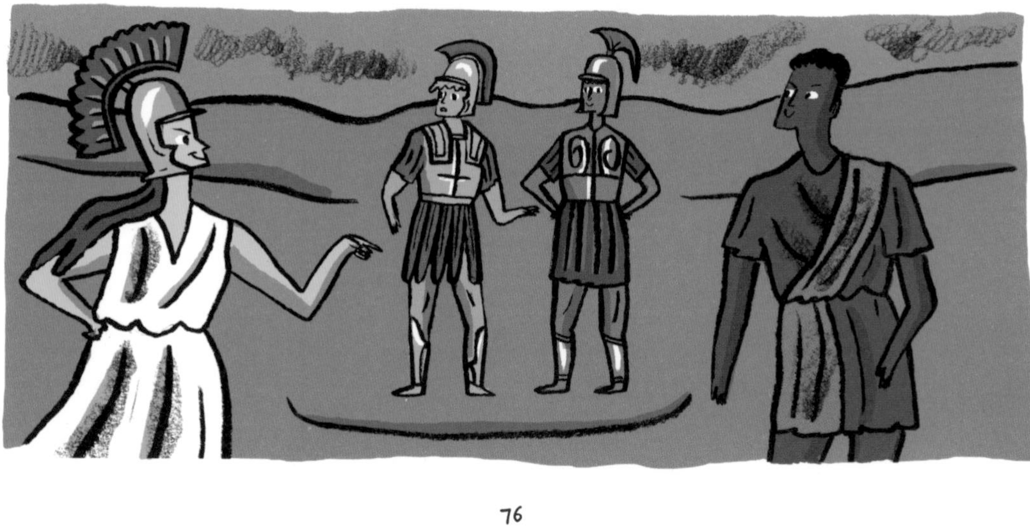

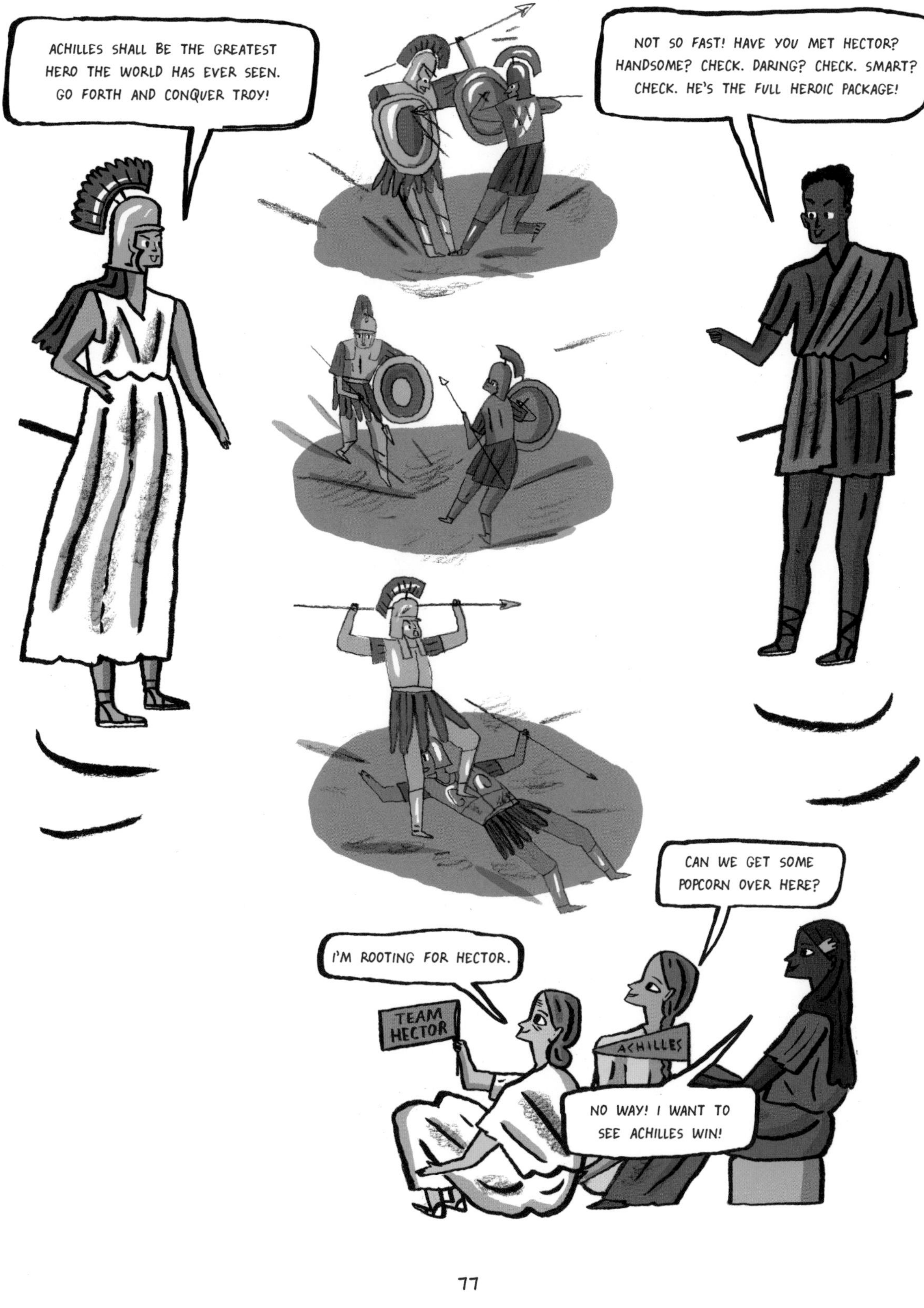
ACHILLES SHALL BE THE GREATEST HERO THE WORLD HAS EVER SEEN. GO FORTH AND CONQUER TROY!
NOT SO FAST! HAVE YOU MET HECTOR? HANDSOME? CHECK. DARING? CHECK. SMART? CHECK. HE'S THE FULL HEROIC PACKAGE!
CAN WE GET SOME POPCORN OVER HERE?
I'M ROOTING FOR HECTOR.
TEAM HECTOR
ACHILLES
NO WAY! I WANT TO SEE ACHILLES WIN!

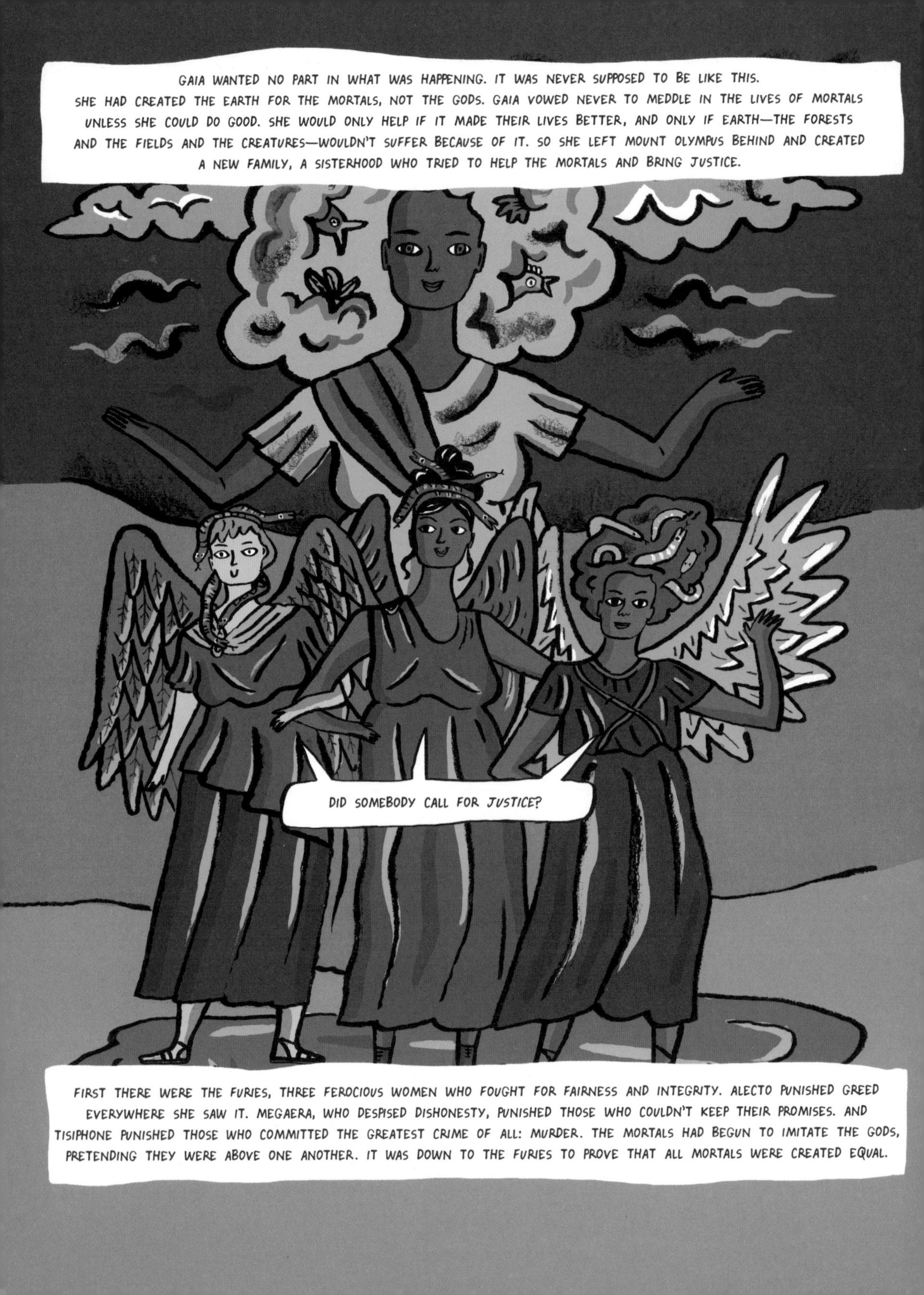
GAIA WANTED NO PART IN WHAT WAS HAPPENING. IT WAS NEVER SUPPOSED TO BE LIKE THIS. SHE HAD CREATED THE EARTH FOR THE MORTALS, NOT THE GODS. GAIA VOWED NEVER TO MEDDLE IN THE LIVES OF MORTALS UNLESS SHE COULD DO GOOD. SHE WOULD ONLY HELP IF IT MADE THEIR LIVES BETTER, AND ONLY IF EARTH—THE FORESTS AND THE FIELDS AND THE CREATURES—WOULDN'T SUFFER BECAUSE OF IT. SO SHE LEFT MOUNT OLYMPUS BEHIND AND CREATED A NEW FAMILY, A SISTERHOOD WHO TRIED TO HELP THE MORTALS AND BRING JUSTICE.
DID SOMEBODY CALL FOR *JUSTICE*?
FIRST THERE WERE THE FURIES, THREE FEROCIOUS WOMEN WHO FOUGHT FOR FAIRNESS AND INTEGRITY. ALECTO PUNISHED GREED EVERYWHERE SHE SAW IT. MEGAERA, WHO DESPISED DISHONESTY, PUNISHED THOSE WHO COULDN'T KEEP THEIR PROMISES. AND TISIPHONE PUNISHED THOSE WHO COMMITTED THE GREATEST CRIME OF ALL: MURDER. THE MORTALS HAD BEGUN TO IMITATE THE GODS, PRETENDING THEY WERE ABOVE ONE ANOTHER. IT WAS DOWN TO THE FURIES TO PROVE THAT ALL MORTALS WERE CREATED EQUAL.

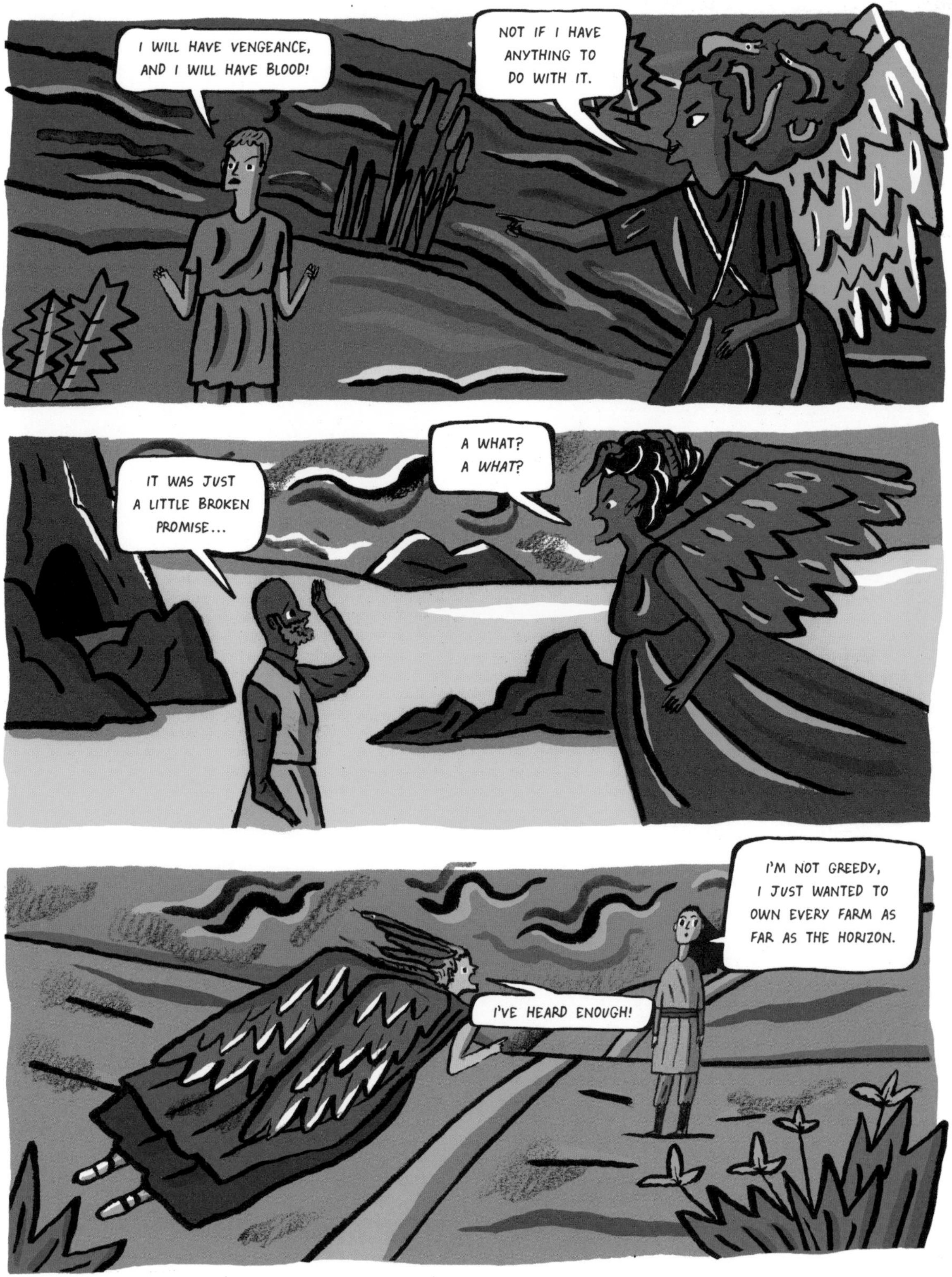
I WILL HAVE VENGEANCE, AND I WILL HAVE BLOOD!
NOT IF I HAVE ANYTHING TO DO WITH IT.
IT WAS JUST A LITTLE BROKEN PROMISE...
A WHAT? A WHAT?
I'M NOT GREEDY, I JUST WANTED TO OWN EVERY FARM AS FAR AS THE HORIZON.
I'VE HEARD ENOUGH!

THE FURIES LIVED UP TO THEIR NAME,
BUT THERE WAS ONLY SO MUCH THEY COULD DO. THE WORLD WAS WIDE AND FULL OF TERRIBLE DEEDS.

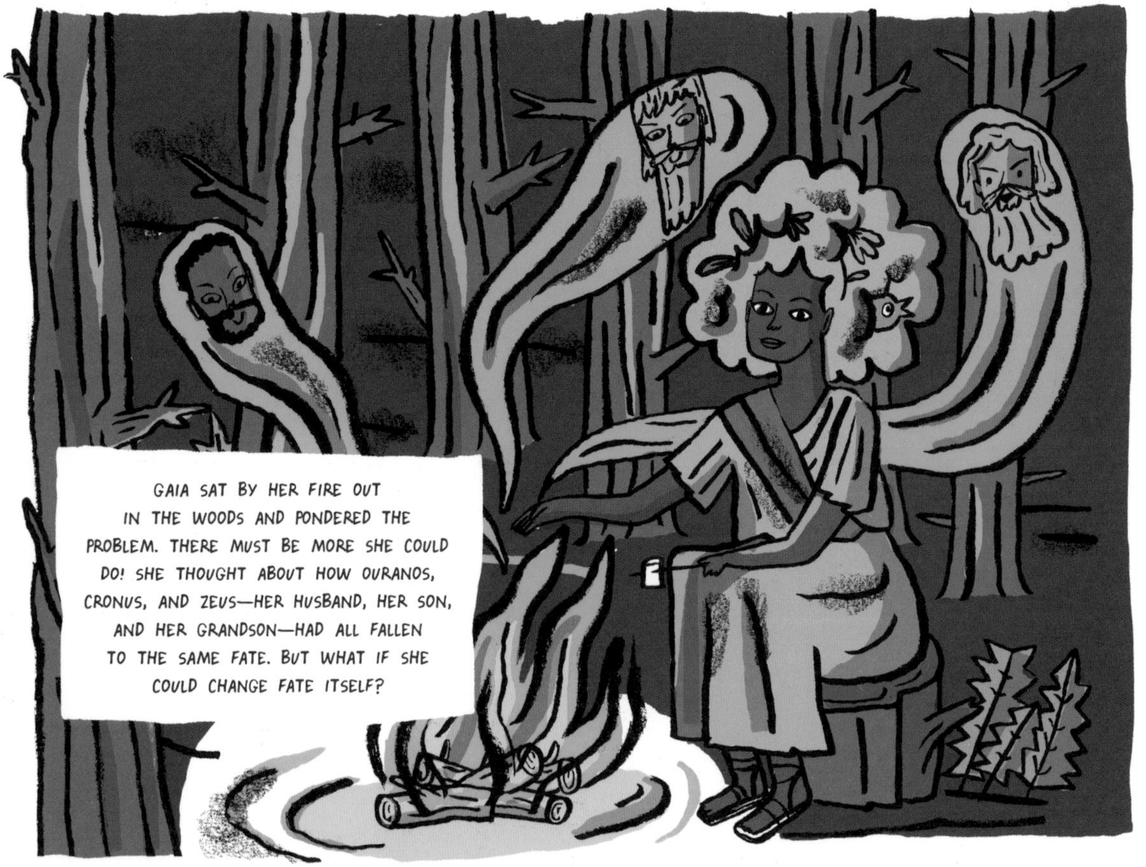
GAIA SAT BY HER FIRE OUT IN THE WOODS AND PONDERED THE PROBLEM. THERE MUST BE MORE SHE COULD DO! SHE THOUGHT ABOUT HOW OURANOS, CRONUS, AND ZEUS—HER HUSBAND, HER SON, AND HER GRANDSON—HAD ALL FALLEN TO THE SAME FATE. BUT WHAT IF SHE COULD CHANGE FATE ITSELF?

SO GAIA CREATED THE FATES, THREE WOMEN WHO PICKED UP THE THREADS OF CHAOS AND STITCHED THEM INTO A PATTERN, SPINNING SENSE INTO THE UNIVERSE. WHEN THE MORTALS UNPICKED WHAT WAS RIGHT AND JUST, WHEN THEY STRAYED TOWARD DARKNESS, THE FATES SET THEM BACK ON TRACK AND OFFERED A PATH FOR THEM TO FOLLOW.

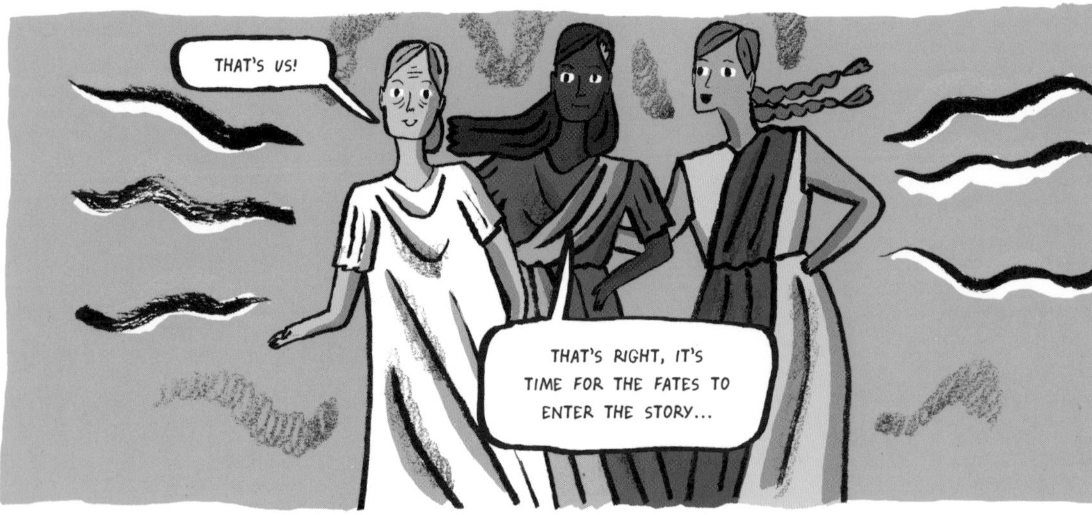
THAT'S US!
THAT'S RIGHT, IT'S TIME FOR THE FATES TO ENTER THE STORY...

CLOTHO TOOK THE THREADS OF CHAOS AND PLACED THEM ON HER WHEEL, SPINNING THE THREAD OF LIFE. LACHESIS TOOK THIS POWERFUL THREAD, MEASURED IT, AND MARKED THE LENGTH IT SHOULD BE. ATROPOS CUT THE THREAD OF LIFE AND SO DECIDED PEOPLE'S FATE, TAKING CONTROL AWAY FROM THE GODS.

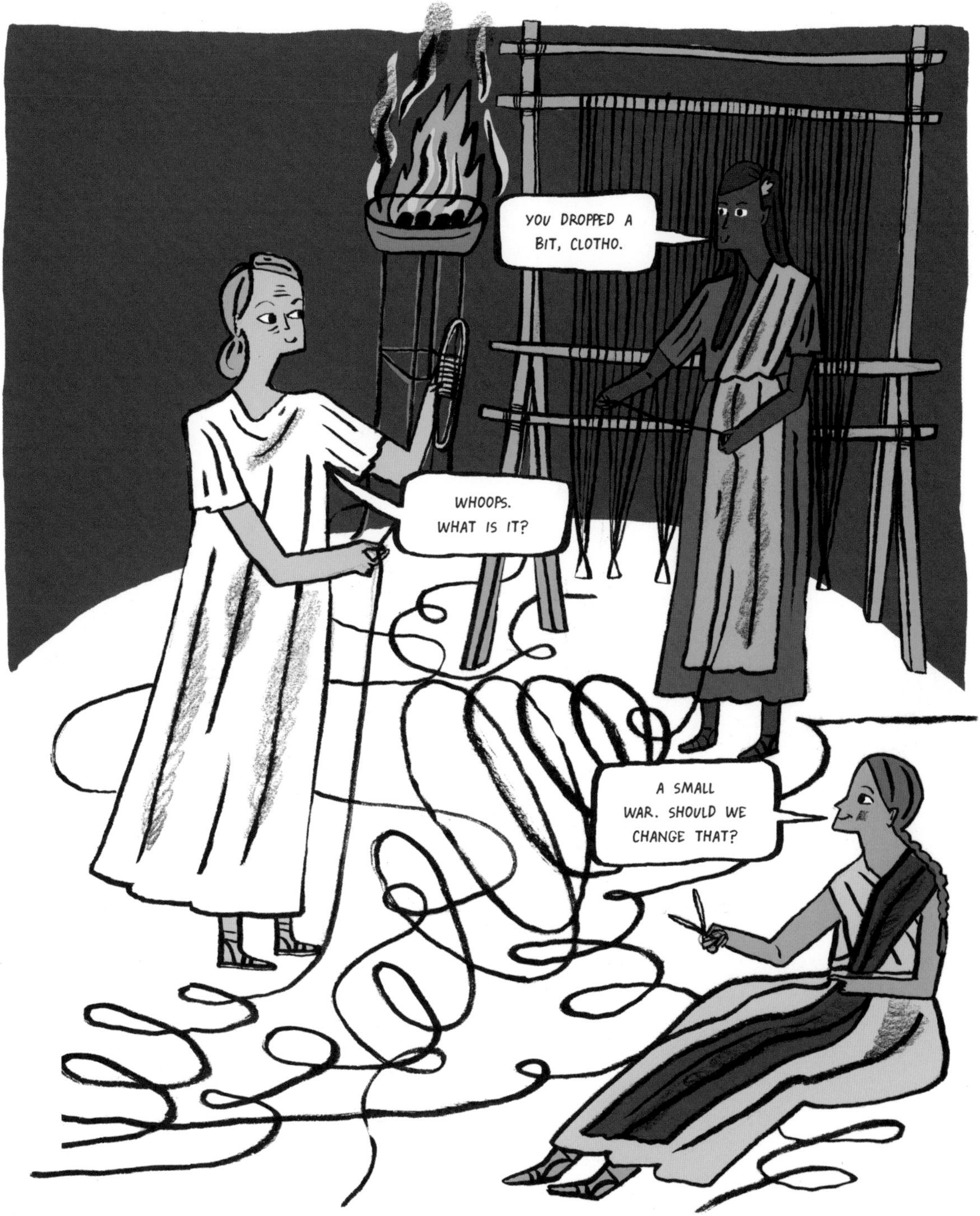
YOU DROPPED A BIT, CLOTHO.
WHOOPS. WHAT IS IT?
A SMALL WAR. SHOULD WE CHANGE THAT?

TOGETHER, THE THREE WOMEN WOVE THE FATE OF THE UNIVERSE.

AND WHAT ABOUT GAIA? SHE WALKED THE EARTH, OFFERING A LITTLE HELP HERE AND A LITTLE HELP THERE. SHE BROUGHT WATER BACK TO WELLS, RAISED HEALING PLANTS FROM THE GROUND, AND NOURISHED THE SOIL IN FAMINE-RAVAGED LANDS. JUST WHEN THE MORTALS HAD LOST ALL HOPE, GAIA FOUND NEW WAYS TO HELP THEM LIVE.

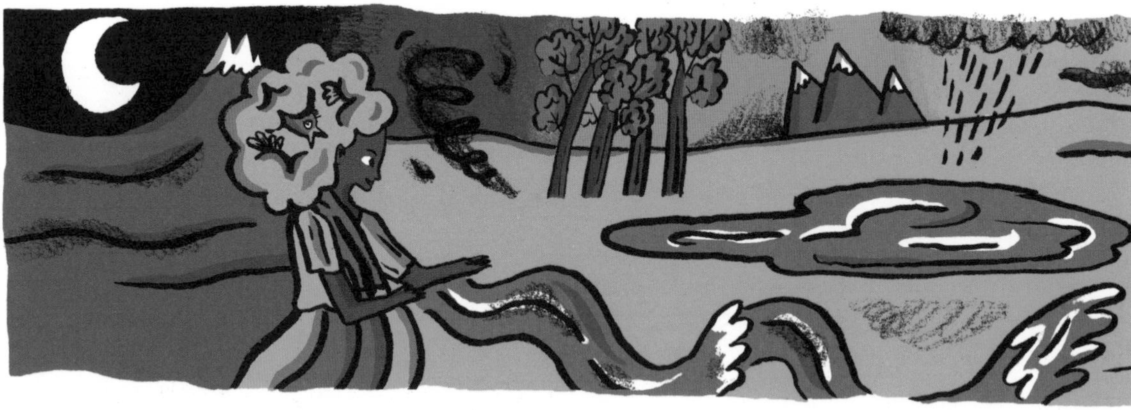

IN THE EVENINGS, SHE SAT AROUND HER FIRE WITH HER NEW SISTERHOOD, THE FATES AND THE FURIES.

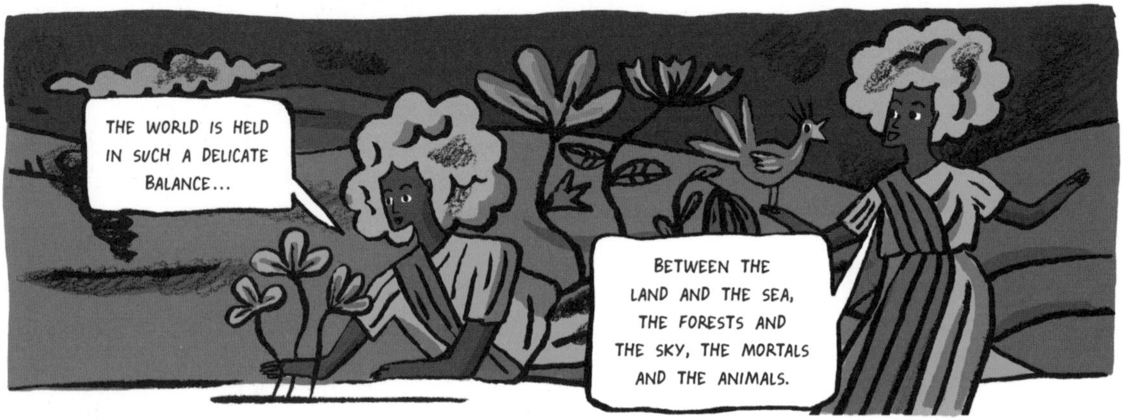
THE WORLD IS HELD IN SUCH A DELICATE BALANCE...
BETWEEN THE LAND AND THE SEA, THE FORESTS AND THE SKY, THE MORTALS AND THE ANIMALS.

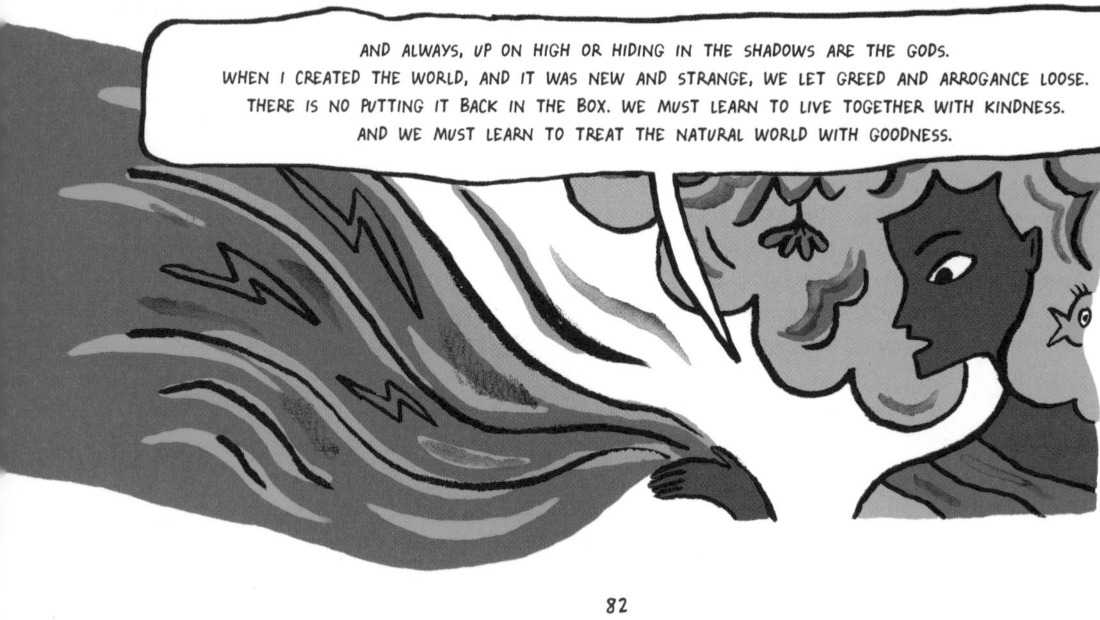
AND ALWAYS, UP ON HIGH OR HIDING IN THE SHADOWS ARE THE GODS. WHEN I CREATED THE WORLD, AND IT WAS NEW AND STRANGE, WE LET GREED AND ARROGANCE LOOSE. THERE IS NO PUTTING IT BACK IN THE BOX. WE MUST LEARN TO LIVE TOGETHER WITH KINDNESS. AND WE MUST LEARN TO TREAT THE NATURAL WORLD WITH GOODNESS.

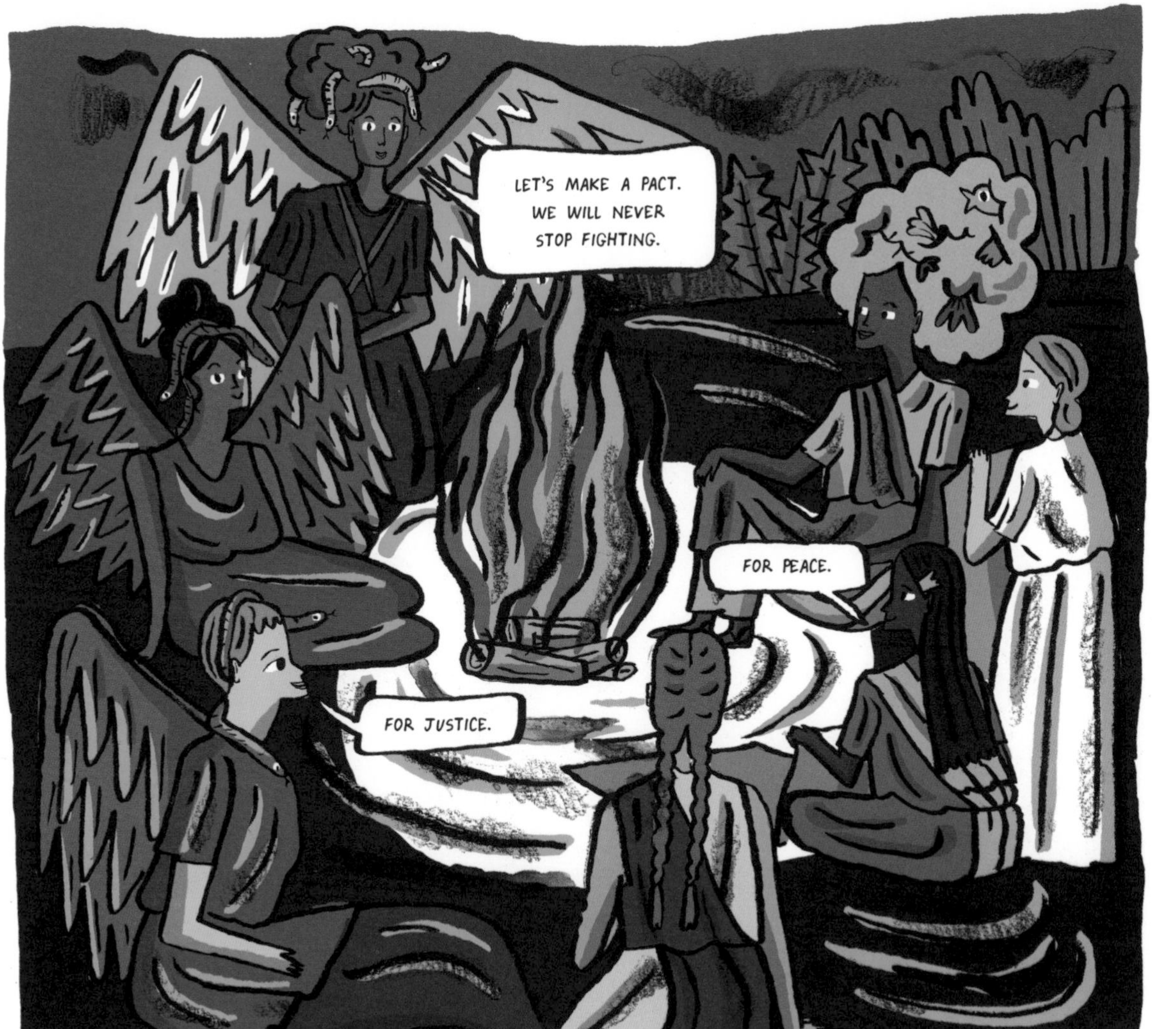
LET'S MAKE A PACT.
WE WILL NEVER
STOP FIGHTING.
FOR PEACE.
FOR JUSTICE.

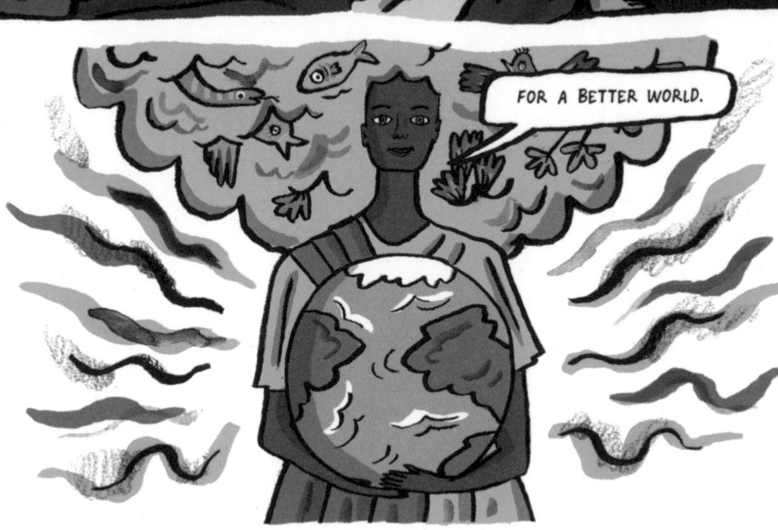
FOR A BETTER WORLD.

THE WOMEN ALL AGREED. THEY HAD CHOSEN A NEW KIND OF WAR. THERE WAS NO FIGHTING, NO SPEARS, AND NO THUNDERBOLTS—ONLY ACTS OF KINDNESS AND SACRIFICE.

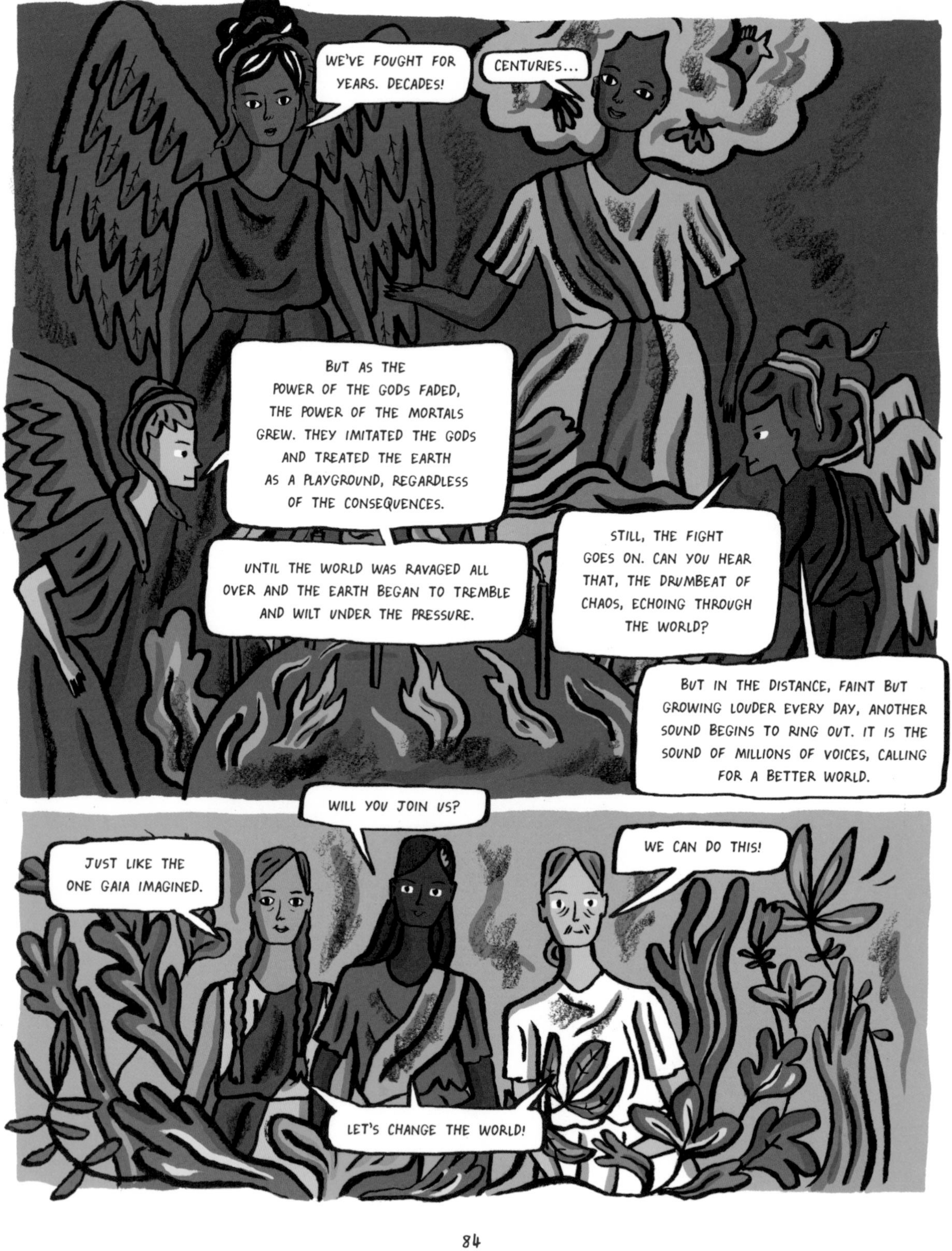

GLOSSARY

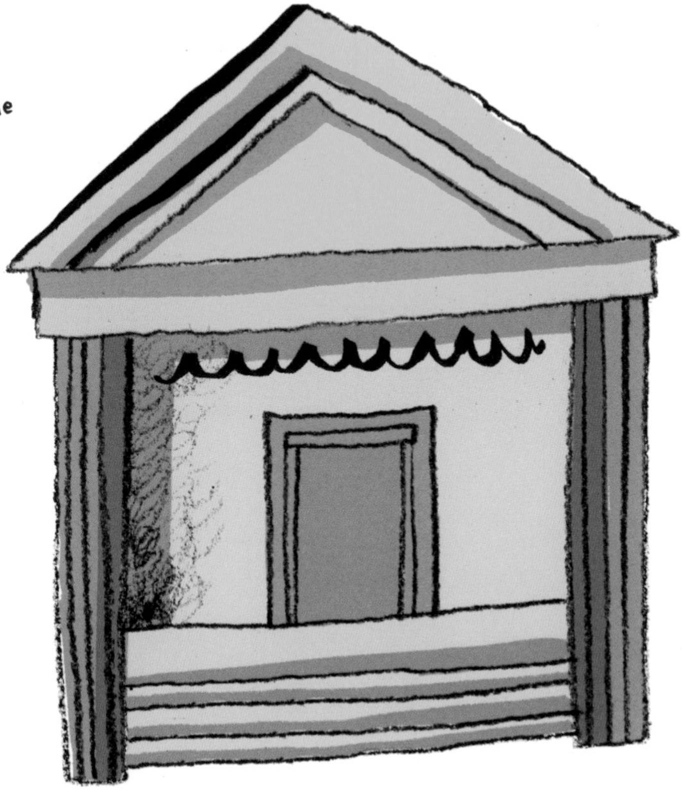

ALTAR: A table or block used for religious ritual and making sacrifices to the gods and goddesses.

CYCLOPS: A one-eyed giant that was originally created by Gaia. When a battle was approaching, the cyclopes forged thunderbolts for Zeus.

DELPHI: A town in Greece that was considered the center of the world and was the home of the oracle.

GIANTS: Enormous creatures who mostly hid in darkness and were feared for their strength and power.

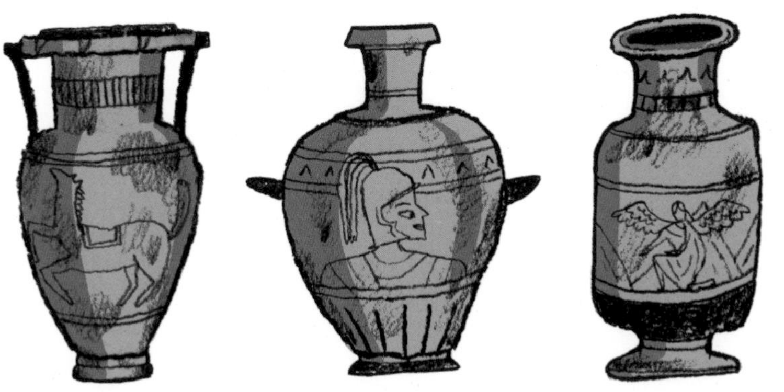

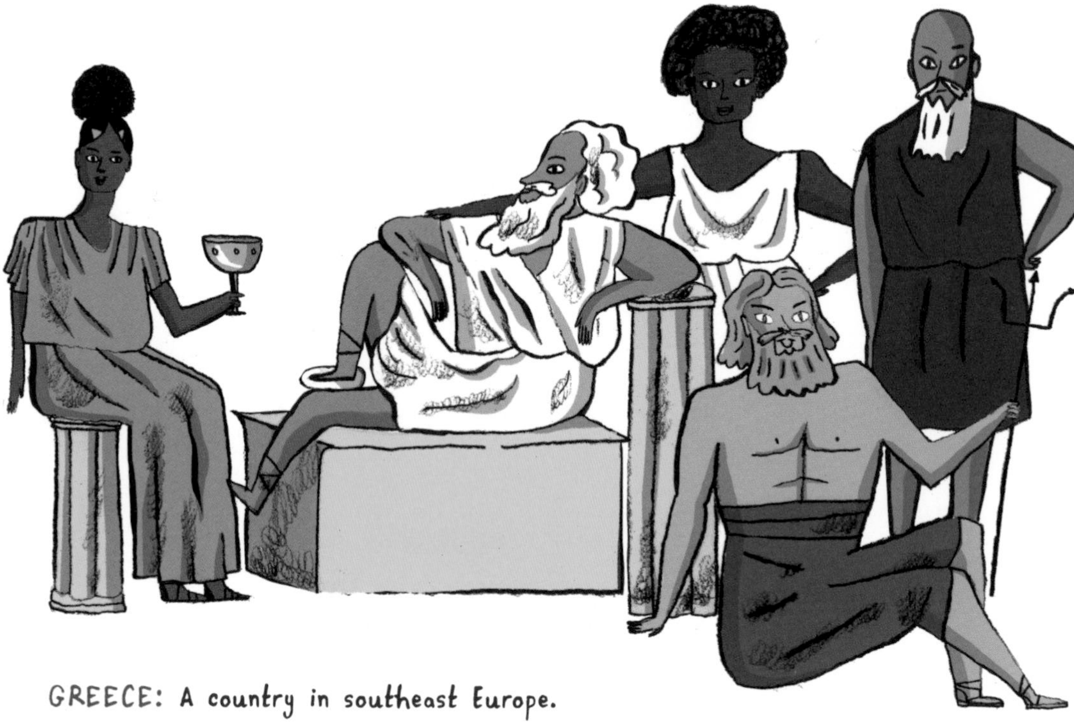

GREECE: A country in southeast Europe. Today, Athens is its capital.

MEDDLE: To interfere in something that's not one's concern.

MORTAL: Someone who is able to die. What the gods and goddesses called humans.

MOUNT OLYMPUS: The highest mountain in Greece, which is home to the gods and goddesses.

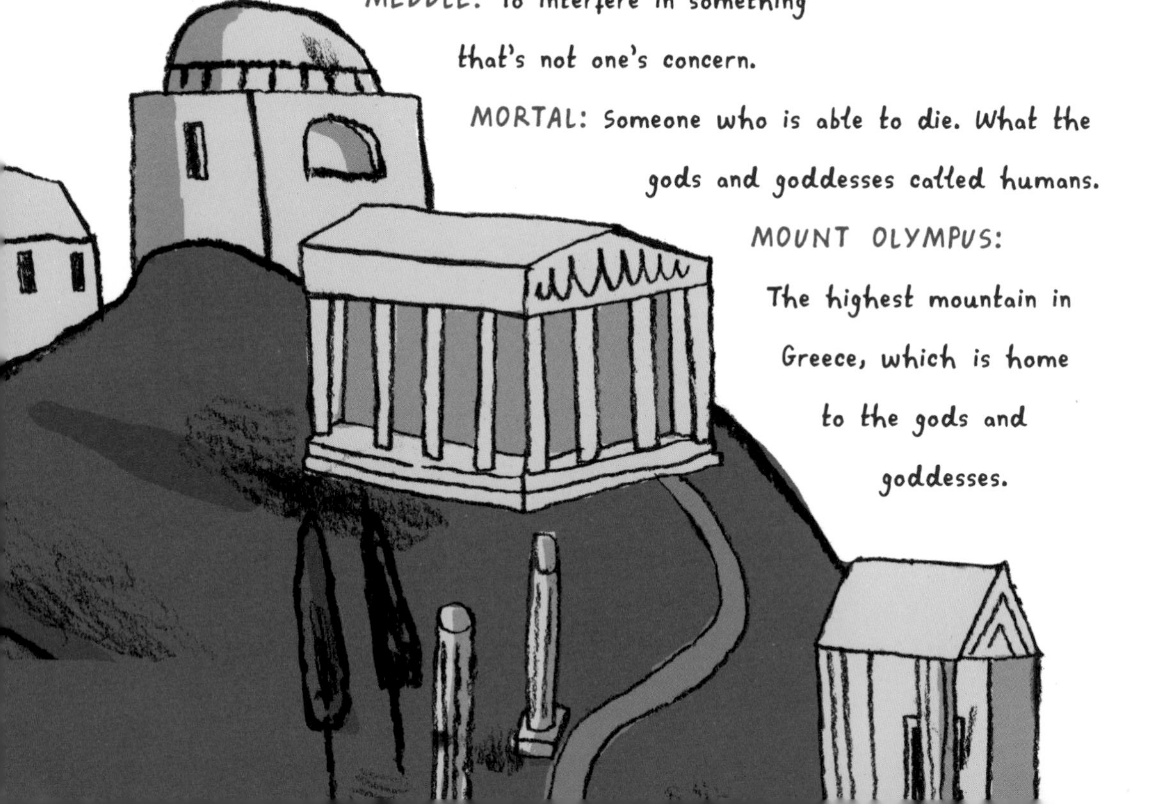

OLYMPIANS: The younger group of gods who came after the Titans. This group consisted of Hestia, Demeter, Hera, Zeus, Poseidon, and Hades.

ORACLE: Someone who is able to predict the future, or a priest who hears the messages of the gods and goddesses and is able to communicate them to the other mortals.

SICKLE: A tool with a curved blade that is often used for cutting grain.

TEMPLE: A building for worshipping gods and goddesses.

TITANS: A group of older gods who predated the Olympians. This group was first led by Ouranos and then by Cronus.

TROY: A city in modern-day Turkey.

TYPHOON: A tropical storm.

TYRANT: An evil or oppressive ruler who wants total control over their subjects.

UNDERWORLD: Ruled by Hades, this is the kingdom where souls go after they die. It's thought to be a darker kingdom than Mount Olympus, and a land of the dead.

SELECT BIBLIOGRAPHY

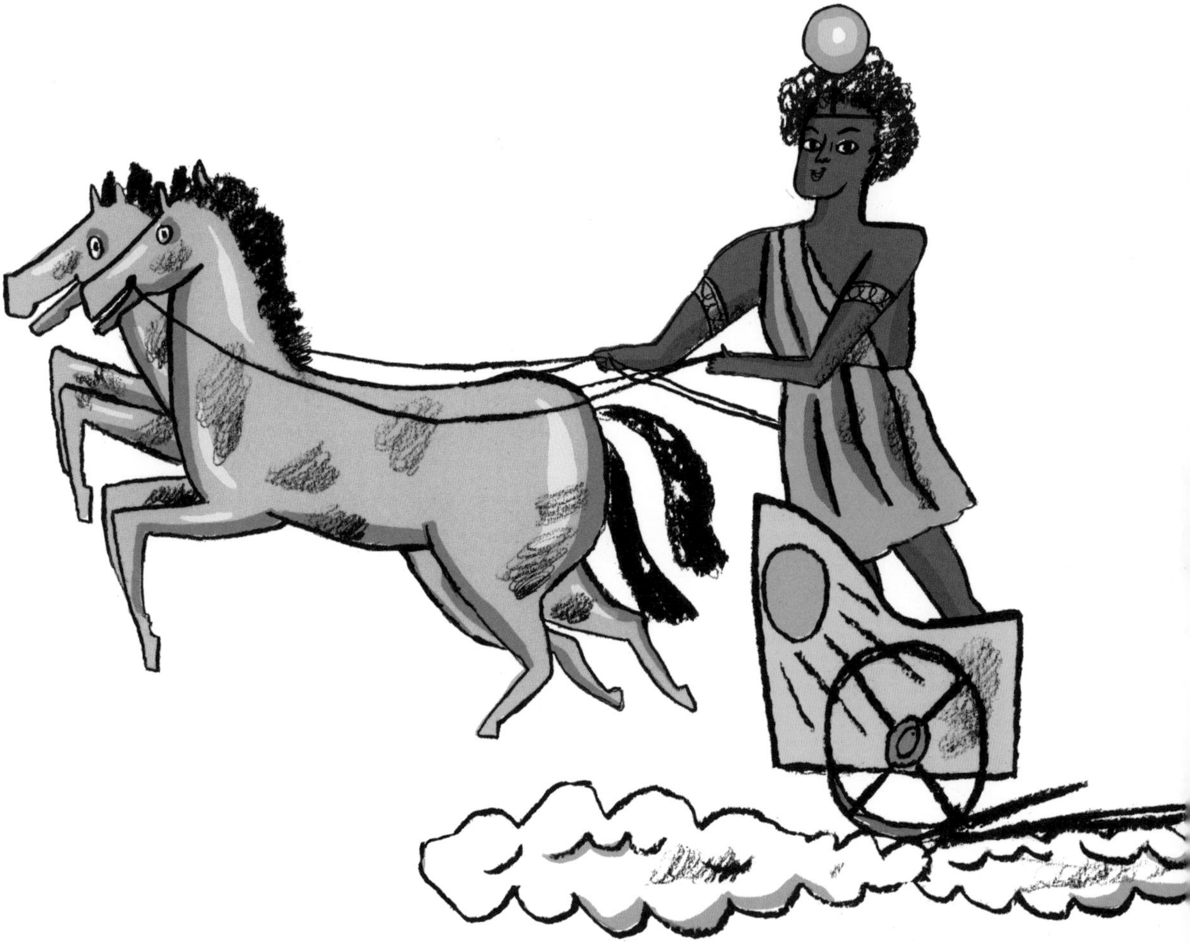

March, Jenny. *The Penguin Book of Classical Myths*. New York: Penguin, 2009.

Matyszak, Philip. *The Greek and Roman Myths: A Guide to the Classical Stories*. London: Thames & Hudson, 2010.

ABOUT THE AUTHOR

IMOGEN GREENBERG is a writer and podcaster who lives in London. She writes about history and myths for children and is also the creator of *Such Stuff*, the podcast for Shakespeare's Globe. The first book in the Tales of Great Goddesses series, *Athena*, received a starred review from *Kirkus Reviews*, who said, "This graphic novel brings plucky illustrated energy to the story of the goddess Athena . . . Three cheers for Athena, smarts, and bravery!"

ABOUT THE ILLUSTRATOR

ISABEL GREENBERG is an award-winning illustrator, comic artist, and writer. Her graphic novels *The Encyclopedia of Early Earth* and *The One Hundred Nights of Hero* are both *New York Times* bestsellers, and her graphic novel, *Glass Town*, was called a "lyrical, endlessly inventive book" by *Publishers Weekly* in a starred review. She is also the illustrator on four acclaimed nonfiction science books by author Seth Fishman. She lives in London and enjoys illustrating all things historical and fantastical.

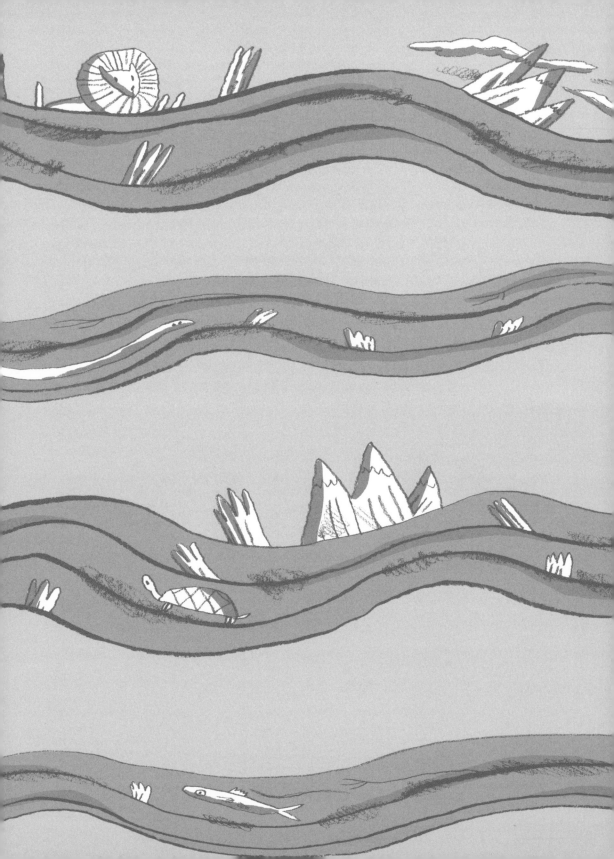

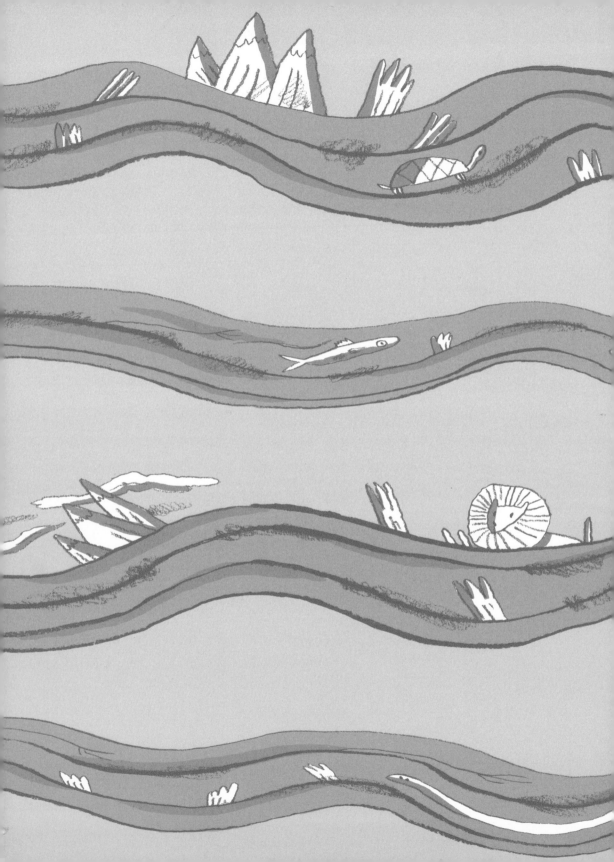